TROUBLE
BREWING

TROUBLE
BREWING

Suzanne Baltsar

G

GALLERY BOOKS

New York   London   Toronto   Sydney   New Delhi

Gallery Books
An Imprint of Simon & Schuster, Inc.
1230 Avenue of the Americas
New York, NY 10020

First Gallery Books trade paperback edition September 2018

GALLERY BOOKS and colophon are registered trademarks of Simon & Schuster, Inc.

For information about special discounts for bulk purchases, please contact Simon & Schuster Special Sales at 1-866-506-1949 or business@simonandschuster.com.

The Simon & Schuster Speakers Bureau can bring authors to your live event. For more information or to book an event, contact the Simon & Schuster Speakers Bureau at 1-866-248-3049 or visit our website at www.simonspeakers.com.

Interior design by Davina Mock-Maniscalco

Manufactured in the United States of America

10   9   8   7   6   5   4   3   2   1

Library of Congress Cataloging-in-Publication Data

Names: Baltsar, Suzanne.
Title: Trouble brewing / Suzanne Baltsar.
Description: First Gallery Books trade paperback edition. | New York : Gallery Books, 2018.
Identifiers: LCCN 2017060564 (print) | LCCN 2018002556 (ebook) | ISBN 9781501188329 (ebook) | ISBN 9781501188312 (trade paper : alk. paper)
Subjects: LCSH: Women brewers—Fiction. | Breweries—Fiction.
Classification: LCC PS3602.A6295 (ebook) | LCC PS3602.A6295 T76 2018 (print)
| DDC 813/.6—'dc23
LC record available at https://lccn.loc.gov/2017060564

ISBN 978-1-5011-8831-2
ISBN 978-1-5011-8832-9 (ebook)

For my personal home brewer.
I'm so drunk in love with you.
#Surfboard

ACKNOWLEDGMENTS

Someone once told me to never be the smartest person in the room, and I make it a point to keep my room packed with people smarter than me.

Starting with the BGW ladies. You are the most beautiful bunch of women I've ever known, and I love that I can call you friends. Brighton, thank you for being my mentor, soundboard, retreat mom, and all-around general badass. Were it not for you, I'd still be using emojis and GIFs to express my emotions. Ellis, you are too brilliant for this world, and I love learning from you. Elizabeth, if there was ever a test I had to take, I'd cheat off you. Esh, my favorite Iowan, you're almost always the first one to volunteer to lend your eyes, and your advice is always perfect. Helen, you've shown me you don't have to be the loudest one to make the biggest splash. Jen, you don't know it, but you've pushed me to let down my guard in writing and in life because of your openness. Ann, you think and do things I could never dream up, and you do it all in the best socks. Melly, you are my third favorite storyteller, only behind my brother and Kevin Hart, which means you are pretty damn funny. And Laura, my long-lost sister, I adore you, plain and simple. When I am old and gray, I'll look back at our many adventures yet to come and smile. Thank you all, ladies, for your laughter and guidance.

Of course, I need to thank Sharon, my agent and dream-maker, for always answering my e-mails even when they're filled with late-night ramblings or drunken ideas, which led to this book. You are a gentlewoman and a scholar, and I never fear with you on my side. Marla, editor extraordinaire, thank you for seeing the possibilities in this manuscript and for being so accommodating while I birthed a human baby and a book baby. My baby and my brain appreciate your patience.

To the PW '15 group, the best collection of writers ever known to meet over the internet, I know there is always someone who can answer any question I have or lend an ear for support. Thanks to my CPs, J.R. and Laura (again), you are the best.

To my family for never making me feel like my dreams were stupid, and for my brother, who I will always thank, for always making sure there was someone smarter than me in the room.

Gratitude, love, and light for Oprah.

And last but not least, I'd like to thank Yuengling, Summer Shandy, Dogfish Head, Brooklyn Lager, Fat Tire, Stone IPA, Sierra Nevada, Goose Island, Lagunitas, Free Will, Hijinx, Funk, the Tavern, Callaghan's, and every other beer, bar, pub, and brewery where everybody knows your name and they're always glad you came.

TROUBLE
BREWING

CHAPTER 1

Piper

It was miserable out. The groundhog saw his shadow this year, and we were all paying dearly for it in Minneapolis. I mean, really, who gave that four-legged, bucktoothed furball that much authority anyway?

While he hid away enjoying the rest of his long winter's nap, we'd been hit with a foot and a half of snow on the first day of spring and were still waiting for it all to melt, even though it was now the last day of March.

I hefted the garage door up another couple of inches so it was off the ground a few feet, despite the outside temperature. Between the heat from the propane boiler and the smell of hops and barley, I needed to get some fresh air. I tugged my beanie farther down on my head before slipping out underneath the garage door, leaving the humidity of my pseudo nanobrewery.

The neighborhood was quiet at this time of day, before

schools let out and people got home from work. I watched the melting snow fall in big clumps from nearby trees and made tracks with my boots in the now-dirty gray mush, contemplating the latest e-mail from my sister. I had asked her to send me some mock-ups of my logo with different colors. My website needed a little pick-me-up; the drab taupe and brown just wasn't doing it for me anymore.

Out of the Bottle Brewery had been my dream for years, ever since I'd learned you could actually earn a living from making beer. And with a couple of cases at a distributor, the reality of making my dream come true was closer than ever before. I wanted—*needed*—everything to be perfect. Including the welcome banner on my website.

I breathed out a big puff of white air, still not used to a Minnesota "spring" even though I'd been there for two years now. Two years of this cold and all of my savings, hoping I could reap the benefits of an expanding craft brew scene.

So far Out of the Bottle hasn't gained much traction, despite winning a few local tasting contests. But that would all change soon. It had to, because there was no way I was ever going back to work for someone else, brewing recipes that weren't mine. Plus, my bank account was in dire need of a paycheck. I had to believe I'd get some of my beer into paying hands. Sooner rather than later.

Before my teeth started chattering, I stomped off whatever snow was left on the bottom of my boots and ducked back into the garage. With five conical fermenters, a lautering tun, three wooden casks, a small utility sink, and a tiny desk, my two-car garage at the back of the house was a miniature brewing kingdom and I was queen.

I couldn't wait to expand and open up a *real* brewery. One with a multiple-barrel brewing system, a tasting room, a couple thousand square feet, and a few workers. A place I could *actually* reign over.

But to get there I needed to sell. And to sell, I needed to get to work.

I pushed up my sleeves and sat down to look back over my sister's e-mail. Unfortunately, the quick jaunt outside hadn't helped in deciding what color to make the funky wording. I dropped my head to the table with a frustrated groan.

"Piper?"

"In here." I turned just as my roommate stuck her head in the side door. Her normally golden-brown skin was tinged pink from the cold. "What are you doing home?"

"My last two clients for today canceled, and Manny heard me sneeze three times. He sent me home to recover," she said, stepping inside.

I snickered. Sonja was the healthiest person I knew. Between her strict workout regimen and constant green juices, I didn't know if she'd ever been sick. Manny, her boxing coach, would have a fit if his star athlete ever really came down with anything more than the sniffles.

"Does this mean you have the night off?"

She lifted a resigned shoulder. Only Sonja would be bereft at having absolutely nothing to do for the night. "Guess so."

"Piper and Sonja's day of fun!" I sang, matching the annoying pitch of Chandler's girlfriend Janice.

She pointed a finger at me. "No, we're not watching *Friends*."

I waved her off as she sat down on a folding chair, extending a pair of fancy leggings out toward me. She always got cool-looking workout gear because of her boxing sponsorship, and the hot pink called to me.

I plucked at them, touching where the black mesh met the pink spandex.

"We could go for a run," she suggested.

"Yes. That's *exactly* what I want to do," I deadpanned.

I loved my friend, but I hated her idea of a good time. She was always on the go, and quite frankly I couldn't keep up. In fact, that's how we met—she literally ran into me. Sonja likes to argue I ran into her, but that's not true.

She had her headphones and *face* on, the one I'd come to learn was her all-business face, and she smacked right into me next to the Landwehr Canal in Berlin. I was brand-new to Germany and happy to bump—literally— into a fellow American. She was there for a month visiting family; I was there studying to become a brewmaster, and we became quick friends. It turned out we were both fish out of water. Me being a student with zero friends, she being reintroduced to her mother's family who she'd only ever met as a child.

Our friendship quickly grew over daily lunches and weekends spent dancing at EDM clubs, forever bonded by bratwursts and a struggle to learn the native language. When she went home, we kept in touch, so much so that when I was moving to Minneapolis, she offered me room and board.

That was almost two years ago. Now we were more best friends than roommates.

"Here." I turned my laptop screen to her. "Which colors do you like for the logo?"

Sonja tied her thick, dark hair on top of her head, a few tiny corkscrew curls sticking out by her temples and at her neck. "Navy with the lime green."

"I like that one, too." I sent off a reply to Kayla to change the header on the website, and before I stood to turn the propane off, I got my sister's response that she'd have it updated as soon as possible. Sonja had seen me brew enough times to know the drill, so she followed me to the sink. I grabbed the wort chiller—a bungle of plastic tubes and copper wire—and untangled it as Sonja screwed one end of the tube to the utility sink's faucet. I dropped the copper wire into the pot, and she let the ice-cold water rip from her end.

Using this method to cool the beer was a bit amateurish, but it was all I had without the money and space for a glycol chilling system. I let the hot water drain out of the garage, carving a steaming path in the snow. My mind went with it, once again losing my thoughts to a future of chrome and steel. I'd had just about enough of these homemade shortcuts.

I was a professional, dammit.

My phone rang in my back pocket, disturbing the mental image of my future kegs. I didn't recognize the number but answered anyway, hoping it wasn't the credit card company chasing down the payment I owed them. I was already up to my ears in interest rates.

"Hello?"

"Hi, I'm calling for Piper Williams."

"This is she."

"Piper, my name is Blake Reed, I got your information from Dave at B&S Distribution."

I'd met Dave a few weeks ago at one of the contests I had won. He'd agreed to stock a couple of my cases at the wholesaler he owned. So far not much had sold, but Dave had high hopes.

"How can I help you, Blake?"

"Well, I was just perusing your website and—"

"You were? What'd you think of the colors?" The question was out before I could stop it, and I slapped my hand over my mouth. Could I be any more desperate?

Blake laughed on the other end, and I could feel my stock in professionalism dropping by the second.

"I like them," he said. "The lime green is different, stands out."

I offered up a silent thank-you to the universe for the unbelievably quick work of my sister and that this guy had a sense of humor.

"I actually called because I was hoping you'd be able to meet with me. I'm opening a gastropub next month, and I'd love to try your beer."

I jumped up, pivoting to face Sonja in a silent scream.

She raised her brows, rushing to my side. I angled the phone so she could listen to the conversation.

"Sure. I'd love to give you anything I got."

Sonja flicked my forehead.

"I mean, I'd love to bring you some samples. When would you like me to come in?"

He laughed again, my nerves no more eased by the sound. "Is tomorrow too early?"

Sonja pumped her fist up and down as I answered, "Not at all."

"How about four o'clock?"

"Perfect."

"Is the e-mail on your contact page okay for me to send you the address?"

"Yes. Absolutely." I knew I sounded way too giddy, but I couldn't help it. Better to be overly excited than to have more accidental innuendoes fly out of my mouth.

"Great. I'll get that out to you in a few minutes."

I danced in place. "Thank you so much. I'll see you at four tomorrow."

I hung up and let loose my scream of joy. Sonja joined me, dancing, ringing her arms around my shoulders.

"Yes! Do you feel amazing?"

I couldn't have wiped the smile from my face if I'd tried. "I do, actually. This calls for a special dinner. What do you think? Pizza?"

Sonja snorted. "Ha. No. I got spaghetti squash. You can finish up out here and I'll get it in the oven."

"Piper and Sonja's day of fun, remember? Pizza's mandatory."

She turned at the door, side-eyeing me. "No pizza, but I'll give you two episodes of *Friends*. Just not the one when Ross gets the spray tan. That one's the worst."

I'd give her that. "Deal."

She closed the door, and I sank into a chair, waiting for the wort to finish cooling before I added the yeast. I watched the temperature gauge with an eagle eye. This batch wouldn't be ready for tomorrow, but it would be perfect nonetheless. Every single gallon had to be.

My first real chance to move out of a converted two-car garage to a bigger place was this meeting. And I was *not* going to screw it up.

I was going to be perfect.

As perfect as my beer.

CHAPTER 2

Piper

I hitched the box in my arms higher and slammed the car door shut with my boot before juggling the cardboard to press the lock button on my key fob.

Carefully, I stepped over the white slush of Satan and held the box steady. This was my future right here, and one wrong step could literally and figuratively be the death of me. I crossed the street to the address Blake had sent me. According to his e-mail yesterday, this was the Public, a new gastropub downtown that would hopefully put my beer on tap and my company on the map.

I gazed up at the dark brick building. Minus the construction releases in the window and the missing signage, it looked ready to open. And I felt ready to puke.

I'd been working toward this for the last ten years. All of my education, my experience, my hours of hard work every day brewing, bottling, labeling, marketing it all myself . . . it had all come down to this.

With a deep breath and one last prayer, I opened the door and stepped into the possible start of my new life.

I blinked, my eyes adjusting from the sunshine to the interior lighting. The Public was fabulous. Exposed brick showcased piping on the ceiling while kitschy light fixtures made out of aluminum cans hung low. The bar in the back off to the left had, on a quick count, about twenty taps. Behind it hung a metal sign made out of bottle caps in the shape of America.

The place was trendy and hip, and I loved it. I wanted my beer to be sold here. Real bad.

"Hey, can I help you?"

I turned toward the voice and found a tall, blond Norwegian statue.

"I'm here to see Blake."

The man pointed in a general direction over his shoulder. "He's on the phone."

I set my samples on a sleek wooden table and met his blue eyes. He stared at me with a curious expression, and I tried not to fidget. Usually you couldn't get Minnesotans to shut up, but this one was silent. Maybe he wasn't a local.

"We have a meeting," I said, feeling silly. Why else would I be in an unopened bar?

From under his Minnesota Vikings hat, the man's gaze drifted to the box for a moment before slamming back to me in understanding. "You're here for the tasting?"

I nodded as a hulk of a man sauntered out from the bathroom, his tattoo-covered arms swinging at his sides. He was enormous—huge shoulders and legs bigger than both of mine combined. Hulk looked between me and the other man, then back to me before a slow smile spread across his face. "Hello, there. How can I help you?"

I pointed to both of them. "Do you guys work here or something?"

Hulk shook his head. "Not officially."

The statue took a few steps toward me. "I'm Connor. That's Bear. We're friends of Blake's."

Bear, aptly named, ducked his head down. "And I am at your service."

This one tiptoed past Minnesota Nice to plant both feet firmly in the flirt camp. "Appreciate that, Bear." I offered him a tight smile. "But I'm here to meet Blake about my beer."

"Your beer?" The surprise wasn't new to me. I was a woman who brewed and sold her own beer. Not quite the norm.

Yet.

But with the way these two were gawking at me, you'd think I was a monkey who'd started explaining the process of evolution in French.

"Yep." I pointed to my T-shirt underneath my coat. "Out of the Bottle Brewery."

Connor's and Bear's eyes grew to cartoonlike proportions.

"When Blake said a craft brewer was coming, I'd assumed you were a dude," Bear said.

Connor looked me up and down as if checking for proof of gender. "Me too."

That's when the kitchen door swung open and all three of us turned at the sound. And my jaw promptly hit the floor.

Months ago I'd found an Instagram account of Hot Dudes Brewing, and I was half-tempted to take a picture of this one and send it in.

This man.

This man deserved an entire Pinterest board. A Twitter hashtag. His own viral meme.

He swept his hand through his hair that wasn't quite brown or blond, straight or curly, but rather an artful mix of all. It flopped to the side in a clumsy sort of style.

His eyes coasted around the room and landed on me. "Piper?"

"Yes," I croaked, and cleared my throat. "I'm Piper Williams." I met his outstretched hand with a smile. His long fingers curled around my hand tightly. My father always said you could tell a lot about a person by their handshake. And his was steady, sure, friendly.

"Blake Reed. Nice to finally meet you."

"You too," I squeaked, reluctantly putting my hand in my pocket when he let go. I wasn't usually such a nervous Nelly when it came to guys, yet I sputtered all over myself with Blake.

Probably because of his hazel eyes. Or the dimple in his

left cheek. Or maybe it was the perfectly trimmed scruff on his angled chin.

He had all of it—the holy trinity of good looks—and, of course, he was the first guy I'd been instantly attracted to since my ex. I had to get myself together and stop ogling him. I was here for Out of the Bottle; a cute guy was *not* going to derail that dream.

"Let's go to the bar," he said in a buttery voice that had me sneaking a peek at his left hand. No ring.

I shook my head. *Focus.* Business didn't mix with plea-sure, and nothing, *nothing* was going to happen between me and a potential buyer.

I picked up my box of samples, but he stopped me be-fore I had a chance to move. "Need help with that?"

"I got it," I said, brushing past Connor and Bear. I sensed three pairs of eyes on me as I set the box down on the bar top, but I kept my spine straight, not willing to be intimi-dated. When it came to my job, I tended to downplay the fact that I didn't fit the mold, trying my best to blend in, to be accepted in a tight-knit community of mostly men. I damn sure hated being "the girl" in "a man's world" and would never dream of using my sexuality to get anywhere in life. But sometimes it was difficult to ignore the obvious dif-ferences, especially when a particular man's smile hatched a few butterflies in my stomach.

"Thanks for coming in today," Blake said as he rounded the bar.

"Are you kidding? I'm happy you called." I took my coat off and hung it on a barstool.

Blake's attention focused on my chest. He smirked, and that dimple carved itself into his cheek again. "Clever."

I glanced down at the heather-gray shirt. The logo of my company was a beer bottle with curves closer to those of a woman. The cap was midair like it had been flicked off, creating a whoosh of air, which looked similar to long hair blowing in the breeze.

I tugged on the hem of the shirt as his gaze roamed from my chest, up my throat, over my face, until finally he met my eyes. My limbs buzzed with nervous energy for more than one reason.

I needed to get ahold of myself. I was a brewer, he was a pub owner. This was strictly business.

I set my shoulders and looked him straight in the eye. "Ready to start?"

"Absolutely." Pint glasses clanked as he set them on the gleaming gray bar top.

Connor and Bear settled on stools next to me, and I raised a brow at Blake in question.

He tilted his head. "I assume you met my friends already."

"I did," I said, grabbing my favorite well-used lime-green bottle opener from my back pocket. I'd had it since I started tending bar in college. It was the closest thing I owned to a security blanket.

Blake leaned toward me, and it took Super Woman effort to ignore the way he focused his eyes on me.

"I bring these chuckleheads in for all my tastings. They represent my patrons." Blake gestured to Connor. "We've got our simple eat-and-drink-anything type, and our arrogant, picky, know-it-all type," he finished, pointing to Bear.

Connor's mouth quirked up into a barely discernible smile. "*Eat* anything? I'm a little pickier than that."

"Yeah, like she's got to—"

Blake cleared his throat, interrupting Bear. His eyes shot to me, clearly censoring his friends for my benefit.

Too bad I didn't do the same to myself. "Are all your patrons going to be single white males?" I teased.

Blake blanched. "No. God, no. I just—"

"I'm kidding. It's just funny." I chuckled, waving my hand out to the three men. "It's like I'm standing in front of the male version of *Sex and the City*."

Blake shook his head in confusion, Connor scrunched up his face in obvious horror, and Bear shrugged. "Just as long as I'm not Miranda."

Connor and Blake both turned to Bear with shocked expressions.

"Shut up. Like you guys've never watched it before."

The other two shook their heads.

"Fucking liars," Bear said, running a big paw over his beard.

Blake slapped the bar. "Dude."

"What?"

"Business meeting," Blake said through clenched teeth. Bear rolled his eyes, and Blake turned to me with a frown. "Sorry."

"He's right. You're both fucking liars. You've at least watched one episode."

Blake stared at me for a half second and I thought maybe I'd ruined everything before he and Connor busted out big laughs. Blake shook his head. "You got me, only one and only once. I'll never watch that show again. So, what do we have to drink?"

Relieved, I lined the bottles up on the bar. "I brought four beers for you to sample today. The first," I said, popping the top, "is an IPA called Platinum Blonde." I poured it into three glasses and distributed one to each man.

Connor slugged his sample before I got any more words out. Bear sniffed, swirled it, and sniffed again. Blake simply held his glass, waiting for me to continue.

"It's got the usual bitter bite, but I used Lemondrop hops, which add a really nice citrusy lemon flavor. It's a good beer for the springtime. If it ever comes," I added with a small laugh.

Connor wiped his mouth with the back of his hand and stared into the bottom of the glass. He didn't seem to have much of a reaction one way or the other. Bear sipped his slowly like a highfalutin wine drinker. Finally Blake took a gulp, and my heart leapt into my throat.

Moment of truth.

CHAPTER 3

Blake

Raising the glass to my lips, I kept my eyes on Piper as I drank. She came highly recommended from Dave, my distributor, and after my first taste of her beer, I wasn't disappointed. The light, hoppy brew was refreshing, and I really appreciated the surprise hint of lemon.

I finished and licked my lips, her attention pinned to my mouth. If I said I didn't relish her eyes on me, I'd be a liar. But truth box?

I'd watched a few episodes of *Sex and the City* with an ex-girlfriend. It wasn't the *worst* show. But Piper never had to know.

"I like it," I told her, holding up my empty glass. "It's different than usual IPAs."

She nodded and turned to my friends, waiting expectantly. Connor shrugged. "Good."

Bear went off on some tangent about the hops, and I

shut down the hearing part of my brain to focus on the seeing part.

Piper was pretty; tall-ish, pale oval face, and freckles on
her nose. But what stood out was her hair, the color of a ripe
red apple. And her eyes. I'd never seen eyes so big and green
before. Innocent and wild all at the same time. When she
looked at me, it felt like a quiet challenge—she didn't back
down when I met her gaze.

"I'd love to be able to grow my own hops," Piper said to
Bear, answering whatever question he'd asked. "I just don't
have the room right now. Maybe when I get a bigger place
with more land." When he nodded, she popped the top of
the next bottle. "I call this one Brunette Beauty. It's an impe-
rial stout." She poured the beer into new glasses and gave
one to each of us with a smile.

"Is that a little bit of coffee I smell?" Bear asked.

She nodded.

Connor finished his in two gulps. "I don't like it."

"Of course you don't, McGuire." Bear elbowed him. "A
thick stout like this is for the discerning beer drinker."

Piper brushed my arm as she walked behind the bar to
rinse out Connor's glass like she owned the place. "Stouts
aren't for everybody. But I think you'll like this next one."
She cracked open the bottle. "It's a classic amber ale. I call it
Natural Red."

Bear snorted a laugh. "Natural Red, huh?"

She pushed the sample toward him. "Yep."

"Like you?"

"Like me," she said, threading her fingers through her hair.

Bear smirked, and I knew that look. The one that said an inappropriate joke was on its way. "You got one named Firecrotch, too?"

My jaw went slack, but before I could speak up, Piper beat me to it. "I thought you were supposed to be the smart one. I expected something more original from you. But if you'd like to discuss crotches further, let's talk about what's hiding in your drawers. Something just as hairy as what's on your head?"

Connor sputtered out a laugh as Bear grinned and nodded. "I like your spirit, Red."

She met his fist bump then looked at me as I tried to hide my appreciative glance down her body, but by the color staining her cheeks, I suspected I wasn't as slick as I thought.

I redirected my attention to my drink. It was crisp, with a nice malty finish. "I love this one."

"I do, too," Bear said.

Connor shrugged. "Eh, it's all right."

Piper wasn't to be dismayed. She bent over closer to him, stretching diagonally across the bar, inching ever closer to me. She smelled like beer and fresh laundry. Who knew that combination smelled so good?

"You're a tough customer," she said to Connor. "But I'm going to crack you. If not with this last beer, then I'm going to come up with one you'll love."

Connor smirked. "You like a good challenge, huh? Me too." He held his glass out. "Do your worst."

She grinned, and I watched both of my friends practically drool over Piper as she poured out the last sample of beer. I could understand how hard it was *not* to become instantly infatuated with her—a woman who loved and brewed her own beer? If I hadn't known better, I'd have thought she was an alien sent down to Earth just for me.

Then again, maybe she was. I'd have to get a closer inspection to be sure.

"This is my Gray-Haired Lady." She handed the glasses out, but Bear and I waited as Connor tried it first. He swallowed one sip, then pitched his head back and polished it off.

"So?" she asked.

His smile grew slowly. "I love it."

"You do?" When he nodded, she did a little dorky dance with her fingers pointing up to the sky. "I did it! I found your drink."

"What is it?" I asked before I tasted it.

"It's a grisette. A dry, golden ale, similar to a saison."

Bear nodded along like he knew what she was talking about. He probably did. He was like a damn encyclopedia.

"Except saisons come from northern Belgium. Grisettes come from the south. They're both known as the working man's beer there. In fact, the grisette was named after the women who'd serve beer to the men who worked in the coal mines. *Gris* means gray in French, and those women wore gray dresses. At least, that's the story I've been told."

She talked animatedly, with her hands, and her excitement about something as boring as the differences between a saison and a grisette was contagious. I could listen to her for hours.

"I like it," I said, pointing to my empty glass. "But the amber ale is my favorite."

She nodded happily, almost bouncing on her toes. "What's your favorite, Bear?"

He scratched his chin through the thick mound of hair. "I really dig the flavor of the IPA, but I'm more of a stout man myself, so I'm going to go with the Brunette Beauty. You don't by any chance happen to have a real life Brunette Beauty in that cardboard box of yours, do you?"

"Plum out of them. Sorry."

"That's all right." Then he grinned. "What are you doing after this?"

I palmed his face. "Excuse this animal. He's not out of his cage much."

Piper patted Bear's arm, her hand so small comparatively. "Thanks for the offer, but I have a feeling you ask out a lot of girls."

"Not a lot . . ." Bear pursed his lips, then reconsidered. "A fair amount."

"There's a lid for every pot, but it's not me, my man."

I laughed, always fond of a girl who could hold her own with a bunch of guys.

"Hey, I've gotta go." Connor stood up and clapped Bear on the shoulder before turning to Piper. "It was nice meeting you," he said as he backed away, slinging on his coach's jacket with a picture of the school's mascot on the back.

Piper stared after his retreating form. "The Otters?"

"Yeah. A couple years ago the high school changed its mascot from the Indians, and they voted on the Otters."

She squinted up at me. "Truly terrifying."

Bear slapped his hand on the bar. "I'm getting out of here, too. Reed, I'll talk to you later. Red, I'm sure I'll see you around."

She shrugged. "Maybe."

Bear shook his head with a knowing smile. "Definitely." He pointed his thumb to her as if to say *Get a load of this one*, and then he was out the door, leaving us alone.

"So, Piper Williams of Out of the Bottle Brewery, how did you get started in all of this?"

She picked up the empty bottles and discarded tops as she began. "I'm originally from Fort Collins, Colorado, and I'm sure you know Colorado is a big craft brew state."

I nodded and leaned my hip against the bar, transfixed by the color of her rosy lips against her pale skin as she spoke.

"I tended bar at my uncle's restaurant during college and fell in love with the industry. After I graduated, I bounced around breweries learning everything I could. Then, about four years ago, I went to Berlin to become a brewmaster."

"Wow." I jerked my head back. "Are you even old enough to be a brewmaster?"

She gave me a funny look. "I'm twenty-seven. I lived in Germany for two years. Six months to complete the course, and another year and a half working in a brewery. Are you old enough to own a bar?" she asked with a twinge of hurt in her voice that had me wanting to sit on my heels like a bad puppy.

"Sorry, I'm just really impressed. I'm thirty, and I don't have a quarter of your experience, so maybe you should be running this place."

She fought a smile, and I thought it a small win. "Maybe."

"What made you leave Germany?"

Her eyes flitted around the room before landing back on me. "Time for a change, I guess," she said with a shrug. "I was offered an assistant brewer position here in Minneapolis. I did that for a while before I quit to make my own stuff. I've put all of my savings into this company, so if I fail I don't know what I'll do. Panhandle, maybe? Sell my hair . . . ?"

I stepped closer, leaving only a few inches of space between us. "I don't see how you can fail. You've made a great product," I said.

"I know it's great. I just have to start selling it."

"You will. I'm going to talk to Dave and buy three cases of each to start with."

"Oh my God. Really?" When I nodded, she launched herself at me. Her arms looped around my neck, squeezing tight. "That's amazing. You're amazing."

I hesitated a few seconds before wrapping my arms around her waist. "I'd be crazy not to sell your beer. It's a perfect fit with the kind of atmosphere I'm trying to build."

She backed away, the smile on her face big enough to power a small city. "Thank you, thank you, *thank you*." She rose up on her toes and laid a kiss on my cheek before gasping and covering her mouth with her hand. "I'm so sorry. That was unprofessional."

"Don't worry about it," I said with a shrug of my shoulder. If she'd known the unprofessional things knocking around in my head from having her in my arms for an innocent hug, she'd have been real shocked.

"Blake, thanks so much for this opportunity," she said, and I didn't care for this more rigid, less bubbly version of Piper.

I shook her hand. "It's my pleasure."

"Good luck with your opening." She smiled, put her wool-lined jacket on, and grabbed her cardboard box.

"Thanks. Maybe you'll be able to stop by some time?"

"Yeah, definitely."

She waved and flew out of the door, her long hair swinging in the wind. Not even ten seconds later, I got a text from Bear.

You think the carpet matches the drapes on that one?

I rolled my eyes.

There weren't many women I could say the first thing that attracted me to them was their knowledge of beer. In fact, Piper was the only one. But after that text, I couldn't help but think of what else I liked about her, including her easygoing personality and the nervous little glance she sent me over her shoulder before she left. Cute woman with good beer? I was at her mercy.

CHAPTER 4

Piper

I was still floating on cloud nine by the time I danced my way through my front door, carrying a shopping bag full of Pillsbury cake mix. Leo, Sonja's orange-and-white tabby, picked his head up from the sofa to blink at me in annoyance before going back to sleep.

"Sonja?" I called out as I kicked my boots off. She didn't answer, and I tried again. "Marco?"

"Polo!" she yelled back from somewhere upstairs.

I set my bag down on the kitchen counter. "Marco?"

Sonja almost never made any sound when she moved, and I didn't know she was behind me until she said, "Polo."

I jumped in surprise and spun around, clutching my chest. Sonja only grinned. "How'd it go?"

"He's going to sell my beer."

She squealed and threw her arms around me, and it took most of my strength to stay on my feet. For all the time I'd been living with her, I still wasn't used to the force of her "hugs." I was taller by a few inches, but with her better-than-Michelle-Obama arms I was almost positive she could bench-press me. I wasn't brave enough to let her try even though she'd asked me on multiple occasions.

"I'm so excited for you," Sonja said, hopping up on the counter with much more agility than Leo could pull off.

"We're celebrating," I said as I held up a box of cake mix. "Are you off sugar this week?"

"For you and for Funfetti, I'm back on sugar today." She grabbed the box and opened it with glee. "So what's the name of this place again?"

"The Public."

"What do you think of it?"

I sighed as I mentally recalled the gastropub, and Sonja laughed. "That good, huh?"

"It's cool and modern. Very hipster."

"You mean very Piper?"

"Very," I said, preheating our dinosaur oven. As usual, I ignored the weird clicking sound it made as it turned on. We ignored lots of little fixes that had to be made.

Our house, a cute little two-story with a trellis and a few hydrangea bushes, had been built in the fifties and sat on the outskirts of Minneapolis. It was the perfect place, and exactly what I'd imagined when Sonja first offered me the second room. Inside, though, the house needed a little TLC. The kitchen was mustard yellow with white cabinets and old appliances. The edges of the grapevine border wallpaper were peeling, and the Formica counter was much worse for wear. But until either of us hit the jackpot, we were bound to this place with our cheap landlord.

"Match made in heaven then," Sonja mused, and for a moment she made me wonder what she was actually referring to. "Out of the Bottle and the Public."

"I hope so," I said, answering my own thoughts as well as Sonja's. "How's your day been?"

She shrugged, making room for the eggs, butter, and oil I placed beside her on the counter. "Same old. Kicked some ass. Took some names."

"Not too tired, I hope." I handed her the mixing bowl and a spatula. "Get those arms to work."

Two hours later, we had twenty-four cupcakes cooled and iced, although thirty minutes in, Sonja had hightailed it out of the kitchen due to boredom and instead gone out for a run. I ended up stuffing my face with two cupcakes before she got home, lest I had to withstand her side-eye at my choice of dessert for dinner. But to hell with it, I was celebrating.

I grabbed my third—and most likely last—cupcake and skipped up to my room to call my parents.

My dad picked up after two rings. "Hello?"

"Hi, Dad."

"Pippi, how are ya, kid?"

My dad thought it hysterical that I had long red hair, was named Piper, and had been obsessed with watching *Pippi Longstocking* as a kid. I thought it only coincidental, but I'd long lost the battle of trying to stop him from calling me Pippi.

"Is Mom around?"

"Yeah."

"Get her on the line. I want to tell you both something."

I heard him call for my mom with a grainy "Chris, Number Two wants to speak to us."

He also thought it was funny to refer to me and my sisters by our birth order. Maybe it was his terrible sense of humor that had cursed him with three daughters instead of that boy he wanted.

I heard muffled rumblings, and I imagined my mother crossing the house in her favorite slippers. The same ones she'd been wearing for ten years. Every year, one of us went to Macy's to buy her a new pair to replace those old ones for her birthday, but they were always the exact same kind: fluffy wool on the inside, red flannel on the outside, and a no-slip grip bottom.

My mother had very specific footwear requirements.

"Hey, sweetie," she said. Her never-ending cheerfulness always put a smile on my face. I looked more like my paternal grandmother than either of my parents, but everyone said I had my mother's temperament. I didn't know if that was true or not. Always smiling and laughing, my mother had a calming influence on everyone around her. I didn't think I personally had that effect, but maybe my beer did.

"I have good news."

"What?" my dad asked.

"A gastropub is going to serve my beer."

My parents' cheers blended together with "That's wonderful, honey" and "Outstanding, Piper, knew you could do it."

"Thanks."

"What's the name of the place?" my dad asked, and I could hear him typing. He was forever Googling everything since he'd gotten a new laptop. Even silly things like *What does WTF mean?* or *Where to find Pokémon?*

"It's called the Public, but you probably won't be able to find anything on it since it's not open yet. The owner said—"

"Here it is," he said over me. "'Downtown Minneapolis will soon have a new pub. The Public, named for the first bars open to the general public in England, will open its doors on April twentieth.'" Dad continued to read while Mom took over the conversation.

"This is exciting, honey. I'm so proud of you."

"Thanks."

"How's everything else going? How's Sonja?"

"Everything's great. Sonja's—"

She barged into the room at that exact moment, wearing a sweaty long-sleeved T-shirt and a headband over her ears.

"Right here," I finished, looking to my friend. "Want to talk to my parents?"

She nodded and wiped her face with her headband before I put the phone on speaker and gave it to Sonja. "Hey, Mama, Papa, what's up?"

I flopped on my back with a laugh. My parents had come to help me when I'd first moved here and had visited twice more since, and somehow Sonja had wiggled her way into my family. She often talked to my parents when they called, and she and my mother were even Facebook friends, exchanging random goat videos since they were both desperate for a pet goat. In particular, a goat wearing a sweater.

"Did you get the recipe I sent you?" Sonja asked. She had my mother on a new paleo kick.

"I did, and I love it. Thank you."

"Hey," my dad said. "Here's a picture of the owner. Blake Reed. Son of politician Jacob Reed."

"He's handsome," my mother piped up.

"Really?" Sonja held the phone closer as if she could see the article through the sound waves. "What's he look like? Wait a minute. What am I saying?" She distractedly passed my cell phone back then pulled her own out.

"Honey, is he as handsome as that in real life?"

I didn't have time to answer my mother before Sonja grabbed my arm to pull me next to her, Blake's picture on her screen. "*Whoa.*"

"His hair is a bit longer, but yeah, he's pretty good-looking," I said as nonchalantly as possible.

Sonja nodded appreciatively while Mom went on about the qualities of his that she apparently had gathered from one picture.

"Mom, I'm not going to date someone I'm in business with."

"Yes," my dad agreed after he cleared his throat. "Pippi knows how to be a respectful businesswoman. She knows what she's doing."

"Well, you're the only one of my girls not married. I thought maybe—"

She thought she could go three for three in the happily-married-off daughters category. I knew my mom didn't mean anything by it, she'd just watched one too many episodes of *Say Yes to the Dress*. I, on the other hand, didn't care much for traditional things like white dresses and marriage certificates, especially after the Oskar fiasco back in Germany. I was fine with my life the way it was. Besides, if I wanted to find a boyfriend, it certainly wasn't going to be the owner of the bar who'd just agreed to sell Out of the Bottle. Major conflict of interest.

"Don't try to *Pride and Prejudice* me, Mom. I'll get married when or *if* I want to. I'll date who I want to date."

"You tell her," my dad said playfully, and I heard a smack on the other end and a laugh from my dad.

"All right, Piper, all right. We'll let you go now. We love you, and we're proud of you."

"Thanks. Love you, too," I said.

"Love you!" Sonja shouted as well.

My parents laughed, giving their final good-byes to the both of us before hanging up.

"Seriously, Piper, Blake Reed is one attractive man," Sonja said, and swooned.

"I know," I said, fluffing up my pillows before lying down

again. Sonja followed next to me, and I cringed. "You're all sweaty."

She ignored me, relaxing with her arms behind her head. "I think you should go for it."

"Go for what?"

She eyed me. "Blake."

"No."

Her eyebrow ticked up a suspicious centimeter, and I waved my hands back and forth. "No. *No.* I can't. My beer is going to be sold at his bar. It would look bad."

"You're being neurotic."

I sat up. "I'm being realistic. I don't need anyone attributing my success to some affair with a bar owner."

"Fine." She flicked her hand out to the side. "But there's nothing scandalous about bringing him a couple of those cupcakes downstairs. There are a few to spare even though I know you ate three."

I ignored her withering stare and thought about what she'd said. I wouldn't wreck my barely burgeoning career, but I could stop by.

For a chat.

With some cupcakes.

As a thank-you.

That's what an appreciative client would do. Build relationships. Totally acceptable.

"That's not a bad idea," I said, tilting my head to the side, convincing myself it would be for business and no other reason.

She elbowed my side. "And maybe you'll wear your good underwear and shave your legs."

I refused to laugh. "Don't push it." I booted her off my bed. "Go before you make a permanent outline of sweat on my sheets."

"Well, somebody should." She wiggled her brows.

I threw a pillow at her, missing by a few feet, as she ducked out of the room. I heard her laughing all the way down the hall.

"All right. You're good to go," one of the installers said as he stood up from the floor in front of the stove. He handed me a few papers to sign, and I caught him watching Piper out of the corner of his eye. I couldn't blame the guy. Piper had this aura about her that made you instantly interested. But for some reason there was a tightness in my chest.

I pushed the clipboard against him harder than necessary, snapping his attention away from Piper. "All set. Thanks for your help."

"No sweat." He shook my hand and gestured for his assistant to follow him out. "Good luck with everything."

I nodded and saw them out the back door before I turned around to Piper. She was leaning on the counter, and I tried, really tried, to keep my eyes off her, but I couldn't. Not off the shape of her legs, the curve of her hips, the line of her back and neck. I catalogued every inch. The small mole on her neck, above the collar of her shirt, and the freckles along the bridge of her nose and cheekbones. Her eyebrows as they rose over her wide green eyes.

I was caught. Staring.

I immediately dropped my attention to the floor. As if that would make me look less guilty. "So . . . you like elephants?"

"Huh?" Piper laughed, and I raised my head.

I pointed to her ears. "Your earrings. They're elephants."

She smiled and touched her earlobes. "They're my favorite."

"Why?" I moved closer to her, watching her fingers play with pieces of loose hair by her temple.

"They're strong and smart. Family-oriented. Did you know elephants mourn their dead? They have funerals and sometimes cry."

"I didn't know that."

She nodded. "They're known to hold trunks like we hold hands."

"That's . . ."

"Totally nerdy that I know random elephant facts." She waved her hands like she was trying to erase the conversation.

"I was going to say it's cute."

She paused and looked down at where our pinkies almost touched, then back up at me. "My sisters and I have matching tattoos." She pushed the sleeve on her right arm up to reveal the tattoo on her inner forearm, three little elephants walking in line, connected tail to trunk.

"You have two sisters?"

"Yeah." She pulled her sleeve in place, her hand back next to mine. "Laurie is older. She's a chemical engineer. Kayla's the baby, she's a graphic designer."

"And you're the poor, unloved middle child?" I joked, and she laughed.

"Exactly."

Another moment of silence descended between us.

"I guess this really wasn't much of a tour," I said after a while.

She shrugged. "It's okay."

I glanced at my cell phone to check the time, and we both spoke at once:

"I guess I better go" and "I'm starving, can I take you out?"

We both laughed and then started to do the same again, only to stop. She held her hands up, offering for me to speak.

"Do you want some pancakes?"

"Pancakes?"

I shrugged. "There's this place down in Edina that's got the best breakfasts you'll ever eat."

"But it's—" She checked her own phone. "Almost three o'clock in the afternoon."

I grinned. "Best pancake-eating time."

"We're working together now."

"I know."

Her green eyes met mine, apprehension behind them. "I can't . . ."

Her words faded, and to be honest, I was glad of it. I was attracted to Piper, and I didn't want to hear it was one-sided. But if her tortured face and nervous hair twirling were signs, I was sure I wasn't the only one feeling this thing between us.

"It's only pancakes," I said, hoping to coax her out.

She wrapped her hair around her index finger exactly three times before she gave in with a sigh. "Okay. Let's go get some pancakes."

"All right." I pivoted toward my office in the back.

Piper stuck her head in the doorway as I grabbed my coat, pointing to the calendar on my wall. "What's that?"

I tossed a beanie on my head. *"Nuns Having Fun."*

She stepped into the office and got up close to the pages, flipping through the pictures of women who'd taken vows of poverty, chastity, and obedience but in the pictures were doing things like riding Dumbo in Disneyworld. "This is the most ridiculous thing I think I've ever seen."

"I know." I put my car keys in my pocket. "It was Bear's birthday present to me. We all went to Catholic school, and he thought it was hysterical."

"I guess it—this one's drinking beer . . . ? I didn't realize nuns could take part in libations."

"I didn't, either, but they do have wine at mass," I said, and ushered her out of the office. "The nuns we had in school were cranky old bats. I can't picture Sister Patricia from sophomore theology ordering a pint." I locked the doors behind us and turned down the street to my car. "Do you mind if I drive?"

"Please," she said with a small smile, and fell into step next to me. Her hands were in her jacket pockets, but every once in a while our elbows tapped against each other. It might've been accidental on her part, but on mine it was absolutely on purpose.

I unlocked my car. "This one's me."

She sat down in the passenger seat of my Ford Escape crossover and touched the dashboard. "Is this new? It smells new."

We buckled up, and I pulled out on the road. "Relatively. I got it in January, as a present to myself. Well, this and the pub."

I realized she hadn't responded after a few seconds, and I turned to her. She gaped at me. "You gave yourself the pub?"

"Well . . ." When she put it like that, it sounded douchey. I tapped on the blinker as I merged onto the highway. "When I turned thirty, I was able to access my trust fund from my grandparents. There was enough money in there to buy myself a new car and open up the Public."

"You have a trust fund?"

I glanced in her direction. "You say it like you've never heard of one before."

"I have, but"—her face scrunched up in confusion—"isn't your dad a politician?"

The little tidbit of personal information she knew had me grinning. "Have you been Googling me?"

"Pfft." She waved me off. "No."

I raised a brow.

She squeezed her thumb and index finger together, mouthing "A little bit," then straightened her smile. "But seriously, trust fund?"

"I've had a lot of good luck by coming into family money, but like you, I put everything I had into my place. If I fail at this, I'll have nothing left. And my parents aren't so happy with me right now."

"Why not?"

"They think the Public is a terrible idea. They think I

should do something respectable, something worthy of our family's name."

"How very old money of them. I'm sorry. That sucks."

I nodded in agreement. "My dad's dad owned a bunch of factories, and his dad before that owned everything on this side of the Mississippi," I said with a sigh. My family's lineage was a long one, and after a while I got tired of hearing and talking about it. That's why I broke away from them, from *it*.

It being that thing. The power-of-God attitude, the passive-aggression, the thinking-that-they're-always-right thing. "My father can be a real dick sometimes, but my grandfather was beyond. I took pleasure in using the old bastard's money to make my dream come true."

Piper patted my shoulder, and I turned to look at her as I slowed for the yield sign at the bottom of the exit. She grinned, a sparkle in her eyes.

"What?" I asked, biting back my own grin at her playful expression.

"Do you still have any more of that bastard's money? There's a new fourteen-gallon fermenter I've had my eye on for a while."

This time I let my smile go. I liked a woman who wanted beer brewing equipment over jewelry. "How about a few siphon hoses or a CO_2 tank?"

She crossed her legs and sucked in air through her teeth. "Oh, I love it when you talk dirty to me."

CHAPTER 6

Piper

You didn't tell me we were coming to the *Original* Pancake House. Now I feel underdressed."

Blake surveyed me as he took his beanie off, dragging a hand through his hair. And it was almost impossible not to stare. But I didn't. These were *business* pancakes.

"Only the best when I take a girl out," he said, gently pushing me in front of him to follow the hostess.

As we walked past the wooden tables and chairs and floral wallpaper, I felt like I was at my grandmother's house. The place was packed, and sounds of chatter and patrons eating surrounded us, but the only thing I could concentrate on was the slight pressure of Blake's palm on my back. When we reached our booth, he moved away, and I immediately missed the feel of his hand as I slid across the worn vinyl seat.

The hostess handed us laminated menus and said our waiter would be with us shortly.

Blake didn't even spare a glance at the menu as he began to play with the sugars, putting them all in the same direction.

"You know what you're getting already?" I asked.

"Two by four," he said, righting the jellies stacked up in their holders.

"What's that?"

"Four pancakes, two eggs on the side." He lifted his eyes to me when I laughed at him. "What?"

I pointed to the plastic jelly holder. "What's with that?"

He tried to suppress a shy grin. "I like things in order."

"I bet you fold your fitted sheet, too." I was kidding him. He looked at me sheepishly.

"No, you don't."

"I do." He nodded.

"How? Why? No one folds their fitted sheet."

"I watched a tutorial on YouTube."

An incredulous chuckle escaped me, and he laughed in spite of himself. "I swear it fits better in the closet folded."

"Okay," I said, shaking my head and looking down at the menu.

"What looks good to you?"

"I don't know." I'd already eaten lunch, but the smells of bacon, cinnamon, and coffee coming from the kitchen made my mouth water.

The waiter, who looked young enough to be in high school, put our waters and coffee mugs down in front of us. "You ready to order?"

Blake raised an eyebrow in question, and I nodded, telling the waiter, "The chocolate chip pancakes, please."

Blake placed his order then turned to me. "You got a sweet tooth?"

I leaned forward with my arms on the table, matching his posture. "More like sweet mouth."

He smirked, his eyes dropping to said sweet mouth, and I replayed those words in my head.

"I didn't mean it to sound like that," I said, hiding my embarrassment behind a sip of water, trying to ignore his teasing gaze.

His hazel eyes, which looked more brown today, had the ability to make me melt, and I didn't want to lose my cool in the Original Pancake House before I even got to try my flapjacks. Though it was hard to contain the flutter in my belly when he smiled and said, "A sweet mouth is my favorite thing."

My cheeks stung with heat, and I knew I turned ten shades of red. I was so out of my element—I hadn't dated since breaking up with Oskar and moving back to the States. My flirting skills were rusty, to say the least. But lucky for me, this wasn't a date.

I didn't have to worry about how I was focused on my career, or that I sometimes didn't bother to shave my legs for weeks at a time. I didn't need to remember that I avoided men in general because I didn't want to have to choose between my job or a nice smile. Nope, I didn't have to bother with any of those things.

I fiddled with my utensils. "Tell me about Connor and Bear. Have you guys known each other long?"

He sat back in his chair and scratched at the bit of scruff on his chin. His fingernails made a scraping sound against his skin, and suddenly I was very interested in the texture of his stubble. What would it feel like against my palm? Against my cheek? My lips?

Was I allowed to fantasize during a non-date? I needed to consult the rule book, if it even existed.

I missed the first thing he said and had to ask him to repeat it. He huffed out a small laugh as if he knew why I couldn't concentrate, and repeated, "We met in high school. We were all on the football team."

"You played football?" I couldn't imagine long and lean Blake, with that pretty boy face, playing football.

"Yeah, I was a receiver. Although I wasn't very good. I did it more for the girls and the recognition."

"I like that you can admit it," I said, adding three packets of sugar to my coffee.

Blake smirked. "You want some coffee with that sugar?"

I waved him off and took a sip, his eyes once again following the movement of my lips. I hated to admit it, on this non-date, that he made my insides go all gooey and I was afraid I'd become a puddle on the floor.

"What position did Bear play?" I asked, since the guy looked like he could terrorize the field.

"I don't remember. Sophomore year, he sprouted up like

five inches and he ended up playing hockey instead. You don't recognize him?"

When I shook my head, he grabbed his phone and pulled up a picture. It was Bear in a Chicago Blackhawks jersey, a closed-lip smile on his face. It was a roster picture, like the ones they show on television when they introduce the lineup.

"Bear played professional hockey?"

Blake nodded. "They recruited him out of high school. He retired last year."

I set my half-empty mug on the table. "I've never watched hockey before."

"But you live in Minnesota. Surely you've seen at least one game."

I shook my head. I wasn't really into sports. "Everything I know about hockey, I learned from *Mighty Ducks*."

"No boyfriend who watched hockey?"

"No." I huffed. "My ex wasn't much of a sports fan. He was . . . the intellectual type."

"You say that like it's a bad thing," he said a bit defensively.

"It's not." I tapped my fingers on the table while I came up with the words to describe Oskar. "But he liked to think he knew better than everyone else."

"Ah." He nodded in understanding. "Well, I'll take you to a game. You'll love it."

I highly doubted I'd love it, but I had a hard time turning

his invitation down. Instead I avoided answering altogether. "And Connor? What's his deal?"

Blake shifted in his seat, making room for his food when the waiter returned. He thanked him and lifted his fork to eat. "He went to a DIII school for football, but tore up his knee and had to quit. He teaches history and coaches at Jackson High."

"And what about you? What happened to you after high school?"

He finished chewing his bite before he answered. "I went to Northwestern, like my father. Got into law school, like my father. Then moved back to St. Paul to work at the same firm my father did."

"I'm sensing a pattern," I said, scraping up a tiny bit of melted chocolate from my plate with my fork.

"One that I broke when I quit to open the Public. He assumed I was going to follow in his footsteps."

Blake rolled his eyes, and I reached out to tap his hand. "You know what you need? A good motivational poster in your office. Something that says, 'Keep your eyes on the prize.'"

His dimple appeared. "Do you have a motivational poster?"

"Yeah," I said. "It's the one with the cat hanging on the rope. It says, 'Hang in there.'"

He laughed, his head bent over his plate, as he said softly, "How have I not met you before?" then shoveled another forkful in his mouth.

I didn't know if it was rhetorical or not, or if I was even supposed to hear it. Either way, his words made something inside me twist all up, and suddenly I couldn't eat another bite.

Instead, I listened to his stories about Connor and Bear, and he asked questions about my family, my sisters. And then when he'd finished his plate, he scooted my leftovers toward him to finish them off, too.

When the bill came, I tried to pay my half, but he wouldn't have it, tossing a balled-up napkin at me, saying, "Let me be a gentleman."

He even went one step further in the chivalry category and held the passenger door open for me when we reached his car. The ride back to the pub was a little longer since we hit rush-hour traffic, but I didn't mind. Blake was a natural speaker, funny and intelligent. I could see how he would've been a good lawyer, holding the attention of the court. Not to mention, he probably rocked a suit like nobody's business.

"Thanks for the second lunch," I said once he'd parked.

"My pleasure. We should do it again sometime."

I nodded, loosening my jacket, suddenly a bit too hot. We went from having lots of room between us to just a few inches when he leaned toward me. And I did the same, like a gravitational force pulled me to him. Some random Top 40 song was playing on the radio, but I couldn't hear it over the rush of blood in my ears as Blake brought one hand up to my cheek and closed the distance between us.

His breath smelled sweet, like maple syrup, and I closed my eyes waiting for the touch of his lips to mine.

It had been a long time since I'd been kissed, let alone given myself permission to let my guard down. I'd worked hard the past few years, forgoing a lot, including romance, to bring my business to life. And now that it was finally coming to fruition—

"Wait. Wait," I said, putting my hands on his chest, realizing I was only two seconds away from crushing my lips to his. No matter how much I wanted it, I knew this was a bad idea. "Hold on a second."

"What?" His eyes were wide with something that was probably reflected back in my own.

"We can't do this," I said. "*I* can't do this."

He backed away, but only a few centimeters. "Why?"

I smoothed my hair and pulled at my jacket like it would protect me. "Brewing is a small community."

His gaze was sweetly patient as he waited for me to continue.

"I can't be known as the chick who sleeps with someone to sell my beer."

That's when his dimple reappeared. "So . . ." He gently wrapped his hands around my upper arms, pulling me toward him again. "That means you want to sleep with me?"

"Blake," I half whined, half warned because, yes, I wanted to sleep with him. I wanted to have his mouth all over me. I wanted to learn the sturdiness of every muscle I knew was hiding under his thin sweater. "Business partners, remember?

I lost my head for a minute, but we can't do this. I refuse to be reduced to a stereotype."

He stared at me for a moment, looking deep into my eyes before he relented and sat back in his seat. "All right. I understand."

Unable to look at him, I dropped my gaze to my lap and picked up my purse. One peek at his dimple or a flash of his charming smile and I'd backtrack.

Instead, I reached for the door handle, but he stopped me with a gentle touch on my elbow. "Will you still come to the opening next week? Bring some friends. Everybody's going to love your beer."

I chanced a glance over my shoulder. My first instinct was to say no, but I was excited for him, for me, to see first-hand what people thought of Out of the Bottle, and I nodded. "I'll be there."

"Great. I'll see you later then."

I hopped out of the SUV and waved to him through the tinted window. I didn't know if he could see me or not, but I got the feeling he was watching me as I made my way to my car.

I hated that I wanted him to watch me. I hated that I really liked him. I hated that for the first time ever my dream was actually a problem.

CHAPTER 7

Blake

I tried to get out of the monthly dinner with my parents at their house in St. Paul. I had too much stuff to do before the opening, but my mother had laid the guilt on thick.

"There are a lot of changes going on right now, and we need you here," she'd said to me on the phone yesterday. "Can't you make a little time to come to dinner? It's important."

But to her, *everything* was important. The luncheons with the girls, the cocktail parties, the every-third-Sunday family dinners—it was all important.

Yet, it wasn't.

None of it meant anything. Meaningless chatter with vapid people. And my mother was the ultimate peacock among all the brightly colored birds.

My father wasn't much better. Sure, he was charming on the outside, but inside he was a son of a bitch. He could be mean to the point of cruel sometimes, especially to his staff. His sharp words had been turned on me often enough that I knew better than to trust his smile.

The problem was they were the only family I had.

But the thought of spending four agonizing hours with them right now, when I could be home or at the Public doing something worthwhile, almost had me swerving my car off the Ford Parkway Bridge just to escape. There were only so many "safe" topics I could stick to before we started arguing. Mostly over my life choices or politics. Sometimes over whether I needed a haircut or if my shoes matched my belt, depending on how much my mother had to drink.

I didn't expect anything different tonight.

I turned down Summit Avenue and parked outside my parents' house, an old Georgian Colonial mansion. The neighborhood was a tourist attraction, filled with big turn-of-the-century homes. The magnificence of the street couldn't be denied, but as I opened my car door and planted my feet on the sidewalk, the beauty turned my stomach. The house I grew up in was representative of my family— beautiful on the outside, cold on the inside. It was huge, much more than what four people needed, but it had been in the family so long I don't think they ever considered living anywhere else.

I checked my phone one last time, praying for an emergency from someone. A come-here-quick! text. But nothing.

Sighing, I walked up the long sidewalk and had only just finished knocking when my mother opened the door.

"Darling," she said, smiling. She put her hands on my shoulders and tugged me down a few inches so she could kiss both of my cheeks. Like she was Parisian or something— my mother grew up on a farm in Northfield.

"Hey, Mom," I said, stepping over the threshold. Soft classical music played in the background, as Sandra, the housekeeper, took my coat. Sandra was relatively new; she'd only been around for the last year or so, since Michelle left.

Michelle was a fantastic woman and single mom. When her kid got accepted to the University of Minnesota, she'd asked my parents for a raise. They'd gotten rid of her instead.

"Hi, Sandra, nice to see you again."

She smiled, but didn't say anything. I guess after Michelle had supposedly "spoken out of turn," my mother ran a tighter ship nowadays.

"Come, Blake, your sister and father are in the drawing room," Mom said with a wave of her hand. Her heels clacked on the dark hardwood floors as we made our way down the hall to the drawing room. Not the living room. The *drawing room*.

"Hey, Dad. Tiff."

Tiffany, my sister, the Kim Kardashian of Minnesota. If selfies were a sport, she'd quite possibly medal in the dimwit Olympics. At one point, I actually thought her face might get stuck in that stupid pout, or maybe she'd eventually go blind from staring at the screen of her phone for too long, but it hadn't happened. Yet.

Neither of them looked up. My dad had his Crown

Royal on the rocks in one hand and his iPad in the other. My sister typed away on her cell.

"Honey, what would you like to drink?" my mother asked from the wet bar by the fireplace.

A fifth of Everclear. "I'm fine for now, thanks."

She nodded and sat down with her own martini.

"How are you?"

I stretched my legs out, my arms resting on the back of the uncomfortable love seat I sat on. "Fine. Getting ready for the opening."

My father snorted.

"Are you coming?" I asked no one in particular.

Tiff lifted her face to me, smirking. "Sure. I'll come support my big brother." It wasn't support she wanted to give, it was free drinks she wanted to get.

"Dad?" I asked, already knowing the answer.

He closed his iPad and sat up. "Your mother and I are going to a fundraiser that night."

"What's the fundraiser for?" I asked less out of politeness or curiosity and more out of trying to fill up the dead air between us all.

"That's what I wanted to talk to you about." He cleared his throat. "Tiffany, put your phone down, this is important."

After a few seconds of her tapping and another prompt from Mom, she finally put it facedown next to her.

"I've been talking to Fred for the past couple of weeks, and we've decided it's time for me to run for Senate."

"But you're already a senator," my brainless wonder of a sister pointed out.

"He means federal senator," I said. "You know, for the United States Congress."

She nodded, but I doubt she got it. My sister floated through life on her looks and sparkling personality.

Dad looked at me. "That means I'm going to be traveling a lot more once campaign season starts. I'm going to need everyone to be at their best."

AKA: Don't screw this up for me.

"It'll look good if I have my family with me at speaking engagements and major events." He put his hand on Tiffany's knee. "We're all under scrutiny here. You need to watch who you talk to, what you say, what you post on your social media." Then he turned back to me. "You might want to think about having someone else run the bar."

"Why?"

Dad patronized me with a simmering look like I was a child. He twiddled his fingers in the air. "You've had your little vacation, but now it's time to get back to the real world. You did what you wanted to do with your business venture, and now hopefully you got it out of your system."

"There is nothing to get out of my system. The Public is what I want, and it's not going anywhere. *I'm* not going anywhere."

"It's a *bar*," my mother said, choking on the word as if it were difficult for her to say.

"It's a gastropub. Not a whorehouse."

Mom put her hand over her heart. "Blake, language. Please."

I ignored her and met my father's gaze. "Wouldn't it be good for you? Your only son opening a business, helping the economy?"

"It's my only son opening a bar to serve alcohol. Lord knows to whom. And whatever else will go on there."

I bent over, my hands in my hair. "Jesus Christ, Dad. You act like I'm selling meth out of the trunk of my car. I'm doing something I'm passionate about. That should be something you're proud of."

"What would make me proud is if you went back to the firm. You had a great job there, on track for partner. Our name's on the sign, for God's sake."

Of course that's what really pissed him off. Me leaving Morris, Jacobson & Reed made him look bad.

"That's not what I want," I gritted out.

"How's it going to look in interviews when next to your name it says *Blake Reed, bartender*?"

"I'm a bar *owner*. And so what? Don't have people interview me then. It doesn't matter."

Dad sighed heavily through his nose, the sure sign he was frustrated. "We've been through this before, in my first electoral bid, and now it will be even more difficult."

"And maybe think about cutting your hair," my mother added as the cherry on top. "There will be lots of opportunities for photos."

"Dinner is ready," Sandra said, just in the nick of time.

I rushed by her to the dining room, hoping to eat as fast as I could. The sooner my plate was empty, the sooner I could leave.

My mother was the last to sit, smiling like she always does, holding out her hands for grace like she was the Virgin Mary. She bowed her head, as usual, murmuring her prayer of thanks, so that when she spoke publicly about her moral values it wasn't all a complete lie.

I dug into the roast like it was my last meal, trying to ignore my sister's chattering about her latest job, this one as an executive assistant to someone at a PR firm, but I couldn't stay quiet any longer. Not after she listed all of her duties: taking care of this guy's day planner, scheduling meetings, setting up for employee lunches . . .

"You're a secretary," I said.

"No. An executive assistant. To the assistant VP."

"That's a fancy term for secretary." I bit into a roll.

She scrunched her face up, nose and cheeks bunching together. Her thinking face.

My mother scolded me with a ruffle of her napkin. "Don't be so condescending, Blake."

"I'm not. I'm just saying, you're getting paid to be the assistant's assistant." I pointed my finger back and forth between my sister and me while I addressed my parents. "You don't like that I *own* my own business, but you're okay with her wasting her college degree?"

I couldn't help but think of Piper. As my sister, no doubt, whiled her days at work away on social media and flirted her way through life, Piper busted down glass ceilings and worked against stereotypes to build her own brand.

My father made that sighing noise again. "Lofty talk coming from you. At least Tiffany has a sturdy, reliable job with benefits and a future."

I ignored his jab as the energy drained out of me. There was no use fighting with them. It wasn't a battle I could win.

Thirty minutes later, I hightailed it out of the dining room, despite my mother's protests to wait for dessert, and brushed by Sandra to grab my coat.

I needed a beer stat.

I texted the guys to round them up, and to my good fortune, they were already at Connor's house drinking. The drive to his place gave me enough time to shake off the worst of my anger toward my family.

I let myself in, gave my friends a brisk head nod, and went straight to the kitchen. I grabbed a bottle of whatever Connor had in the fridge before going back into the living room.

Bear inclined the neck of his bottle toward me. "What's got your panties in a bunch?"

"Dinner with the family."

Bear huffed. "What happened this time?"

"Jacob Reed is running for U.S. Senate, and I apparently need to find a respectable job to make him look good."

"The usual then?" Bear laughed to himself, then motioned to Connor. "At least this kid has some good news."

I turned to Connor. "What?"

"Nelson is retiring," he said, readjusting his hat.

I almost spit out my beer, partly because it wasn't good, but mostly out of shock. "Really?"

Dick Nelson had been the football coach for something like thirty years. He was a legend, although in recent years the team's record had been horrible. "Are you gonna get the job?" I asked.

"Don't know," Connor said, around a sip of his beer.

"You'll get it," Bear said. "You're the offensive coordinator and a great coach. You're the logical choice."

I nodded in agreement, and Connor shrugged. "I hope so. I could use the money, and the boys could use a winning record."

I threw my feet up on an ottoman as *SportsCenter* returned from commercial break, and my mind wandered back to Piper for what was probably the hundred and fifteenth time today.

Piper was fresh. Sharp and witty, not afraid to speak her mind. In the few hours I'd spent with her, she'd never censored herself. She didn't wear a lot of makeup and wore the ugliest pair of worn combat boots I'd ever seen. She didn't even tie the laces up. She was carefree, and I was hopelessly attracted to following wherever the wind blew her.

Unfortunately, the wind wasn't blowing in my direction.

I'd told her I'd take her to a hockey game one day, and I wanted to keep that promise. Trouble was, she wasn't super-keen on continuing to see me in a nonprofessional manner.

I had to respect her wishes, much as I didn't like them.

I understood where she was coming from. It must be tough to be a woman in a business of men who tended to be pompous know-it-alls—I'd experienced their upturned noses firsthand at a conference when I confused a witbier and hefeweizen. They were a tough crowd to please and even tougher to be accepted into. I could see how it might look bad if we were to develop a relationship, but on the other hand, who gave a shit?

I wanted Piper.

"Hey." Bear knocked his foot with mine. "You look possessed or something. Your eyes are all glazed over."

I shook away thoughts of Piper and took a sip of my beer. God, Piper's beer was so much better than this crap. I told my friends so.

"Then get her to give us some. In fact, does she need a taste-tester? I'll gladly volunteer," Bear said.

I put the bottle down on the coffee table. "She's coming on Friday. You can ask her then."

He raised his brows. "Oh, I can make her come on Friday. You betcha."

"Shut up," I said, throwing a pillow at Bear.

"Dude. Saying 'you betcha' doesn't make what you said any less sleazy," Connor said.

"Seriously, though, does she have a boyfriend?" Bear asked, with a ridiculous eyebrow wiggle.

I rolled my eyes. "You're not her type."

Bear propped the pillow up behind his head. "And I suppose you know what her type is?"

"Well, I figure it's me since we almost made out the other day." As soon as the words were out of my mouth, I mentally smacked myself. I was sure Piper wouldn't want these guys to know what went down between us, and I sure as hell didn't want their curious stares now.

Connor eyed me from under the brim of his hat. "Almost?"

I shrugged, not answering his question.

"As usual, you couldn't close the deal," Bear said with a shake of his head.

"Hey." I sat up, garnering both of my friends' full attention. "It's not like that. Piper is great." Connor and Bear nodded, their faces a little taken aback by my sudden change in attitude. "And we're in a professional relationship. So . . . you know . . ."

"No." Bear circled his hand for me to continue. "We don't know."

"No mixing business with pleasure."

Connor smirked. "Would've been more convincing if you hadn't touched your eyebrow."

"You always touch your eyebrow when you lie," Bear agreed.

"I need new friends," I grumbled, pushing as far back into the couch as possible to cover up whatever truth I couldn't hide from my oldest buddies.

Bear huffed out a laugh. "Nah. You'd never replace us. Who would you braid your hair with then?"

CHAPTER 8

Piper

There were no parking spaces left on the same block as the Public, and I took that as a good sign, so instead of complaining about having to walk three blocks in these heeled boots, I reveled in each sloshy step. The closer I got to the bar, the more noise I heard, the more people I saw milling about outside. Opening night, and Blake had a smash hit on his hands.

After our almost-kiss in his car, I'd waffled back and forth about whether to come tonight. I didn't want to give him the wrong impression that our relationship was anything other than professional. But in the end, Sonja talked me into it and these boots. Although she couldn't come with me because she was a big loser who'd scheduled an early morning workout session tomorrow, so I was stuck by myself. In these toe-pinching boots.

The place was packed, and I held my bag close to my side

so the poster I'd brought wouldn't get bent. I slowly made my way to the back, hoping to find Blake. He wasn't there, but Bear and Connor were laughing with a group of other guys.

"Hey." I tapped Connor's shoulder for his attention, and he offered the smallest of smiles to me.

"Hey, Piper."

"Have you seen Blake anywhere?"

"He's around somewhere." He lifted his glass. "The Gray-Haired Lady," he said with a salute to me.

"There she is!" Big burly arms snaked around my middle, lifting me up with a shake before putting me back down. "Girl of the hour." I turned around and did a double take. I knew it was Bear from his meaty arms, but without his bushy beard I couldn't be sure.

"You shaved." My words came out more like an accusation than a question.

He ran a hand over his jaw. "I go into hibernation for the winter and grow a beard. Once the weather starts to warm up, I shave it off."

"Makes sense," I said, staring at him. Without the beard, you could see how handsome he was. The gnarly-tattoos and dirty-looking-man-bun kind of handsome.

He pointed to the rest of the men surrounding us. "I've got them all drinking your beer. They love it."

They all nodded at me, and I smiled. "Awesome."

Bear introduced me to a Danny, Johnny, and Tyler, I think. With their plaid shirts and facial hair, it was hard to keep them straight.

"Take your jacket off, stay awhile," Bear said, motioning to an open seat at the bar.

I sat down and ordered my amber ale from a pretty bartender with purple streaks in her hair.

"Put it on my tab," Bear said before a voice rang out.

"No, put it on mine."

I turned to find Blake just a few feet away, his dimple winking at me. He held up one finger, silently telling me to wait as he put away some clean glasses and took care of a customer's tab. He made his way around the bar, wiping his hands on his jeans before holding his arms out.

"Thanks for coming," he said in my ear when I hugged him.

I knew I probably shouldn't have, but between my excitement over his success and my delight at seeing his face again, I couldn't help it. I hung on to his shoulders, making sure I didn't wobble when I stepped back. He looked me up and down. "You look pretty tonight. Taller than usual."

His compliments never failed to make me feel a twinge in my belly like I was thirteen again and talking to the cutest boy in class. I lifted my foot up to show him the three-inch heels. "I never wear shoes like this. I'll be lucky if I don't break my neck."

"Why'd you wear them?"

"My friend said they made my legs look good."

One side of his mouth slanted up sinfully. "I can't argue with that." He held on to my hand as I sat back down on my stool. "I'm happy you're here. Everyone is loving your beer."

My cheeks hurt from all the smiling. "Glad to hear it." I picked up the bag I brought. "For you."

"Another present?" He unwrapped the plastic around the poster and unrolled it, laughing. "You actually bought me a poster."

"I did." It pictured a giraffe and the words *Stand Tall and Dream Big* next to it.

"I love it," he said with another chuckle, showing it to his friends. They didn't find it funny, not being in on our joke, and went back to their conversation. The only thing that mattered to me, though, was Blake's smile.

"Thank you." He leaned down a fraction of an inch, as if he was going to kiss me, but then straightened, rolling up the poster.

I immediately felt at a loss. This was what I'd wanted, right? I wasn't going to date him, or kiss him, or engage in any other physical activity that I dreamed up when I let my guard down.

"I'll be back," he told me, and headed in the direction of his office. I spun on my stool, taking in everyone at the bar. A good number of businesspeople looked as if they'd come right from work, but there were also a lot of denim and flannel shirts on hardy Minnesota types. And there was what looked like an even amount of men and women, a good mix of a crowd that would only be positive for the future of this place.

I saw Tim, who I used to work for at Twin Cities Brew Company, sitting at a high-top table in the corner. Deep in conversation with two other guys who looked vaguely familiar, probably other brewers, he didn't see me. I was once again reminded how small the brewing community was, and how reputation meant everything. We were all friendly with one another, helped each other along with tastings and festivals, and I would never want to do anything to jeopardize the others' support. If they got a whiff of anything happening between Blake and me, I knew it could be my downfall. I walked a tightrope, being the only woman around here who brewed, and I didn't need anything to push me over the edge.

And, of course, that's when Blake came back into my view. Because the universe hated me.

He was being his charming self, smiling and shaking hands. There was no job, too big or too little, that he didn't do. He helped the bar back clean up and restock, hopped behind the bar to pour, and never once failed to have a conversation with every patron who approached him. His parents were crazy for not wanting him to do this.

Seeing him here, in his element, it was obvious this was what he was meant to do.

"Hey, boys."

The sultry voice lifted me from my daydreams about Blake, and I glanced over my shoulder. A beautiful woman stood among the men next to me. She playfully put her head on—was it Tyler's shoulder? Or maybe it was Johnny's—and tugged at long dark hair that curled over her shoulder. She leaned forward, the slinky material of her dress showing off her near-perfect cleavage. It didn't seem to escape the attention of any of the guys.

"Haven't seen you in a while," the woman said to Bear with a hand on his back.

He looked down at her briefly. "How's it going, Tiff?"

"Fine. Fine. How 'bout yourself?"

He nodded but sipped his drink, ending the conversation. Connor plain ignored her, his eyes on the television above the bar.

Clearly they weren't fond of her, but I didn't know why. She was model beautiful, with a tiny waist and endlessly long legs in heels higher than mine. But she knew how to walk in them. I looked down at my own outfit, feeling like a troll in the long tunic top and black skinny jeans. This *was* my dressy outfit.

A man next to me offered the woman his seat, and she sat down with a smile then looked over at me, giving me a quick once-over. Clearly, I wasn't any competition for her, so she didn't bother with me. She sat up against the bar, typing on her phone, barely looking up when the bartender asked, "What'll it be?"

"Dirty martini, extra olives. And put it on Blake's tab."

My eyebrows rose in curiosity. This woman obviously knew Blake well. From her familiarity with everyone and the way she looked, I assumed maybe they were together. But it didn't matter to me.

Not really.

I had no claim on Blake. We weren't together. We were partners in business, that was it.

Although . . . I had to find out who she was. You know,

for curiosity's sake. When I cleared my throat and she didn't acknowledge me, I tried another tack. "Excuse me?"

She didn't take her eyes off her phone. "Yeah?"

"You know Blake?"

She nodded, answering distractedly. "He's my brother."

Oh. A little bit embarrassed, a little bit happy, a little bit confused. Ever since my relationship with Oskar, I'd had a bad habit of underestimating myself. Most of the time it was in this career that I'd chosen, but sometimes with men, too. I didn't think I was good enough, and it snuck up at the worst times, like now, next to a woman I didn't think I could compare to.

With a heavy sigh, I took a big gulp of my beer and kept myself busy with my cell phone. I pulled up Twitter and read through a couple of things before I found an interesting tweet from @BeerasaurusRex. He was a local guy who ran a blog on craft beers. And he was apparently at the Public tonight. He'd posted a picture of a flight, listing the names of each one. And there at the end was my Natural Red!

I smiled to myself, giddy inside. My leg bounced as I continued to read the reviews of each beer until he got to mine.

@BeerasaurusRex The Natural Red is from @OutOfTheBottleBrewery and a little too malty for a real Amber. Seems it isn't so natural after all. Should go back in the bottle.

My gut flopped. He didn't like it. My first review was a thumbs-down, and if I hadn't been in front of so many people I'd probably have cried. I tried to shake it off, but the longer I sat at the bar, the more edgy I became. I turned back to Tim's table, noticing that all of the men there had their heads bent together. To my left, some random guy was staring at me, and I tried to think if I recognized him or not. A couple directly behind me whispered. Was BeerasaurusRex one of them?

I felt claustrophobic.

I needed to leave.

I stood up and waved to Bear, Connor, and their friends. "It was nice seeing you again."

"You're leaving already?" Bear asked, wrapping his arm around my shoulders. "You just got here."

"Past my bedtime." I smiled, hoping that it seemed genuine. I didn't want Blake's friends to know I was the tiniest bit humiliated.

"Are you sure?" Bear scanned the bar. "You barely had time to talk to Blake."

"It's fine," I said, stepping away from him. "I've gotta go."

But Bear wasn't paying attention to me anymore. He motioned to Blake, who was quickly approaching. "Yo, your girl here is leaving already."

"What?" Blake whipped his head to me, his hand on my waist. "Really?"

I shouldn't have liked him touching me, but I did. Still, I stepped away from his embrace. A girl had to hold her ground. "Yeah. You've got your friends here . . ."

"I don't care about them," he said, dragging me away from the group. "It's still early yet. Not even nine o'clock."

"I know. I had a long day," I lied. "And there's so many

people here it's kind of like . . ." I extended my fingers and pretended to scream.

Blake actually smiled. "It's crazy, right? It's packed, but that's great."

I nodded and put my jacket on. "Thanks for inviting me tonight." I slung my purse over my arm. "I had a great time. I'm sure you're going to have a ton of success here."

I tried to run-walk as fast as I could out of the door, but with my heels I was more like a toddler learning to walk for the first time, and Blake easily caught up to me just outside the door. He grabbed my elbow.

"Hey. *Hey.*"

I turned to him, and he took his time staring at me, his gaze bouncing all over my face. It was my favorite quality about him. When he looked at me, he really *looked* at me.

"Piper, I wish you didn't have to leave yet, I'd like to—"

I don't know what came over me, but I stood up on my toes, leaned in to his cheek, and kissed the place where his dimple usually resided. His breath caught, and he held on to both of my arms, keeping me in place, then suddenly his lips were on mine.

And I traveled to a different world. One where no one else existed but Blake and me. I felt myself falling further and further into this universe where there was no noise, no other people, no light or dark, just us, kissing forever.

Then reality crashed in on us when the door to the bar opened with a loud bang. I jolted back, feeling the weight of eyes on me. And they didn't belong to Blake.

I turned to my left and there was Tim. He did a double take at me, his eyes narrowing when he realized what I was doing. I dropped my head down, desperate to come up with an excuse. Anything to explain away this kiss. But before I could come up with something, Tim cleared his throat. "Going to introduce me?"

I took a breath and met his stare. "Blake, this is Tim, head brewer at Twin Cities Brew Company and my old boss. Tim, this is Blake, my . . ."

Blake reached for Tim's outstretched hand and filled in the blank. "I'm the owner," he said, pointing to the Public.

"Oh." Tim looked between the two of us before saying to Blake, "Nice place."

"Thanks."

I shifted my weight during the awkward pause that lasted a lifetime, until Tim broke it up. "I had your Brunette tonight. Working on anything new?"

"Not right now. Just focused on getting my name out there," I said.

Tim nodded, his silence saying more than any words could. He'd been somewhat of a mentor to me when I worked for him, and I knew whatever it was he'd seen tonight, he didn't like. I trusted Tim; he was smart and honest, sometimes a little too honest. He was hard on me, but in a good way. He'd forced me to be strong, to not back down when I was faced with criticism. He'd also introduced me to a lot of people and pushed me to go out on my own. If he thought something fishy was going on, I'd lose the faith of not only him, but a lot of other people he had influence over.

"Well," he said after a while, putting his hand on my shoulder. "It was good seeing you." Then to Blake, "Nice meeting you."

He gave me one more look, a warning. It told me to focus. Stay in my lane. Avoid drama. Basically the opposite of what I had been doing just now.

As soon as Tim was out of earshot, Blake wrapped his hand around my wrist. "Piper, I—"

"Don't."

"You don't even know what I'm going to say."

"Whatever it is, don't. You can't say it. I can't hear it. And we certainly can't kiss again."

Blake let go of me with a curt "Fine."

But I didn't have time to be bothered with petting his bruised ego. I needed to rescue my own. Keep my train from falling off the tracks. Not only had I kissed Blake when I'd expressly said it wouldn't happen, but I'd done it out in the open, where anyone could see.

I darted away, headed home to my bed and hopefully a new start tomorrow.

CHAPTER 9

Piper

"Sonja!" I slammed the front door. "You'd better be awake!" I ran upstairs, tripping over Leo, lounging below the top step. "Seriously?"

He eyed me, unmoving, as I stepped over him into the hallway and down to Sonja's room. I barged in without knocking, and she looked up at me from her spot on the floor, legs straddled. "Are you *trying* to wake the neighborhood with your screaming?"

"If it wasn't for your incredibly fit body, I'd think you were a ninety-year-old, in bed by eight o'clock."

"I'm not in bed," she said, pointing to the carpet. "And it's not eight o'clock."

"Nine-twenty-three. Close enough." I flopped on her bed, looking up at her ceiling.

"So how was it?"

"Horrible."

"Why? What happened?"

I turned onto my stomach, watching as she shook her legs out and brought them straight in front of her, flexing and pointing her feet. "BeerasaurusRex hated my beer and Blake kissed me."

"What? Wait." She hopped up onto her knees, face screwed up. "One thing at a time. What is a Beerasaurus?"

"He's a beer blogger who tweeted about me. He didn't like my beer."

She sneered. "His name is Beerasaurus?"

I nodded. "Rex. BeerasaurusRex. And he didn't like me."

"He gave your beer a bad review, not you."

"Same thing."

She rolled her head in a circle before looking at me. "*Not* the same thing. He doesn't like your beer. And he's stupid. Next." A laugh escaped me when she waved her hand at Beerasaurus like a gnat. "You kissed Blake."

"Well . . ." I bit my lip. "Technically he kissed me."

"You say that like it's a bad thing. Was it bad? Does he kiss like a Saint Bernard?" She visibly shivered. "Remember that guy, Rob, who looked like Steph Curry? He was a sloppy kisser. A real shame."

I shook my head. "No. It was good. Fantastic." I laid my head on my arm. "Probably the best kiss I've ever had."

Sonja scooted closer to the bed, laying her head near mine. "Explain. Are you sure you know the definition of horrible?"

I let out a groan along with some of my worry. "Tim saw us."

"What? I can't understand you when your face is smooshed in the mattress."

I propped my chin on my hand. "We were outside having this *moment*, and Tim walked out."

"Tim as in your boss from Twin Cities, Tim?"

"It was so embarrassing."

She tilted her head to the side. "Again I ask: did you have spit hanging from your mouth or what?"

"Ew, no. Why do you think everyone kisses like an animal?"

"So what's the big deal?" She shrugged. "You kissed a cute guy. You should be excited." She poked my arm. "You need to stop worrying about what other people think. God forbid you act like a woman and not a robot who brews beer all the time."

That was the pot calling the kettle black. Sonja was 100 percent focused on her goals, rarely leaving time for anything else, including men. "Oh, okay, Miss I-can't-go-out-because-of-my-6-a.m.-workout."

She narrowed her eyes at me. "Hey, there's nothing wrong with being *scheduled*. I make time for guys; they just need to fit into the fifteen minutes I have free."

"A real wild thing you are."

"Come on. Meditate with me, it'll make you feel better." When I groaned like I was in pain, she pulled my hand, and I ungracefully rolled off the bed and into her lap. "It'll relax you," she said, looking at me upside down.

It didn't. Not the meditation I did with Sonja, not the hot bath I took, and not the white noise I tried listening to so I could fall asleep. After midnight, I gave up and grabbed my phone to stalk Blake on every social media platform there was. He was a popular guy, and there were plenty of pictures to look at, Facebook statuses to decipher.

When I finally forced myself to turn my phone off hours later, I tossed and turned, my brain unable to shut down. My mind couldn't stop replaying tonight. I remembered the way he'd held me and the scent of his cologne. I could still feel his lips on mine and where his fingertips had touched my cheek.

In any other place, in any other time, I would've jumped at the chance to go out with Blake. But at this point, when I had four tastings lined up for bars, and a brew festival, I needed to keep my head down and to keep working. Now wasn't the time to start a relationship, especially with someone who could influence my career in a particularly negative way.

By the time I fell asleep, the sky had started to turn gray with the rising sun, so I only got about three hours of shuteye. I dragged myself out of bed to make a cup of coffee. I wasn't much of a caffeine person, but I needed it to help me get through the next couple of hours while I brewed.

When I went to open the refrigerator, I saw a note stuck on with a bumblebee magnet, written in Sonja's loopy cursive. "'I'll be home around noon,'" I read out loud to myself. "'Don't eat the chicken.'" It was signed with a smiley face.

I was half-tempted to eat the chicken just to piss her off. Sonja was a terrific cook, and always made extra for me, but she stuck to a specific meal calendar. One too many complex carbohydrates and her whole day was thrown off. And she told me I needed to relax?

I laughed to myself and stepped outside to start my day. Opening up the garage, I took a deep, calming breath. Brewing was my real meditation. With music on, I didn't have to think as I got to work sanitizing my equipment in order to brew another batch of Platinum Blonde.

From start to finish it took about six hours until I got it into the fermenter, but I got a little break as the wort boiled. I set my timer for sixty minutes and sat down, intending to cut out labels for bottles. I had only gotten through a few pages when my cell phone rang. It was Tim.

And like that my zen was gone.

I punched the green Accept button, ready with a cheerful greeting, hoping he was calling to congratulate me on my first sale, but I had a feeling that wasn't the case. "Hey, Tim, miss me since last night?" I joked. He hummed a hello, and I braced myself for this conversation. "So, what's up?"

Tim was never one to pull punches, and he certainly didn't pull any this time. "I gotta tell you, I was really surprised by what I saw between you and Blake last night."

I didn't say anything. I didn't know what to say.

"You know you're the first and only woman to ever work at Twin Cities," he said.

"I know."

"You're very talented at what you do."

"Thank you."

"So why would you think it's a good idea to get wrapped up with Blake Reed?"

I didn't necessarily think it was a good idea, but the way he seemed to be scolding me only made me want to argue. "To be honest, Tim, I wasn't thinking about much last night when you walked out of the Public. But it's really none of your business, is it?"

"I've vouched for you."

"So?" I huffed.

"Your beer is good. You don't need any help from anyone."

"That's a backhanded compliment if I ever heard one. I'm not getting help from Blake or anyone else." I began to pace, my pulse picking up with the need to defend myself.

"You have to understand how it looked from my point of view, Piper. What if someone else walked out? What if it was another bar owner, and he expected the same thing to stock your beer in his bar?"

"That'd be a pretty awful person, wouldn't it? I don't associate with awful people or men who sexually harass women."

He was quiet for a few moments while my temper rose.

"Piper, I don't care about your personal life. Truly, I don't. But I do care about you."

I breathed in my nose and out my mouth, like Sonja told me to all the time. Yes, Tim had been my boss, a really good one at that, but I'd earned my position at Twin Cities. The fact that he, of all people, would insinuate anything else was beyond insulting. I didn't appreciate him treating me like I couldn't decide for myself what I should or should not do. Like I didn't know what it was like to be a woman in this field.

"I shouldn't have to tell you that when you're the sole proprietor, everything comes back to you. You're the creator *and* the salesperson. You need to be above the fray at all times."

"I also don't need this business mansplained to me."

"I don't know what that means."

"Of course you don't." I laughed. "You said it yourself, I was the only woman to ever work at Twin Cities. I'm usually the only woman anywhere when it comes to brewing, so please don't tell me about how things look from your perspective. I'm well aware of what men think about me, no matter what I do, whether it's true or not."

"Piper, I didn't mean to—"

"Just forget it." I sliced my hand through the air. "I appreciate your concern, but I can take care of myself. I don't make any decisions lightly."

He hummed again. "Well, I guess that's it then. It was good seeing you, Piper. Good luck with everything. Really, I mean it."

"Thanks." I hung up and sunk into my chair, my adrenaline wearing off. I doubted myself sometimes, struggling with my confidence, but when push came to shove, I was able to fight when I needed to.

I went back to cutting labels, trying to blow off steam. With each snip of the paper cutter, my anger dropped a notch. I was almost even-keeled, but when my alarm went off it skyrocketed again.

"Son of a—" I jumped up, going to the boiling pot. I'd missed my hop schedule, throwing off this batch. "Dammit!"

I created my recipes after a lot of tests and had them down to a science. But because I lacked automatic equipment, I had to manually be precise in every detail so each beer from the same line tasted the same. One too many malts or not enough fermentation time would affect the flavor. Or in this case, missing the time to put the Lemondrop hops in the boil would completely change this Platinum Blonde batch.

It might be good to drink, but if it wasn't consistent with my brand, I couldn't sell it. It was a complete waste of money, time, and resources.

I wanted to scream or pull my hair out.

But I did neither as I turned the boiler down. Maybe I could gift this off-brand beer to my friends as birthday presents. I chilled the brew and poured it into the fermenter before cleaning up and heading back inside, cursing Tim, the phone call, this day, the whole weekend.

I wasn't in the right head space, too jumbled up with thoughts of Blake and Out of the Bottle. Sonja walked into the kitchen right after me, tossed her Beats headphones on the counter, and plopped her gym bag on the floor.

"Why, don't you just look chipper as a daisy today," she

said when I bent over, my elbows on the counter. "What happened?"

I shook my head, reluctant to answer.

She washed her hands in the sink before grabbing a banana from the hanging fruit basket. "Tell me."

I relayed my conversation with Tim and how I'd screwed up my beer because of it. "And it all comes back to *him*," I said. "If it weren't for Blake, I wouldn't have argued with Tim, which made me miss the hop schedule. It's all his fault, really."

Sonja let out a dubious laugh. "Did you ever think maybe if you let yourself give in, you wouldn't be a walking mess? Ever since you met him, you've been second-guessing everything. Go with your gut. You like him, see what happens." She slung her arm around my shoulders. "If you don't, you might end up burning the garage down."

I had a strong fight-or-flight response. When it came to Out of the Bottle, I always fought. But when it came to my personal life, I always flew. Maybe it was about time to put my dukes up.

"Yeah. I guess."

Sonja shook me until I smiled. "You want to go to the movies? I'll buy."

"You know just what to say to a girl, don't you?" I laughed.

She turned away with a sly wink over her shoulder. "If only everyone were as easy as you."

CHAPTER 10

Blake

It had been almost two weeks since the Public opened, and it had gotten only positive reviews so far. Day and night, I searched for criticisms, reading Yelp, TripAdvisor, and blogs for what people thought. I'd become addicted to it, needing the reassurance that the pub was going to be okay. That the risk was worth it.

I was in Connor's car when Bear batted my phone out of my hands from the back seat. "Put that away, dude. You're going to go crazy."

"I already am crazy," I said, pocketing the device.

"I think it's safe to say you'll be making back three times your investment soon enough," Connor said, turning into the State Fairgrounds parking lot. "I think it'll be our new coaches' hangout after games this season."

"You hear anything else about the position?" I asked, pointing to an empty parking space.

He shook his head. "Just trying to get the team ready for next year. Working them hard in the weight room is all I can do for now."

I knew the head coaching position was really important to him, and I patted him on the shoulder, hoping for the best, as he shut the ignition off.

Chilly air hit me as soon as I opened the door, but the cold didn't seem to have deterred anyone from turning out for the craft brew festival. With three tents set up, hordes of people were huddled together drinking inside and outside. Over one hundred beers were available to sample from around the country, a good opportunity to taste different brews and possibly pick some for the Public.

Connor, as usual, went to the line with the shortest wait, while Bear and I were a little more particular. I got a double IPA from a brewery in Milwaukee, Bear had a porter from Devils Backbone, while Connor went with a lager.

We milled around for a while, shooting the shit, drinking different beers. Bear even got stopped for a photo. It didn't happen that often anymore, but apparently the fan hailed from Chicago and recognized him right away. As Bear finished up talking, I spotted a sign in the last tent boasting a familiar-looking logo. And underneath it was Piper.

I strode toward her before I'd even made the conscious decision to do so. I hadn't seen her since she ran away from my pub like she was on fire. And it was my fault.

I had kissed her.

I couldn't help it. Not after she leaned into me, pressing

her sweet lips against my cheek. She'd smelled so good and felt so warm against me. She was everything I liked best, and I wondered if she knew it when she looked up at me.

"Hey there."

"Hi." Her eyes softened the slightest bit before glancing away when she grabbed a rag to wipe up a few drops of spilled beer from the table. "What can I get for you?"

I looked over the choices she had. The Platinum Blonde or Natural Red. "I'll take the Blonde."

She filled my cup and handed it back to me, our fingers brushing in the exchange. That's when I noticed she still hadn't smiled at me, and before I could try to make her, a woman elbowed her in the side.

"Hi, I'm Sonja," she said, sticking her hand out. Sonja was small with pretty features. Her skin and eyes were the same warm brown, and she had a sweet smile that belied the strength of her handshake.

"Blake," I said. "Do you work with Piper?"

"Friends and roommates." Sonja briefly glanced at Piper. "You the owner of the Public?"

When I nodded, she leaned forward, hands on the table in front of her, and I noticed the boxing logo on her hoodie. Before I could ask about it, she went on, "Pipes tells me your gastropub is pretty awesome. I'll have to check it out, especially if you're serving her beer. It's the only kind I drink."

I smiled at Piper. "Good friend you got here."

That earned a grin, but it wasn't at me. It was aimed at Sonja. "The best."

That's when Bear and Connor caught up to us and greeted Piper, who in turn introduced Sonja.

She pointed at Bear. "You look familiar. Do I know you from somewhere?"

"I used to play pro hockey," he said, and Sonja snapped her fingers.

"Yeah. You're Thomas Behr. You played for the Black-hawks."

Connor huffed out a laugh. "Recognized twice in one day. You gonna be on the cover of magazines now?"

"Shut up," Bear said to him before turning back to Sonja. "You a big fan of hockey?"

She shrugged one shoulder. "As much as the next Minnesota girl is. You mind if we take a picture?"

"Yeah, sure."

Sonja sidled up next to Bear, though she had to balance on her tiptoes with more than a foot of height difference between them. She tossed her phone to Connor, who stepped away to take their picture, and suddenly it was only me and Piper.

My eyes fell to my now-empty cup. "Can we talk about what happened at the opening?"

She stopped me with a halting gesture. "I wasn't lying when I told you it wasn't right for us to . . . date. I've got a lot riding on this," she said, pointing to her booth. "I can't screw it up."

I wanted to argue with her, but now wasn't the time, especially since we were surrounded by everyone else in her

field. It'd be a terrible time to say *Forget them and kiss me
again*.

A group of four guys approached the table, and Piper's
demeanor changed. Her lips tipped up into her happy-go-
lucky smile and her shoulders rounded back into a friendly,
confident posture.

"So, you run this place?" one of them asked.

"I'm the owner and brewer," she said with a proud grin.

One of the other guys, obviously tipsy, leaned over the
table into her space, offering what he probably thought was
a flirtatious smirk. In reality, it was smarmy.

"Well, color me surprised," he said. He might as well
have been a dog for the way he drooled over her. "I've never
met a woman brewer before. Are you sure you're the one in
charge, and not just the pretty girl they put up front to sell
the beer?"

Piper's jaw clenched. "I'm sure."

And then this douchebag proceeded to point to the logo
on her shirt, his finger way too close to her chest for my lik-
ing. She brushed him away with a congenial laugh and took
a step back as she filled their cups with samples.

I wanted to say something, save her from this guy, but I
didn't have to. His buddies pulled him away as they moved
on, and I breathed a sigh of relief. Piper's eyes met mine, and
her cheeks were flushed. I didn't know if it was from anger
or embarrassment, but either way I didn't like it.

"Does that happen to you a lot?"

She shrugged her answer, but I knew the truth. A beautiful woman hanging out with drunk guys all the time, I could only imagine what kinds of things were said to her.

"That's shitty," I said.

She waved it off, setting her shoulders. "Whatever."

I stepped to the edge of the table, getting as close to her as possible without going to her side. "It's not whatever. Nobody should be saying crap like that to you. It's not right."

"Listen." She tipped her head up to me. "I've got thick skin, all right? He didn't hurt my feelings. I'm fine. If I weren't, I wouldn't still be doing this after all these years."

I nodded, proudly. "Like a boss."

She grinned widely. "Like a motherfucking boss."

Damn, I wanted to kiss her even more after that line. I settled for a high five.

I wrapped my fingers around her palm, squeezing every last second out of this small contact as possible. She finally pulled away from me, and I didn't try to fight it.

"Looks like they're getting along," she said, pointing over my shoulder.

I followed her gaze to find Bear curled over Sonja's shoulder looking at her phone. "Guess so."

"Good," she said, turning into me. Probably a little closer than she'd expected, since her eyes widened. "Maybe they can do all the sporty things together that she tries to force me to do."

I tilted my head, admiring the freckles on her nose. "You're not into sporty things?"

"Not with that one," she said, motioning with her head

toward Sonja. "She takes all the fun out of hikes. She's like, 'Oh come on, let's run to the top, it'll be fun. Oh, why don't you come to the gym with me to box, it'll be fine.'" She held up her right hand. "That's how I broke my middle finger. Do you know how hard it is to brew with your fingers all bandaged and taped together?"

I ran my thumb over said middle finger. "I'm guessing pretty hard."

She didn't answer, her eyes trained on where I touched her. After a moment, her attention flashed around me, clearly trying to avoid eye contact. "Wonder where Connor got to."

I scanned the crowd and spotted his ratty high school football hat. I narrowed my eyes to get a better look at the woman he was speaking to. She was older. Pretty, but definitely older. "Over there," I said, motioning with my empty cup. "He's got a thing for cougars."

Her eyebrows rose. "Really? Didn't expect that. From Bear, yes. Connor, no."

"It's the quiet ones you gotta watch out for," I whispered, conspiratorially.

She smirked. "I'll remember that."

Sonja skipped up to the table, while Bear meandered behind her.

Another group approached Piper's table, and I stepped out of the way. "Maybe I'll see you later?"

She tossed me a quick nod and smile, and I wanted later to be now.

CHAPTER 11

Piper

I'm all dressed up with nowhere to go," I shouted from the living room. I ran my fingers through Leo's thick fur, making sure none of it clung to my jeans or favorite shirt. It was a special occasion, so I'd broken out the clingy V-neck. Paired with one of Victoria's secrets, I actually owned some cleavage.

"Grab the tequila. Let's do a shot." Sonja flitted down the stairs.

I turned to her, dressed in a cute romper with tights—a style I could never pull off. "You want to do a shot?"

She threw me a look and waltzed past me to the kitchen. "It's my birthday. I only turn twenty-seven once. I'm doing a shot—shots—of tequila."

I pushed off the sofa and followed her. "Alrighty then."

She grabbed the bottle of the rarely touched Patron and two small glasses, then poured an overflowing shot into each one.

I picked mine up, wiping the excess liquid off with my thumb. "To my best friend."

"To my birthday."

"To a hundred more."

"To staying twenty-seven forever," she said, and I clinked my glass to hers then swallowed down the clear liquor, grimacing at the burn. Sonja immediately filled up the glasses again. She saluted me and downed the second shot.

When Sonja wanted to do something, she went all in. And tonight—

"I'm getting drunk!"

I echoed her cheer with my own and swallowed the tequila. I couldn't let my best friend get drunk by herself, but I stopped her from pouring me a third shot and pulled up Uber on my phone. "Where do you want to go?"

I hoped she'd say the Public. The last time I saw Blake, at the beer festival, he'd had this cute hopeful look on his face; he told me he'd see me later, then leaned in close to whisper, "Sooner rather than later, Piper."

And then I'd died.

My heart felt like it had stopped for a good five seconds after he said my name and offered me a quick glimpse of his dimple before he slipped into the crowd, pulling Bear and Connor along with him.

Since then, I'd been itching to see him and his lopsided smile again. And hear his voice. And stare into his blue-green-brown eyes. But, whatever, it's not like I was desperate.

Not really.

"The Public, obviously," Sonja said, and took shot number three.

My best friend, she never let me down.

"We gotta see your boyfriend."

I typed the address into the app. "Not my boyfriend."

Her voice lifted to an annoyingly high lilt in a spot-on impression of a ten-year-old. "But you want him to be."

I didn't have an argument there, so I took the middle schooler's way out and echoed her words back with just as irritating a nasally voice, then showed her my phone. "Our ride will be here in four minutes."

"Enough time for one more shot."

I filled up a glass of water. "Or to chug this down." She begrudgingly drank it as I put the liquor away. "I'll get ya drunk, but I won't clean up your puke."

"Some friend you are."

I pushed her shoulder. She retaliated with a pretend right hook. God forbid she actually landed that thing, or I might not be going out tonight.

We grabbed our purses and headed outside to meet Lucy, our sixty-six-year-old driver, who regaled us with the time she snuck backstage at a concert on her twenty-first birthday and gave a blow job to Peter Frampton. She was apparently a well-known groupie in the Midwest.

"Thanks a lot," I said, stepping out of the car.

"No problem."

I waved and pivoted around.

Sonja swiped some lip gloss on. "Lucy is kind of awesome."

"Right?"

It was a Friday night, and the weather was warm enough that a lot of people were barhopping downtown. And from the number of patrons inside, it seemed a lot of them were hopping to the Public.

"There's Bear." Sonja pointed at the bar, and it didn't escape my attention how she ran a hand over her hair.

"Sonja," I said, halting our steps. "Do you have a thing for Bear?"

She snorted. "No."

I eyed her.

"No. We just have a lot in common. We text sometimes. I don't have time for a man, you know that."

I nodded, but my suspicion went up a notch when Bear turned around, and her face split with a big grin.

"Hey, birthday girl." He gave her a high five then threw his arm around her shoulders, pulling her close.

Connor stood behind Bear. He offered me a wave, his face somewhat hidden behind his ever-present baseball hat. "Hey."

I leaned my elbow on the bar. "What is this? *Cheers?*"

"Where everybody knows your name," Bear said.

Blake suddenly appeared at my shoulder behind the bar.

"Does that make me Sam?" he asked no one in particular, but his eyes ended up on me. He checked me out from head to toe, and when his eyes lit up, I'd never been happier that

I'd spent half an hour digging through the clearance bin at Express for a top.

I nodded in answer to his question, and he gave me one of his cocky grins. "Are you going to be my Diane?"

I bit back my own smile, fighting the resounding voice in my head shouting *Yes! Yes! Yes!*

"How about getting this lady a birthday drink?" I said instead, pulling Sonja to me.

"What'll it be?"

Sonja almost never drank, but when she did it was usually vodka with a twist. Something about drinking alcohol straight without mixers for less sugar and carbs and blah blah blah. But tonight she threw caution to the wind.

"I'll have your finest beer, please."

Blake rapped his knuckles on the bar twice before grabbing a glass to pour her a Natural Red. He placed it in front of her. "Only the best."

He looked to me then for my order. "I'm going with the Brunette tonight."

He poured expertly, just a touch of foam at the top. "Brunette Beauty, straight out of the bottle." He handed it to me, and I had a feeling he brushed my fingers on purpose. "You know, this is one of my top sellers."

My face felt like it was going to split in half because my smile was so big, and I turned in a circle, doing a little dance. One of my beers was a top seller. *I* was a top seller.

And BeerasaurusRex could kiss my ass.

I caught Blake staring at said ass over my shoulder, and I

savored the attention. The more I hung around him, the harder it was to control my desire. I knew it was a bad idea to want to be with him, yet as long as his heated gaze was on me, I didn't care.

"If it's selling, I'm happy."

"Me too. Listen," he said, bending to put his forearms on the bar to speak quietly to me. "I know this isn't the best time to talk shop, but I was thinking for the summer, I could get—"

Bear butted into the conversation. "Hey. No business at the dinner table."

"Not a dinner table," I pointed out.

He held up a fry from the plate of whatever sandwich he'd eaten. "Close enough."

Sonja stole the fry and ate it.

Bear flicked his finger back and forth between himself and Sonja. "So, that's how it's gonna be between us?"

"Yup."

"You better watch it," he said, teasing. "Next time you might lose a hand."

Sonja waved his warning off. "It's my birthday."

"That's actually a good idea," I said. "Base layer to soak up the alcohol." I turned back to Blake. "Can I have an order of fries?"

"Sure. Anything you want."

"And a shot of tequila!" Sonja added.

Before I could say any different, Bear circled his index finger. "Round of shots for all of us."

Connor clapped his hands once and turned his hat backwards. "Bear's paying."

Bear nodded. "Line 'em up, Reed."

Blake checked with me, his eyebrow raised, and I shrugged. "You heard the man. Line 'em up."

He set five shot glasses on the bar and poured from a bottle that came from his top shelf. I handed them all out, and Blake came around to our side of the bar, right behind me.

We all lifted our glasses in the air, and Blake surreptitiously slipped his arm around my waist, tugging me back against him, making it nearly impossible for me not to sigh out loud in contentment.

He said something but I missed it, too enthralled by the feel of his chest against my back and the citrus-and-cedar smell of his cologne. I wanted nothing more than to taste his lips again, and out of the corner of my eye, I caught the way his mouth quirked up as if he knew exactly what he was doing to me.

Bear brought me out of my trance with his deep "Happy birthday!"

We all followed suit and clinked glasses before drinking down our shots. Sonja threw her hands up in the air, bouncing up and down. "The champ is here!"

That was shot number three for me in under ninety minutes—I was still clearheaded enough to know it was my last, but tipsy enough to not second-guess it when I spun around in Blake's arm and put my hands on his chest.

He was solid underneath my fingers, and I somehow resisted dragging my nails down to his stomach.

We were just a few inches away from each other, and he ducked his chin down. "Feeling good?"

"Feeling fantastic."

He started to step back from me, but I stopped him, latching my fingers around his wrists. He pursed his lips, gazing down at me like an adult would indulge a child. "What?"

"You're not staying to hang out with us? With me?"

The side of his mouth tipped up. "You want me to stay with you?"

My body buzzed with excitement, my insides warmed. "Yes."

He ran his fingers through my hair and tucked it behind my ears, then rested his hand on my shoulder. "I like when you wear your hair down."

"I like . . ." My words faded when his thumb skimmed back and forth over my throat.

"You like . . . what?"

Between the alcohol buzz and Blake's hands, I couldn't think of one thing. Nothing. Completely blank.

He smiled knowingly. "Lemme grab you some french fries. Don't let anyone take my spot."

As soon as he was out of earshot, Sonja was on me. "Those are some major heart-eye emojis you're giving off."

I brought my drink to my lips, taking a sip to give me a moment. "Am not."

She shot me a look. "I'd say you're a few hours away

from the one with the heart between the heads." She paused to take a gulp of her beer. "You know which one I'm talking about?"

"Get out of here with your emojis." I laughed. "Go be your own." I pushed her back toward Bear before turning into the bar to drink my beer. Less than a minute later I got a text from Sonja. A couple of heart-eye emojis, flamenco ladies, beers, cats with the heart eyes, and approximately fifteen eggplants and cherries. Subtle she was not.

CHAPTER 12

Blake

It was well after midnight by the time we all moved over to a table and decided to play a drinking game. First it was quarters, which Connor won with single-minded focus. Then categories, but we were all too buzzed to think of anything good, so we kept naming animals you find in a zoo. It was arguable that you could find any animal in a zoo. Because it was a zoo.

We were all pretty drunk when someone—I don't know who—suggested I find a deck of cards. I tossed the small cardboard box on the table and sat next to Piper. She was lovely. I didn't know if I'd ever used that word before, but I started to think it was underutilized in modern society.

I wrapped my hand around her neck, underneath her sheet of soft, red waves. "Did I tell you, you look lovely to-night?"

Her mouth turned up in a lazy smile. "No."

"You look lovely tonight."

She let out a giggle and rested her temple on my shoulder. I moved my hand down to her waist and pointed to the deck. "What are we playing?"

Sonja, who had lived up to her self-proclaimed name of "The Champ" by keeping up with Bear drink for drink, shuffled the deck. "Bullshit?"

No one disagreed, and she dealt. Piper didn't move from my one-armed hold, which made it difficult for me to arrange my cards, but I didn't have it in me to let go. Our close quarters also made it easier to see her cards.

She tossed a trio of cards facedown on the table. "Three fours."

While Sonja yelled out the accusation, I whispered it into her ear. "Bullshit."

She turned into me so my lips scraped the shell of her ear and temple, and I noticed her slight tremble.

She sat up and grabbed the stack of cards with a grumble, then realized how well I could see her hand when she looked at me over her shoulder. When she couldn't hold her scolding face any longer, she broke out into a laugh as she settled back next to me, her left leg pressed against my right. Her hip along mine, her shoulder tucked under my arm.

By the time last call rolled around, we were all slow to move. Piper was the first to stand, pointing at the bathroom, soundlessly letting us know where she was going. Connor, with his hat on sideways, sat up. His eyes were bleary and red as he threw his car keys on the table. "I'm done. Some-one call me a cab."

Sonja frowned. "Where's the after-party at?"

Bear tapped on his phone. "Want to share an Uber?"

Connor mumbled his answer into his elbow when he put his head back down. Sonja agreed, drinking the dregs from her glass.

"Car will be here in a minute," Bear said.

Sonja's face brightened. "Is it Lucy?"

"Who's Lucy?" I asked.

In her drunken state, Sonja ignored me, dancing with her hands up, singing "Lucy in the Sky with Diamonds."

"All right, you. I think this party has officially come to a close." Bear threw her over his shoulder, heading to the door, but I jumped out to stop them.

"What about Piper?"

Connor trudged past me. "She's in the bathroom."

"I know that. I mean, you're not waiting for her?"

"Nope." Sonja picked her head up, her face red, most likely from the mixture of alcohol and hanging upside down. "She's all yours. Get that eggplant," she said amid drunken giggles. Bear pretended to drop her, and she shrieked. "Your hands can't hit what your eyes can't see!"

Bear gave me a salute before they left in a blur of arms and legs, with Connor dutifully following. He patted me on the arm on his way out, mumbling something about "Don't screw this up."

And coming from Connor, who rarely commented on his own love life, let alone anyone else's, it was the best advice I was going to get.

I walked behind the bar just as Piper came out of the bathroom. "Where is everybody?"

"They headed out. Sonja was pretty plastered."

Piper's head swiveled to the door and back, a confused expression taking over. "How's she getting home?"

"The guys are sharing an Uber with her." At her suspicious eyes, I held my hands up in defense of my friends. "They'll get her home safe."

"I don't doubt that. Even drunk Sonja could break your jaw." She plopped down on the barstool in front of me, her eyes still narrowed.

"We can hang out a bit here or you can go home if you want. Whatever," I said, but it wasn't *whatever* for me. I wanted her to stay.

She cast her eyes down to where her fingers played with a few drops of condensation from an empty glass, but she hadn't moved so I figured she wasn't leaving anytime soon. I helped the bartenders clean and close up. Then Piper and I were alone.

"It's so quiet," she said, and I plugged my phone into the stereo system to put music on before I sat down next to her.

I grabbed the deck of cards. "What do you think? Up for another game?"

She eyed me over her beer bottle as she took a sip, and

one more time tonight I was tempted to kiss her. "What are we playing?"

"Pick a card," I said, setting the deck down between us. "Low card has to tell a secret."

She leaned toward me, giving me an eyeful when her shirt gaped open. Her bra was purple with tiny pink bows on each strap, and it took Herculean effort to pick my eyes up.

"You're on."

We each reached for a card at the same time, our fingers crashing together, but I backed off, letting her go first. She showed me a three. I picked a nine.

"I hate cooked vegetables."

"What?" I huffed. "That's not a secret."

"Yes, it is."

"Hating soggy carrots is an aversion, not a secret."

She ignored my protests and picked another card. This time it was a jack. I pulled a six. "I'm going to go your chickenshit route and say I don't like milk."

She looked at me like I was crazy. "You don't like milk?"

"No."

"But what do you put in your cereal?"

I swallowed a gulp of beer. "I don't really eat cereal."

"You don't eat cereal?" When I laughed at her incredulous squeak, she smacked her palm on the bar. "But what do you have for breakfast?"

"Coffee. Sometimes a protein shake or eggs. Pancakes, if I feel like making them."

She gawked at me, her hand on her heart. "I'm obsessed

with cereal. It's one of my favorite foods. Cocoa Puffs, Apple Jacks, Cheerios, Frosted Flakes, Boo Berry at Halloween time."

"Boo Berry." I slapped my thigh in delight. 'Cause I was drunk. "I forgot about that."

"I love Boo Berry. More than Count Chocula or Franken Berry."

"Are you some kind of cereal connoisseur?"

She nodded seriously. "Yes. Yes, I am."

My smile was uncontrollable around this girl, and I had a hard time keeping my hands to myself tonight. She didn't seem to mind at all, though. I drew my fingers down her cheek, then rested my hand on the outside of her thigh, moving us so we sat facing each other, both of her knees between mine.

"Your turn," I said, motioning to the cards.

She picked a ten. I got a queen.

"Make it a real secret this time."

Her eyes went to the ceiling, her index finger scratching absently on the bar. "Okay." She focused on me. "I don't know how to swim."

I cocked my head, surprised. "You never learned?"

"A kid pushed me into the pool when I was really little, and I almost drowned. I've been afraid ever since."

"Wow." I spread my fingers over the top of her thigh. "You don't go in water at all?"

"I go in but only until about my waist, where I can stand."

"Just enough to get wet," I said as lasciviously as I could.

She laughed, pushing my shoulder. "Go home, you're drunk."

Instead we both pulled another card. This time I had the low four. "I know all the lyrics to *Big Willie Style*."

"The Will Smith song?"

I hesitated to answer. "The Will Smith album."

She busted out with a big snort, clapping her hands. "Please. Please rap something."

I sat back and cleared my throat, ready to put on my finest performance of "Gettin' Jiggy with It." I threw out the first couple of lines, but as I really started getting into it, Piper stopped me when she doubled over in a fit of giggles. "Oh my God. That's excellent." She sat up and wiped the tears from her eyes. "You're really tough. Very hardcore."

"It was the first CD I ever bought. At the time I thought I was supercool. I practiced the dance moves in my mirror every night." I showed her, bouncing my shoulders, emulating the one and only Fresh Prince.

She broke out in laughter again, and this time I joined in, our heads bent close together. It seemed like ages until we could control ourselves.

We each picked another card, and I ended up with the low card again, and admitted, "I peed the bed until I was five."

"Sure you've grown out of that one?"

I smirked. "Why? You planning on sleeping in my bed anytime soon?"

She blinked slowly and shook her head so her hair hung forward, but I caught the blush on her cheeks. "Pick again, Tinkle King."

I clucked my tongue at her and pulled a queen. "Aha! High card."

She closed her eyes tight and picked a card. She opened her eyes and grinned. "A queen. What now?"

"We both drink and pick again?"

She agreed and clinked her bottle to mine before going back to the deck. She held up a seven, and I yet again was stuck with the low six.

"I think you're rigging the deck," I said, tossing my card down.

"I'm not." But she smiled evilly. "Ante up. Give me another secret."

I sighed. "In college, I was at a party, some kind of luau or something, and I dressed as a hula girl with a grass skirt and coconut bra."

Piper was already giggling before I even got to the good part.

"I thought it'd be a good idea to play Tarzan and grabbed onto a string of lights to swing into the little pool they had set up. Turns out Christmas lights don't hold a grown man, and I ended up busting my face into the pavement. Got a trip to the emergency room in my grass skirt, and this scar." I touched the faint line on the bottom of my chin.

"And an awesome story." She traced my scar with her thumb when I dropped my hand, and with our heads bent close together it wouldn't have taken much for me to kiss her. I think she realized it, too, because her attention fixed on my lips for an eternity before lifting up to meet my eyes.

"You're up, Giggles McGee," I said quietly.

"Hold on to your underpants, Tinkle King." She laughed at her own joke and that made me chuckle as she pulled a card. An eight. This time I beat her with an ace.

"So, when I was younger I was flat as a board." She made a face and added, "Still am."

I held back from saying *I like your boobs* and instead settled for "I like you exactly the way you are."

She flicked my nose. "You're sweet. What was I saying? Oh, yeah. Boobs. So, in ninth grade, for the homecoming dance, I stuffed my bra with socks—real creative, I know— and this senior, Tyler Haas, who was sooooo cute, asked me to dance. We were dancing"—Piper danced in her seat— "having a great time. So when he asked me to go out in the hallway, I went. We made out a little and he pulled me into one of the classrooms and got a bit handsy. Lo and behold Tyler Haas did not appreciate my sock boobs and left."

She frowned at her memory. "I was devastated and cried, like, all night. And Monday morning, when I tried to talk to Tyler, he'd told all of his senior friends about what happened. I ate lunch in the library for the rest of the year after that."

A totally irrational anger coursed through my veins. This was something that happened to Piper years ago, yet how dare this immature dickweed make her cry?

"I hate Tyler Haas," I said.

She laughed at me, but when I didn't budge, she leaned in close. "I hate him, too."

I breathed her in, the lingering scent of beer and a perfume she'd never worn around me before, but even that couldn't keep the exhaustion at bay. It was well after three, and I thought it was about time to head out. "What do you think? Time to hit the road?"

She checked the time on her phone. "Oh my God, yeah." She brought up the Uber app, but I didn't feel comfortable with her riding alone with someone this late.

"I'll go with you."

"No way. That's silly."

"Piper, it's late. I wouldn't feel comfortable about you going home by yourself."

"I'll be fine," she said through a yawn.

An idea popped in my head, but I didn't know how well it would go over. "My place is a quick walk. You can stay over if you want. Or go home, but I'm not letting you go alone. Your choice."

Her feet danced under her as she considered it, indecision clear on her face. "I don't want to put you out."

"You're not."

She typed out a quick text before saying, "I'll go to your house. But only because I'm beat."

"Understood." I grabbed my phone and jacket from behind the bar and turned the lights off. I locked the front door then held on to Piper's hand as we made our way out the back door. It was the middle of the night, and the temperature had dropped low enough that our breath puffed out in clouds. But with Piper's fingers laced between mine, I didn't feel the cold at all.

"It's only a couple blocks this way," I said, leading her toward my apartment.

Just a few steps in, Piper said, "How much farther?"

"It's six blocks."

"Oh my God. It feels like ten miles. I'm sooo tired. I can't walk anymore."

"Yes, you can." I tugged her along.

"I can't. My feet are falling off. My toes are numb."

"You're just drunk."

"So are you," she said, poking me in the side.

"Exactly. I'm drunk, too, so quit your bitching." There was no heat in my voice. In fact, I laughed again because so did Piper.

"*You* quit *your* bitching." She let go of my hand to stand still.

"What?"

She didn't move, apparently protesting walking any farther.

"Want me to carry you?"

"Yes. Piggyback. One, two, three."

My reflexes were terrible after a night of drinking, and Piper slid down my back after jumping on me like some kind of wild animal. I told her so and she slapped my arm, but we tried again, this time with me counting. She jumped for the second time, and I caught her legs around my waist as she locked her arms around my neck. Drunk Piper was awesome and hilarious. Sleepy Piper holding on to me with her body pressed up against me was incredible.

"This is much better," she said into my neck, then went silent for two blocks.

"You still with me back there?"

"Mhmm. Just enjoying the ride."

There was a sexual innuendo joke to make in there somewhere, but I wasn't with it enough to find it, and instead kept my mouth shut, feeling Piper's slow breaths on my cheek.

Just as I got to my apartment complex, she said, "You know what I like about you, Blake?"

"That I'm devilishly handsome?"

"No." She yawned. "You give good piggybacks."

I set her on her feet and turned to face her. She was basically asleep standing up, her eyes halfway closed, but I bent my knees and laid a chaste kiss on the corner of her mouth anyway. "And you give terrible innuendo."

CHAPTER 13

Piper

I woke up with the driest mouth known to man and a horrible thumping in my head. It took a few minutes to become fully conscious, and when I cracked open my eyes, I didn't recognize where I was. The walls were light gray, unlike the cream color in my own bedroom. The two windows displayed a beautiful view of downtown between striped curtains, not the pitiful view of my backyard. And the bedding I lay under was a plain navy, not my colorful paisley.

I smacked my lips together, trying to swallow over my sandpaper tongue, and turned on my side, only to be greeted with the bare chest of Blake. I instantly forgot about my confusion for a minute and admired Sleeping Beauty. His arm was thrown over the top of his head, his hair a mess. He breathed evenly through parted lips, and I cuddled closer into his side, matching my inhales and exhales to his.

I remembered our walk home and how I'd forced him to

carry me. But once we'd made it inside, I had pretty much passed out as soon as I'd sat down, so I didn't know how I'd gotten to Blake's bed, but I still had my clothes on.

Blake Reed, gentleman.

Even though I knew nothing happened between us last night, I'd happily waltzed across the line I'd drawn to keep myself from him. To keep it strictly business.

But I wasn't fooling anyone when I said I wasn't interested. I wanted Blake.

I just didn't know how to reconcile that with my goals of continuing to sell my beer in his pub. There was no way to make it all okay. Appearances were everything, and if I appeared to be untoward in my business dealings, no one would take me or my beer seriously.

I couldn't begin to solve any of that now. The hangover made sure of that. It also made sure that my hands did whatever they damn well pleased.

I traced Blake's stubble-covered jaw with my fingertip. When he stirred but didn't wake up, I continued my exploration. I gently dragged my finger down his throat, over his Adam's apple to his collarbone, lightly scratching at his skin there until he woke up.

"Morning." His normally velvety voice was groggy with sleep.

"Hi."

He dipped his head down, blinking a few times, then reached over to the nightstand for a pair of thick-framed glasses. "How did you sleep?"

"Good. I passed out cold."

He shifted to his side, his left hand holding his head up, his right hand under the covers on my hip. "Yeah, you did. I was barely able to get your shoes off before getting you into bed."

The thought of him having to take care of me while I was drunk had me cringing inwardly. Waking up in his bed after a night of drinking was not the impression I wanted to leave, personally and certainly not professionally. "Thanks for letting me crash here."

"Of course." His fingers expanded over my hip, and he studied me for a long time, letting me know he wasn't thinking about me in a professional manner *at all* right now. The trail his gaze left as it blazed down my body felt like I might never recover. I was fully clothed but felt naked under his observation.

His eyes were wide, pupils dark, and when he slowly lifted his hand I anticipated a kiss, but instead he dragged his index finger across my bottom lip. It was an intimate touch. One where we spent endless moments breathing each other's air, staring into each other's eyes.

He dropped his finger down to my chin, softly cupping my jaw with his palm. "If you don't have to rush out or anything, do you want to stay for breakfast?"

"I thought you don't eat breakfast."

He smiled and tapped my nose before rolling over to grab his cell phone from somewhere on the floor, offering me a glimpse of the sleek muscle on either side of his spine.

"Lucky for me, it's ten-thirty. Just in time for brunch. How about some hair of the dog? I have bagels. A few pieces of fruit if you'd like."

He was adorably rumpled, his eyes wide behind his glasses, and I eagerly said yes, wanting to make him just as happy as I wanted to make myself. He sat up and threw the covers off, but as I did the same, my headache came back.

"Oh." I put my hands on either side of my head and bent over. "I could do with some ibuprofen."

"You like orange juice?"

"Yeah."

With my eyes downcast, I heard him leave and return a minute later, his bare feet in my line of vision.

"Here."

I looked up, momentarily stunned when I learned Blake slept in cutoff sweats that hung low on his hips. Those shorts were threadbare and practically pornographic. If he noticed my staring, he didn't say so. He simply waited with his palm up, holding two gel capsules in it and a glass of OJ in the other hand. I took his gifts gratefully and swallowed them down. I coughed at the burn of alcohol mixed with the juice.

"And some vodka, too," he said with a smile. "Ya know, hair of the dog."

"Right." I stood up, but my eyes drifted back over his un-fairly delicious body, and I couldn't help but think how good he looked while my own clothes were wrinkled, the waist-band of my jeans cutting into my side. I imagined my makeup had probably run down my face during the night, so I probably looked like a clown, too.

"I think I'll just freshen up. Where's your bathroom?"

He led me a few steps down the hall to his bathroom, white tile walls with clothes and towels on the floor. He mumbled something under his breath and slid past me to pick everything up and dump it in a laundry basket hiding in the closet. "Do you want to shower? There're towels in here, if you want."

I checked myself out in the mirror. My raccoon eyes and ratty hair were complemented by the pillow crease across my cheek. "I think I might."

Our eyes met in the mirror, and a few moments passed where we both seemed to realize how awkward this was. We were doing the morning-after thing after a night of absolutely no debauchery.

His lips curled into a slow smirk, and he backed out of the room. "Let me know if you need anything."

He shut the door behind him, and I sat on the closed toilet lid. I didn't know whether to be mortally humiliated or excited at my morning with Blake. If memory served me correctly, Drunk Piper was overly touchy-feely. I recalled how I had tried to kiss him last night after he had locked the door. He'd turned around, and I threw my arms around his neck, but he'd held me back and smiled gently. "Not like this. I want to kiss you when you'll remember it."

Well, I remembered it. And I wanted to slap myself. Thank God Blake was too much of a nice guy to bring it up.

I swallowed thickly, dehydrated beyond belief. I bent over the sink and drank straight from the faucet before reaching for the toothpaste. A red-and-white toothbrush was next to it, and I hesitated only a second before grabbing it. I didn't know what toothbrush rules were, but if I'd slept in his bed, I thought I was allowed to use it.

I used gobs of toothpaste to wash the bad taste out of my mouth, then turned the shower on and stripped down. In the middle of washing my hair with his manly smelling shampoo, I heard a knock on the door. A moment later, the door creaked open.

"Piper? I heard the water running and thought you might want different clothes to put on. I'll set them here." When I poked my head out of the curtain, he smiled at me. "Okay?"

I wiped the suds away from running into my left eye. "Just making myself right at home."

"Good." He stepped up to the shower, a wicked gleam in his eye, and held on to the curtain just below my hand. "Need any help?"

I had no snappy comeback because, yeah, I needed help putting my scrambled brain back together from his flirtations. "I think I'm doing fine for now."

He leaned in close and wiped a drop of water from the tip of my eyebrow. "Sure?"

"Sure," I said, but it came out all ragged and breathless.

"All right. You let me know."

I nodded and dragged the curtain closed before he

could see how my body reacted to his playful smirk. The door closed a moment later, and I finished showering in peace before drying off. I fretted for a minute over whether or not I should put my underwear and bra back on from last night, but became distracted when I saw what he'd left for me to wear: a Mumford & Sons concert T-shirt and a pair of women's leggings. I left my clothes from last night balled up on the floor and got dressed. Curiosity was killing the cat.

The first thing out of my mouth when I met him in the kitchen was "Why do you have patterned pink-and-gray women's leggings in your possession?"

He lazily perused my body. It took him a long second to answer, but when he did I knew he wasn't lying. "A couple months ago my sister crashed here. She was out drinking and came knocking on my door in the middle of the night. She left those here when I sent her home in a cab and sweats." He closed some of the distance between us, just barely brushing my side when he reached behind me to open a drawer. "But I kind of like how jealous you sounded just now."

I guffawed. "I'm not jealous. I have nothing to be jealous for. I don't get jealous."

He nodded sarcastically and opened a tub of cream cheese. "Sure."

I folded my arms, watching like a petulant child as he carefully took each bagel from the toaster oven. "By the way, I used your toothbrush."

He took his eyes off smearing cream cheese on the bagels for a second before going back to it. "Okay."

I figured he'd be more offended by it. Like I could get him back for calling me jealous. This guy was way too unflappable.

He tilted his head toward the living room. "Come on. Come sit."

I followed him to a spacious area with two overstuffed couches and a big television. He was quick to place coasters and napkins on the coffee table before he set the plate of food down. I plopped next to him, noticing a couple of books neatly stacked up on a small shelf and sneakers on a shoe rack in the corner. He really did like things in order. I made a mental note to see how he folded his fitted sheet.

He grabbed the remote and turned the television on. "What do you want to watch?"

"Anything, I'm not picky."

He surfed through a couple channels as I picked at slices of apple. He settled on ESPN and sat back, grabbing a bagel on his way. "*30 for 30*. This is one of the best," he told me, pointing to the television. "It's about Mike Ditka and the 1985 Bears."

"Awesome." I dragged out the word so he knew just how I felt about watching Mike Ditka and the Bears.

"You said you didn't care."

I picked up my own bagel and bent my legs into a comfortable position on the couch, my feet a few inches away from his thigh. "I didn't think you were going to make me watch some stupid show about football."

"It is *not* some stupid show," he said, pointing his half-eaten bagel at me. "It's educational."

I eyed him for a moment before giving in. Call me spineless, a defeatist, or a coward, I wouldn't care. Just put Blake's hand on my calf, and I'd give in to whatever he wanted.

"Okay."

He kept his hand on my leg, his thumb lightly rubbing over my ankle, making it really difficult to concentrate on whatever the narrator said about Mike Ditka. Eventually he hauled my feet into his lap without any warning, and that was the end of my caring about the Bears.

"What did you think?" he asked when the credits rolled.

I had no idea. The best part was when he excitedly squeezed my toe at the commercial for a new movie he wanted to see. And I couldn't let him think he could pop on a sports show all the time and I'd be okay with it.

My brain screeched to a sudden halt.

All the time? Since when did I think I'd be over here all the time? My mind was three steps ahead of me, planning out our future television habits.

I didn't hate the idea, but I had to seriously cool it. Even though something was happening between the two of us, I was nowhere near ready to dive headfirst into a relationship. Oddly enough, with Oskar, I'd had no problem jumping right in. It bit me in the ass later on when he asked me to give up more than I wanted. All Blake had asked me for was some time, and I just wasn't ready.

"Want to watch a movie?" he asked, moving my feet from his lap to go over to the stack of DVDs on the entertainment console. "I have *Ocean's Eleven*, the new one and the original, all the Godfathers, *Tombstone*, *Mission: Impossible*, *Young Frankenstein*, *Sandlot*—"

"*Sandlot*. *Sandlot*." I pointed excitedly at the DVD he held. "That's my favorite movie."

He cued it up, then tugged me to his side with an arm around my shoulders. "Mine, too."

As soon it began, he quoted every line until I backhanded him on the stomach. "You're killing me, Smalls."

He chuckled softly into my hair. "We should go out. On a date."

It wasn't a question, and I didn't know what to say.

A minute passed, then, "Piper? Date? Tomorrow?"

I shook my head. My mind was all over the place; even though my heart was on a straight and narrow path right to him, I didn't think it was a good idea to say yes unless I was absolutely sure it was worth the risk of my business's reputation.

Blake slunk farther down into the cushions, positioning me more fully against him, and I let my head drop to his chest with my arm across his stomach. I realized how weird it was to cuddle like this after I'd left the date suggestion hanging between us, but I was too comfortable to move. And he didn't seem to care, especially when his fingers began to trace up and down my spine.

We laughed over the same parts of the movie, sometimes saying the lines with the characters, until Squints jumped into the pool for Wendy Peffercorn's attention. That's when Blake asked me again. "How about next week? Dinner? Maybe a late-night movie?"

He was too cute. Honestly. But the thought of dating him, and another potential client or bar owner finding out and assuming things, made me nervous. "I don't think so."

"You already used my toothbrush. You're wearing my T-shirt. We're practically married. You might as well go on a date with me."

I huffed out a laugh and tipped my head up to look at him. He wore my favorite Blake smile, crooked and dimpled.

"No."

He playfully rolled his eyes then wrapped both of his arms around me, dropping the subject until just about the time Benny pickled The Beast. "Go out with me, pretty please with a cherry on top?"

I sat up. "You're relentless."

He ducked his head down to my neck and scraped his mouth along my skin as he said, "When I want something, yes."

My arms broke out in goose bumps at the feel of his lips pressing gently against my throat.

"Please, Piper."

I closed my eyes, knowing I wouldn't be able to hold him off for long, especially when he lowered his voice and said my name in that raspy way. My brain, and my ovaries, wouldn't be able to handle much more of it. "Okay, I'll make you a deal."

He lifted his head, listening intently to me.

"The Public is selling my beer, but it would look bad if word got out about us, and you're the only bar with my beer. So I won't go out with you until two more bars pick up accounts."

He narrowed his eyes, then nodded slowly, extending his hand. "You've got yourself a deal, Miss Williams." Just as I curled my fingers around his for a handshake, he jerked me into him and whispered sinfully, "And you better believe I'll be pulling out all the stops. I want to be your best first date ever." His lips hovered close enough to mine that I could feel the heat from his breath. "I want to be the best of a lot of things for you."

I closed my eyes, waiting for a kiss, a kiss I was frantic for, but it never came. I opened my eyes to find he had sat back against the cushion. He cocked an eyebrow. "If I have to wait, so do you."

I huffed and threw myself into the corner of the couch. Well damn.

CHAPTER 14

Blake

After my blissful weekend, I was back at work. Grouchy and upset. Bear teased me during our workout. He said it looked like I was constipated. Really, I missed Piper.

Cheesy, I know, but we'd spent the entire day together Sunday, Netflix and chilling, minus the sex. And I didn't even care. I'd Netflix and chill—really chill—with Piper every day if I could. What irked me the most was that I didn't know when I'd see her again. Two more bars had to pick up her beer, and *then* we could go out.

It would happen, I was sure of it. Especially after I talked up her beer a bit to some friends. They'd no doubt want to buy in. I just had to be patient.

Problem was, patience was not my strong suit.

So here I was in my misery, in the middle of slogging through payroll in my office, when my cell phone rang. My mother's number was displayed on the screen. I didn't really have time to stop and chat about whatever crisis she was experiencing right now, but I couldn't ignore it, either. She was my mother.

"Hey, Mom."

"Hi, darling. Do you have a moment?"

No. "Sure. What's up?"

"Your father and I are just coming back from lunch, and we wanted to know if we could stop by."

"I'm not home right now. I'm at the bar."

"Yes. That's okay. We wanted to . . . to see it."

Shocked, my jaw flapped open and closed. They wanted to see it, meaning my place, my bar. I knew it was crazy to think they might change their minds about what I wanted to do, but my hopes lifted anyway. I was an eternal optimist. "Sure. I'll be here."

"See you in a little while," my mother said, and I hung up, but just as I went back to QuickBooks on my laptop, Darren, the chef, knocked on the doorjamb.

"Hey, Boss. I'm making a ham and cheese for lunch. You want one?"

Darren was at least ten years older than me, and I still wasn't used to him calling me "Boss," but I appreciated the sentiment. Without looking up from the spreadsheets in front of me, I nodded. "Yeah, thanks. That'd be great."

Minutes later, Darren had made himself at home in a chair across from my desk after handing me a plate.

I'd taken it gratefully. "How're things going on your end?"

"Good."

"Kitchen staff is working well together?"

Darren had carte blanche over the food and his staff. The draw of the Public was the alcohol, but everyone knew the food had to match the beer—that combination was what kept customers happy. I'd hired Darren because he had enough experience to run the kitchen on his own, allowing me to focus solely on the business, but also because he had an appreciation for beer. When I interviewed him, we'd bonded over our mutual affection for a few drafts, spoken about other bars we enjoyed in the area, and found we shared a common sense of what the Public could be.

We didn't have a big food menu, but what we did serve was delicious, the usual pub fare with seasonal modern twists, paired with coordinating beers. Currently the biggest sellers were grilled cheese with bacon and tomato, shrimp skewers, and our specialty homemade chips.

"Yeah. Everybody's meshing really well together, but I wanted to talk to you about hiring someone else. Maybe just part-time to help out on the weekends to start. We need somebody else on the line. I need help expediting."

I couldn't answer right away—I'd taken a huge bite of the sandwich. It was the first thing I'd eaten all day, and I was devouring the simple ham and cheese like it was Darren's delicious braised brisket. Good thing my mouth was full, though, because it gave me a chance to do the mental math.

Sure, it was good we were so busy that we needed to

hire another person, but I had to be diligent about how and where I spent my money, especially in the first year of business. The first few months after an opening were always good because the place was a novelty; it was the following years you had to watch out for. But there could be worse problems than to have too many orders bogging down our kitchen.

"Okay," I said, brushing my hands free of crumbs. "Do you have somebody in mind?"

Darren glanced down at the floor before meeting my eyes. "Actually, I do. My nephew is starting culinary school in the fall. He could use some hours on the line."

I nodded and swallowed a gulp of water from the aluminum bottle I kept with me. "Bring him by so I can meet him."

He smiled. "Will do. Thanks."

He stood up and grabbed his plate. I stood up, too. "Thank you, Darren. You're doing a great job. The Public wouldn't be doing as well as it is without your touch."

He shook my hand and backed out of the door. "I'll be prepping in the kitchen."

I didn't have time to sit back down because I heard my mother's nasally voice calling my name. For the love of God, I needed to have my payroll submitted before 4 p.m., otherwise my staff wouldn't get paid this week.

I headed out into the main room, where my parents were standing with Missy, the bar manager. My father looked bored, with his hands stuffed in his pockets, while my mother seemed horrified, staring at Missy's new fuchsia hair streaks and sleeve of tattoos.

"Hey," I said with a wave.

Missy frowned apologetically. "They were waiting outside when I came in."

"It's okay. Thanks."

She seesawed between me and my parents before correctly guessing she should head for cover. She always came in early to prep the bar, but today, she pointed toward the back. "I'll be in the kitchen."

After she was gone, I led my parents to a high-top table by the window. My mother walked on her tiptoes like she was sidestepping shit on the sidewalk. My floors were immaculate. I should know, I'd personally mopped this morning. They took a seat, but my dad didn't remove his coat.

"Relax, Dad," I said, purposely pushing his buttons. "Stay awhile."

He stared out of the window, pointedly ignoring me.

"Can I get you something to drink?" I gestured to the bar.

Dad shook his head, but Mom piped up. "I'd love a Chardonnay, darling. Thank you."

"I don't have wine."

She glanced around, her brow furrowed. "This is a bar, isn't it?"

"A gastropub. I've got a list of fifty craft beers and a small choice of liquors."

Her nose turned up. "Water. Do you have sparkling?"

"Tap."

My mother nodded begrudgingly while my father huffed. It didn't take a rocket scientist to know he wasn't impressed. I turned to fill up two glasses of water and poured myself a beer before having a seat with them. "So, what brings you to my humble abode?"

Mom folded her hands in her lap. Sunlight streamed in from the window, painting rainbows on the walls from the reflection of her diamond bracelet. "Well, your father and I wanted to talk to you."

She narrowed her eyes at my dad, obviously ordering him to speak up. He cleared his throat and moved his glass of water a few inches away. "You missed dinner last weekend."

"I told Mom I was really busy here."

He held his palms up. "It's empty now."

"Because we don't open for another two hours." He knew we weren't open. Missy had to unlock the door for him.

He folded his arms back up, one on top of the other. "It's our one standing appointment every month," he said, referring to the family dinner as if it were a business meeting. "Did you lose your respect for your mother when you went off on this tangent? She spends a lot of time making those dinners for you."

"Sandra makes the dinners," I said, unmoved by his withering glare. But after a solid ten seconds of staring, there was no way he was backing down. I sighed and turned to my mother. "Sorry, Mom."

She patted my cheek. "I miss you when you don't come

over." Her fingers dragged through my hair by my temple. "You still haven't gotten it cut yet."

I shook her off and focused back on my dad. He readjusted one leg over the other, his face wiped clean of any emotion. That was the worst part, his happy face—if he had one—was the same as his aggravated one. It proved beneficial in his political career, but as a father, it was pretty shitty.

"I'll be making a public statement next month to announce my run. I want you there, beside your mother and Tiffany."

It wasn't a question, request, or suggestion. It was an order.

I traced the top of my glass, not listening to his instructions that I should wear a suit because it would be televised. I hadn't even agreed to go, but I guess I didn't need to. I was a Reed. There were expectations.

He never once said thank you or showed any sign of gratitude, and even though I wasn't surprised, I hoped he spoke more kindly to his constituents than to his son.

"Yeah, all right, I'll be there," I said, out of nothing more than pure familial loyalty.

He nodded once and stood, buttoning his coat. My mother followed him, lowering her voice. "This place is . . . nice, but I think it could use some brightening up. Maybe some color on the walls."

"Sure. I'll think about it." I helped her with her coat and ushered her to the door.

My father gave one last sweeping look around, and I witnessed brief disdain pass through his eyes. Even with his obvious contempt for what I was doing, I had to acknowledge that he'd showed up. It was the very least he could do. "Thanks for coming in."

"Well, I had to see what you've been wasting all your time on."

I smiled, holding back the string of curse words on the tip of my tongue and clenching my fists. "Well, we can't all be senators."

"No, you can't."

He pivoted, stalking out of the door. My mother kissed my cheek and followed him out, again walking on her tiptoes. I let out a breath, spotting Darren and Missy poking their heads out of the hallway.

Missy winced. "Those your parents, huh?"

"Yep."

"They seem . . . pleasant."

Darren took a few steps toward the bar. "I didn't know your dad was Jacob Reed, the politician."

"The one and only," I said, sitting back down at the table to finish off my beer.

"Didn't want to follow in Daddy's footsteps?" he teased with a grin.

"Nah. I didn't want to grow up to be an asshole."

Missy snorted and headed behind the bar to begin her duties as Darren went back to the kitchen.

Fifteen minutes with my parents, and my day had gone from bad to worse.

"You want a refill?" Missy asked.

"Yeah, I think I do." I grabbed the untouched waters and my empty glass from the table to place on the bar. I took my new cold beer back to my office, determined to finally finish payroll, but as soon as I sat down my phone chimed.

I growled. "Can't I catch a break?"

I snatched my phone up, and suddenly the dark cloud that had been hovering above me all day disappeared. Piper's picture flashed on the screen along with a text message.

Good news.

I chuckled at how she'd demanded to take my picture when we'd exchanged numbers. I'd turned my camera on her in return, but she'd ducked her head back, wiggling away from me. I did the only obvious thing then—I tackled her. I'd snapped a photo of her mid-cackle, her mouth open wide in laughter, eyes closed shut. Wild and beautiful.

I typed back.

Oh yeah?

Monkey Bar just purchased 3 cases.

I knew I probably looked like a grinning idiot. But this was the best news I'd heard all day. I sent back:

1 down, 1 to go.

Is that a threat?

Believe me, you'll be begging soon enough.

We'll see about that.

I huffed out a laugh. We *would* see. And I couldn't wait.

CHAPTER 15

Piper

I turned my back toward the mirror, checking out how my butt looked in these new pants. "I don't know. What do you think?"

"They're very blue," Sonja said from her spot on my bed. "But I like them." She stood up. "Put your shoulders back. You're always slouching. When you stand up straight, it makes the shirt fit better."

I followed her directions and set my spine straight, making the bottom hem of my white T-shirt lift up to show a tiny sliver of skin at my waist. Between the new outfit, my dark makeup, and the soft curls Sonja had put in my hair, I looked far sexier than I had in a long time. But it was my first date with Blake, and I wanted to show him a different side of me.

I had texted Blake two days ago to let him know Pete's Tavern in St. Paul had bought two cases of the Platinum

Blonde, with the promise to buy more if it sold well. I was beyond excited to have another bar pick up my drafts, but I suspected Blake was just as happy that I was going to deliver on our deal.

No matter how much I fought my attraction to him, I'd been looking forward to this date for a lot longer than I liked to admit.

The doorbell rang, and Sonja grinned. "I'll get it."

"I can get it." I stopped her with a hand on her shoulder, but she slipped out of my grip and went out to the hall.

"Sonja, don't," I said, failing to edge her out of reaching the steps. She was halfway to the door when I hissed, "Sonja, do not say any—"

She turned around, her back to the front door, with her hand on the knob. "Don't say anything about how you're so nervous you sweat through your first shirt? I'd never."

"I hate you so much," I yelled in a whisper as she opened the door with a wink to me.

I sank into the wall, listening as Sonja greeted my date with a cheery "Hey, Blake."

"Hey."

"Big date night, huh?"

I imagined she shot him a couple of finger guns when she clicked her tongue, and I quietly slunk down another two steps just in time to see her dig her fingertips into his shoulder.

"Do I need to give you the *Hurt her and I'll kill you* speech?" Before Blake could answer, she cut him off. "Because you know I can. One good punch to the kidney, and I'd have you down for the count."

"I'd prefer to stay in your good graces and keep Piper happy."

"Good, good." Sonja smacked his arm.

Her whole display was over the top, but I appreciated how much she cared. She was, after all, the one who had taken me in when life was at its bleakest. In the last two years, she'd witnessed how I'd picked myself up from the pit I was in after Oskar's blow to my self-confidence. I'd turned down blind dates and a few odd phone numbers, not ready to let go again. Until Blake.

Sonja understood what this date meant—a new beginning—and she certainly wasn't going to let Blake go without a warning.

"Piper," Sonja called, "Prince Charming is here."

I tucked back into the shadow of the staircase, unmoving, pretending I was upstairs and not eavesdropping on their conversation like a creep.

I heard the door close and Blake say, "Prince Charming, eh?"

"You know you ooze charisma, don't try to act all modest," Sonja said, and I smiled to myself. Blake was a tad cocky, but I liked that about him. Sure of himself without being arrogant.

I ran my fingers through my hair before making myself known. Blake turned to me with wide eyes, slowly looking me up and down.

Sonja nodded to me with a knowing smile before heading off to the kitchen.

"Hey, gorgeous," Blake said after a while.

"Handsome," I said against his ear as we leaned in to kiss each other's cheeks.

"Here." He presented me with a gift that he'd been hiding behind his back.

"A cactus?" I scrunched my nose up. Cacti were not particularly known for their beauty.

"Yep. A cactus is hearty and strong, and it blooms flowers even in harsh conditions." He handed it to me. "Reminded me of you."

My confusion melted at the explanation. "So much better than stupid old roses." I placed it on the square side table in the living room before crossing back to Blake. "Thank you. That was really sweet."

I grabbed my purse and jacket and left with a wave to Sonja. She waved back, a piece of lettuce stuck to the fork in her hand. "Have fun." Then she looked past my shoulder to Blake and flexed a bit. "Best behavior, Charming."

He laughed good-naturedly behind me. "See you later, Mayweather."

I closed the door on her resounding laugh and followed Blake to his car, but when he opened the passenger side door for me, his eyes stayed glued to my body. Even after he climbed in on his side.

"You're staring," I said, once he was behind the wheel, his eyes on my legs.

His attention shot to my face. "Sorry."

"No, you're not."

He laughed. "No, I'm not."

As Blake turned the ignition, the car filled with an expectation, a tension in the air. We weren't fooling around anymore. We'd crossed over the getting-to-know-you phase, and even though this was only our first date, it certainly didn't seem like it.

It was more like a second, or even third. And if it was a third date . . . I shook my head. I couldn't get ahead of myself.

"So, where are we going?" I asked.

"How do you feel about seafood?"

"Do I get a lobster bib?"

He briefly looked at me when he stopped at a red light, a goofy smile on his face. "I'll see what I can do."

The drive to Stella's Fish Cafe wasn't long, and he'd only just finished the story of his parents visiting the pub before he parked. I didn't hesitate to reach for his hand on the short walk through the parking lot, and he didn't let go as the hostess led us to the rooftop.

The cotton candy sky was wide open above our heads, and a slight breeze danced with the umbrellas over every table, the perfect atmosphere for a date. I spotted a guy with a lobster bib around his neck, and I tugged on Blake's arm, gesturing to it.

He shook his head in amusement.

"Anything look good?" he asked after I'd had a chance to look over the menu. "Want any appetizers?"

"Do you like oysters?"

"Sure. You know what they say about oysters, though."

I kept my eyes down, ignoring his obvious ploy. "That they're an aphrodisiac? I'm pretty sure that's an old wives' tale," I said, and picked my head up, trying to look as bored as possible, "but I'll try to control myself from jumping your bones."

He grabbed my hands. "It's actually scientifically proven. I saw a show on it . . . something about the omegas, so don't try to hold back on my account. Just let yourself feel whatever it is you need to feel."

I fought my smile hard, but it came through, contradicting my eye roll. Blake gave my fingers a satisfied squeeze before looking over the menu again.

After a minute, he asked, "Where'd we land on the oysters?"

"Get them. Obviously," I said breezily, meeting his gaze. I was going to just let myself feel whatever it was I needed to feel.

Our waiter, Brian, showed up to take our drink orders, and I perused the long list. Apparently I'd taken too long because Brian cleared his throat. "If you like wine, the Tavo pinot grigio is very popular."

"No, I want a beer," I said, looking up at him.

"We have a spiked cider you might like."

I shook my head. Wines and ciders, that's what they thought women always wanted to drink.

"Do you like light or dark beers? I can pick something out for you if you tell me."

"I'm kind of picky," I said, and coughed to cover up a laugh across from me.

"How about a Heineken?" Brian offered.

I tossed the menu on the table and leaned back in my chair to fully face him. "The best way to drink a Heineken is to pour it out, so no, I don't want a Heineken. I'm going to have the Deschutes IPA."

Brian's eyebrows hiked up—either at the bite in my tone or the choice of beer—and I hoped he didn't always look so dumbfounded when taking orders.

"I'll have the same," Blake said.

Brian nodded and turned on his heel.

Blake waved him off. "What a turd. I don't know why guys feel the need to be so condescending toward women. Who said you can't tell the difference between an ale and a lager just because you're a girl?"

"Oddly enough . . ." I sighed. "A lot of guys."

"Guys are assholes," he said, straight-faced and per-turbed.

I stared at him for a moment then busted out a big laugh. His indignation on my behalf was cute. "Totally."

Brian returned a few minutes later with our drinks and took our food orders with nothing more than a few words. Between Blake and me, though, the conversation never stopped.

"I've been thinking about your fear of swimming," he said as he dropped a bit of horseradish sauce onto an oyster.

"Oh yeah?"

He nodded and sucked down the oyster. "It just so happens I found some of those kids' floaties on sale on Amazon. I'm going to buy you a pair, and we'll head out to Lake Calhoun."

"What kind of floaties are we talking about?"

"You can pick: whales, turtles, or fish."

I took a sip from my pint before frowning. "Damn. I was really hoping for dolphins. Guess I'll have to pass."

"Make you a new deal," he said, and I leaned forward, curious. "If I find you dolphin floaties, you have to come swimming with me. Preferably in an itsy-bitsy bikini."

I made a show of thinking about it. "Make it pink dolphin floaties and a one-piece and you got yourself a deal."

He agreed and held out his hand for me to shake. Then I put on the lobster bib delivered with my meal, and Blake proceeded to snap a picture of me.

Before we knew it, our plates were cleaned and the sun had set. The stars twinkled above us, and as Blake paid the check, I regretted the date coming to an end. "Thanks for dinner. It was delicious."

Blake wrapped his arm around my shoulders as we made our way out of the restaurant. "You ready to dance?"

"I told you I don't dance." When he let out a disbelieving huff, I elbowed him. "I'm not kidding. I really don't dance."

"Really?"

I shrugged. "I mean, I dance, sure. But I'm not any good at it."

"We'll see about that."

"O-k-a-a-a-ay." I dragged out the two syllables into three.

Once we got into the club, it was difficult to see anything between the crowd and the low lights. Blake held on to my waist as we trudged through the sea of people. He guided me to the bar, where we agreed on shots of tequila. We clinked glasses before downing them, and I suspected Blake thought the hard liquor would get me to loosen up, but when he made his way onto the dance floor, I didn't follow.

He turned, tossing me a cheeky little look before breaking into a two-step. I watched him dance. He wasn't exactly Michael Jackson, but he had rhythm, enough to catch the eye of another woman dancing close to him.

I saw her eye him up and slowly make her way toward him, "accidentally" brushing up against his side. He congenially acknowledged her, and she took that as an invitation to dance with him.

It wasn't.

I didn't consider myself a jealous person, but I got out on the dance floor faster than a sprinter in the Olympics. I took Blake's hand, dragging him away from the girl. The bass of the music beat in my chest, and the heat from the crowd immediately made my skin slick, but I wouldn't have pulled away from Blake if an earthquake had rocked the floor beneath our feet.

"Come on, Sunshine, let me see what you got." Blake turned me in a circle, then gestured to the space between us, daring me to dance.

I did, but not on beat. I guess he thought my awful dancing was cute, because he wrapped his arms around my waist, laughing into my neck.

He guided me through each song, pressing our hips together and moving my arms. Sometimes his dancing was silly, sometimes it was sensual, but no matter what he did, he made me have fun. And that was the sexiest thing of all.

We were wrapped up together when Blake bent down, his mouth close to my ear. "Can I take you home?"

"You want to take me home?" My heart dropped. I thought we were having a good time.

"I want to take you to *my* home," he said.

My heart soared, and I leaned back, catching his smirk and meaning. I wrapped my arms around his neck, speaking my answer into his ear. "Yes."

The minutes between leaving the club and arriving at Blake's place raced by, and then time slowed down as we stood inside of his door. The click of the lock sounded like a gunshot in the silent apartment, and he turned to face me, his movements like a panther hunting his prey. My nerves ratcheted up a few notches with his lazy once-over, desire clear on his face. His hands skimmed over my shoulders then down my sides before landing on my waist.

"Okay?" he asked, his mouth hovering over mine.

With one simple word he was giving me an out, but I

was under no illusions of what was about to happen, and my pulse raced at the thought because I wanted it. Wanted *him*.

I just didn't know how this would affect my future, and that made me nervous.

The longer I thought about it, though, the more I didn't care. As long as I was here, in this place with Blake, I had no room in my mind to think about more. There was only him, his hazel eyes, and the soothing motion of his thumb circling my side.

"Yes."

His lips were on me then, better than I remembered, and I couldn't get enough. I licked at his tongue, nibbled at his lip, tugged on his shirt.

He pulled away from me with a twinkle in his eyes. "How are those oysters working out for ya?"

I shoved at his shoulder, laughing. I didn't need shellfish to put me in the mood, particularly when he caught my hand, yanking me to him. He curled his fingers around my neck, kissing me sweetly as he backed me down the hall to his bedroom, where he held me at arm's length. "Still okay?"

"More than okay." I smiled.

Then he smiled.

And then we melted into each other.

CHAPTER 16

Blake

I woke up to the sounds of a chainsaw. A soft, feminine, crackling chainsaw. I picked my head up and looked to my right. Piper was fast asleep, cheek on her pillow, lips parted. That slow rumble sounded from deep in her throat.

"Sunshine."

She didn't wake up.

"Piper," I tried again, louder.

The snoring didn't stop.

I pinched her nose. "Piper, wake up."

She waved my hand away and slowly opened her eyes. "Hi."

"Hey. You snore."

She blinked the sleep from her eyes. "No, I don't."

"Yeah, you do." I turned onto my back and slid my glasses on, getting a good look at her. Even with pillow creases across her cheek and with her tangled hair, she was the prettiest girl I'd ever seen.

"I think someone would've told me."

"I think maybe they were trying to be nice by *not* telling you."

She curled up into a ball and snuggled deeper into the covers. "Yeah. And you pointing it out isn't nice."

I stayed quiet for a few seconds before imitating her snore with a loud snuffle.

Her hand poked out of the comforter, blindly trying to smack me. "Shut up and spoon me."

I laughed and draped my arm around her, pulling her into my chest. I rested my chin on the top of her head. "You're pleasant in the morning."

"Only when I'm exhausted and someone wakes me up to tell me I snore."

"Sorry." I hummed, running my hand over her hair and down her naked back. "Go back to sleep."

"I can't when you're doing that," she said, but when I stopped, she whined, "No, keep going."

I stroked my fingers up and down her spine. "Tell me a secret."

"We already played that game."

"I mean a real secret. Something that you never told anyone else." I gently tugged on her arm so she turned toward me.

She lay on her back, her eyes on the ceiling, her mind clearly on something else. "Remember when I said I lived in Germany for a while?"

"Yeah."

"The program was only six months. I didn't plan on staying there any longer, but I met a boy."

I twisted a lock of her hair around my finger, and she dropped her attention to me, saying, "His name was Oskar. We had mutual friends and met one night at a bar. He was cute and smart, an architect who spoke a couple of languages."

"Never mind," I said. "Maybe I don't want to hear this."

She poked me in the side. "Jealous?"

"No-o-o-o." I dragged the word out, denying the truth.

She smiled.

"What? I'm not. Go on."

She shifted onto her side so we faced each other. "Well, this was a couple of years ago. Laurie was off and married, Kayla engaged, and I guess I was feeling a little left out, because when he asked me to stay I didn't hesitate to say yes."

My hand on her hip tensed involuntarily.

"We moved in together, and he bought me a stunning yellow-gold engagement ring."

I looked at her barren ring finger, imagining the fat diamond that once sat there. "But . . ." I prodded when she didn't continue.

"But as soon as I said yes, he changed. I still had so much to learn, but he wanted me to stay home and be a housewife. He wanted me to be what he called a real woman, and give up my"—she put the word in air quotes—"hobby."

I snorted. "What an ass."

She nodded. "He made me feel silly for wanting my own life. Whether he knew it or not, he did a number on my self-confidence, always dropping these passive-aggressive one-liners, like shouldn't I be happy he wanted to take care of me. What kind of woman didn't want her man to be *the man*?"

"Sounds insecure."

Her eyes skipped down for a few seconds before meeting mine again, her tone more serious than before. "I wasn't willing to give up my dreams for a man. I packed up my stuff and left the ring on the dresser, ending an engagement no one knew about. Not even Sonja knows," she whispered.

"I don't mean this to come off as insensitive, but good. This Oskar character was an idiot. If he truly loved you, he should've helped you achieve your dreams, not put them down or call them a hobby." I moved my hand to her jaw. "Plus, it's worked out well for me, so I can't be too upset with him."

I kissed her cheek with a loud smack and kept going until she broke out into a fit of laughter. I knew it must've taken a lot out of her to be put down by someone she loved. Knowing this secret made me want to back her more fully because I understood the feeling of not being supported. My parents did that as an art form.

"I'm afraid of turning into my father," I said, confessing my own secret.

"What?" Her smile turned to a frown.

I took a deep breath. "It's the main reason I quit. Sure, I love the Public, but I saw what was happening to me at the law firm. I was turning into my dad."

"What do you mean?"

"I worked all the time. I had my assistant, Beth, on speed dial, and I was calling her on weekends. I could hear it in her voice how she didn't want to come in when I asked her to, but she was too afraid to say no. I was tired all the time and snapping at people. I wasn't trying to be a dick, but it just sort of happened, you know? I'm not making an excuse for myself, but when you're stressed and tired, and the partners are breathing down your neck, you lose yourself. I almost never saw Connor or Bear, and when I did, all I did was get plastered. One day I realized I had a choice. I didn't have to be miserable. I didn't have to turn into my dad. So I left."

"Wow," she said, surprise coloring her voice. "I'm happy you did. I think a lot of people don't recognize things in themselves, and they keep getting deeper and deeper until they're so miserable, they can't see a way out."

"Exactly. I wasn't going to be one of those people."

"Well," Piper said, echoing my words from earlier, "you quitting worked out well for me, too."

I kissed her forehead. "We're working out pretty good for each other." I traced a finger down her cheek. "Want a couple more minutes of sleep?"

"No. I'm awake now. I want breakfast." She sat up, her legs straddling my waist.

I'd become intimately familiar with her body, and among the many things I'd learned, I knew she'd break out in goose bumps from head to toe if I kissed her really lightly under her jaw, right by her ear.

I sat up and kissed a line across her throat, knowing last night would probably be etched into my memory forever, feeling the skin of her thighs pucker under my hands.

"Come on." She pushed herself off from me, and I wanted to whimper at the cool air when our hot skin parted. "I'm hungry."

I supposed there was time for more sex after sustenance. "Fine."

"I need clothes."

"Do you?"

She put her hands on her hips, trying on an irritated face, but it didn't last long. The corner of her mouth kicked up. She helped herself to my dresser, opening up each drawer until she found what she wanted: a plain white T-shirt and black shorts.

I was sad to see her beautiful body disappear, but got a good show as she flipped her long hair over her shoulder and strutted away. I threw on a pair of sweats before heading to the bathroom. Piper had my toothbrush in her mouth.

"I hope you don't have any germs," I said, squeezing green mint toothpaste on the bristles once she was finished with it.

"If I did, I definitely gave them to you last night." She propped herself against the doorway as I brushed. "I don't think you really care about a couple of bristles. Which, by the way, are a bit soft. I think it's time for a new brush."

"I'll add it to the grocery list." I had half a mind to add

one extra for her, but I didn't want to get ahead of myself. I knew Piper was skittish about our relationship, and no matter how well I thought it was going, I didn't want to push it. Especially after she'd told me the Oskar story. I finished up, and we went to the kitchen, where I opened the refrigerator. "What do you want?"

She peered over my shoulder. "Pancakes."

I shut the door and pointed to a cabinet, where I kept the Aunt Jemima box mix. She found it and shook the nearly empty bag at me. "Seriously?"

"What?"

"You're one of those people who leaves the smallest amount of *whatever* in the container and puts it back for the next person. Like, the tiny bit of orange juice or the scraps of peanut butter you can't get without a knife, and there isn't enough to put on a cracker." She shook the bag of mix once again. "You can just about make one pancake out of this." She crumpled up the bag, shoved it in the box, and threw it away.

I'd been living alone for so long, I'd forgotten some of my habits might be annoying to someone else. "Well, there is no next person so . . ."

"There is now," she said offhandedly, and I froze with my hand on the refrigerator.

She let the lid of the trash can slam shut before rambling an explanation. "I mean, not me . . . I just meant . . . you can't leave crumbs in a bag."

I bit my lip to hold in my laugh.

"It's not . . ." She shook her head, her hair covering her face as her words trailed off.

I tucked her hair behind her ears and tipped her chin up to kiss her. "I'll try not to leave crumbs in the bag, but I'll probably need you to remind me. A lot."

She smiled shyly. "I guess I could do that."

And with that simple agreement, our relationship solidified a little bit more.

"Want to go out?" I asked. "We could go to the Original Pancake House."

Her face twisted in horror. "Then I'd have to put pants on."

"Right. Bad idea." Keeping Piper in the least amount of clothes possible was task number one.

"I can make them from scratch. I need eggs, flour, baking soda. Do you have that?"

I held my arms up. "Sunshine, I'm a thirty-year-old guy living alone. Do you think I have flour or baking soda?"

She waved me off. "How about bananas?"

"Those I have."

I handed her the bunch, and she grabbed the egg carton from the fridge. With a fork, she created some kind of yellow concoction in a bowl. "I saw this on Facebook. They made pancakes out of a banana and two eggs."

I got her the pan and butter and let her do her thing while I took a seat at the breakfast bar. Watching her in my kitchen gave me more enjoyment than it probably should have, because she had this pixie kind of aura, constantly flitting around. She bounced on her toes as she poured the lumpy batter into the pan and hummed while she flipped the pancakes.

She placed a steaming mug of coffee down in front of me, along with a plate of brown goo. She sat next to me with the same breakfast of what looked like an overcooked egg-cake-thing. We both poured syrup on it, but I doubted it would help.

I took a bite, and she raised her eyebrows expectantly. I chewed and swallowed what was essentially burnt banana.

"How is it?"

"Not good."

She ate her own bite and cringed. "Yeah. Not good."

We threw away the "pancakes" and settled on a breakfast of Cheez-Its and grapes with the promise that I'd go to the store real soon.

I gave the remote to Piper to pick what she wanted on Netflix, and we ended up watching some show called *Gilmore Girls*. I didn't understand the humor, but the mom was hot, so I couldn't complain.

After the first episode, I lifted Piper's feet off my lap and took her mug to refill. That's when I noticed the time. Almost noon. I had my dad's public announcement at four. Unfortunately.

"Hey, I've got this thing I have to go to today." I pressed the brew button on the Keurig.

She turned to me, one eyebrow raised. "Are you being evasive on purpose?"

"No. It's my father's coming out."

She took her mug from me when I sat down. "Oh, the congressional running thing."

She said it so breezily, I wished that was how everyone treated it. "I have to be there by three-thirty."

"Oh." She sat up. "Okay, well, I'll just—"

"I didn't mean that you had to leave." I fixed her feet back on my lap, forcing her to lie back down. "I said it because we've only got another three hours to get a couple more episodes in."

"That means you like it? You're hooked on *Gilmore Girls*?"

I wrapped one hand around her ankle. "It's all right."

We stared at each other, and an idea popped into my head for a millisecond to ask Piper to go with me today. But that was stupid. *I* didn't even want to go. Staying in our bubble was much more appealing.

But something flickered in her eyes, like she was waiting for me to invite her. Or maybe she wanted me to press play on the next episode. Either way, I wanted to keep Piper to myself a little while longer. The next episode began, and I tried not to notice the clock as it ticked closer and closer to three—the absolute latest I could shower, change, and drive to the auditorium in time. But before I knew it, time was up.

I turned the television off and cleaned up the kitchen as Piper went back to the bedroom. She returned a few minutes later in her outfit from last night.

"Gimme like twenty minutes to get ready, and we'll go, okay?"

She pointed her thumb behind her to the door. "I was going to call an Uber."

"No way. I'll drop you at home."

"You don't have to." She tapped on her phone. "You've got stuff to do. Don't worry about it."

"Piper." I held on to her shoulders, forcing her to focus on me. I didn't know why she tended to fight me on simple issues like letting me drive her home instead of a total stranger. I could only guess she still wanted to keep her guard up, stay strong and independent, but what she didn't understand yet—and what I supposed I had to prove—was that I didn't want her to change. Her fierce self-determination was one of the first things that had attracted me to her. I only wanted to spoil her a bit, treat her the way she deserved, and give her a ride home, for God's sake.

"I picked you up, I'm going to drop you off." She opened her mouth to argue, but I cut her off before she could. "Ten minutes. Ten minutes, and we're out the door."

I kissed her to keep her from saying anything. "Go sit your pretty little butt down."

I waited until she was seated to head to the bathroom. I got into the shower, thinking about what made her so antsy to leave. After what she'd told me about Oskar, I could understand why she'd be hesitant to get serious with someone, but it didn't seem to me like either one of us had a choice in the matter.

Our paths in life seemed destined to cross because of the choices we'd made. But as much as it felt right to me, I had to tread lightly. I wasn't going to force her to move any faster than she wanted.

I skipped shaving, already hearing my mother's complaint, and changed into something suitable for the son of a senator. After a drag of my hands through my hair, I was ready to go.

Piper looked up from her phone when I walked into the room. "You clean up nice."

"Thanks." I reached for my keys and wallet.

"Keeping the glasses on is a good touch. Very academic. Sexy."

I pulled her to me, laying a kiss on her that seemed to go on for hours because my hands had a mind of their own. Her tongue tasted faintly of coffee while her hair still smelled like my sheets.

When we finally broke apart, I cleared my throat and shook reality back into my head. "Kissing you is dangerous. Especially when I have to be somewhere in"—I checked my watch—"eighteen minutes."

She opened the door. "You started it."

I nodded after her, taking in the view of her body as she walked down the hall. Yeah. I totally started it.

CHAPTER 17

Piper

After my date-turned-sleepover with Blake, I hadn't seen him all week. We'd talked a lot via text, with one phone call Monday night. We were still on the phone when Bear and Connor showed up at his house to watch whatever game was on. I ended up on speaker phone with all of them, learning the ins and outs of baseball.

Bear had asked when he could try some of my new beer, but I was stuck on the recipe. I needed some clarity, and to drink some good beer that wasn't my own, so I decided to check out a brewery in St. Paul, and asked Blake to tag along.

And truth be told, when he pulled up to my house I was at the door waiting. I'd missed the guy. His model look was off the charts, and I couldn't be happier for the warm weather because Blake in a snug V-neck T-shirt had me looking forward to summer.

I stumbled mid-step as the thought hit me. Blake. All summer. I wondered if we'd be together. I hoped so.

"All right?" he asked, meeting me with a hand on my elbow when I staggered.

"Fine." I didn't think it would be the coolest move to describe my mind ramble about whether we were an official thing or not.

"You look stunning, as always."

The denim shorts and loose top didn't quite scream *stunning* to me, but I loved that he always complimented me. He made me feel confident even in ripped shorts I'd cut up myself from a pair of jeans.

"I was thinking the same thing about you," I said as he kissed my cheek.

He tugged on my ponytail. "That why you tripped? Blinded by my exquisite good looks?"

I scratched at the couple days' worth of scruff on his jaw. "Yes. Obviously."

"Careful," he said, opening the passenger door for me. "You'll break an ankle that way."

We set off toward St. Paul with the Avett Brothers as our soundtrack.

"Tell me how the thing went last weekend."

He opened up his window and hung his elbow outside. "Fine," he said, easing the car onto the highway. "We were at this middle school auditorium since he's running on an education platform."

"That's good."

"I guess. But I've learned just how many of your principles you have to give up in order to get a little bit back." He snuck a brief glance my way. "Politics is all show."

He scrubbed his hand over his mouth and took a deep breath as if it was difficult to even remember the event. "The campaign manager is an asshole, and even more condescending than my father, which is a feat."

I hadn't met his father yet, but from everything Blake had said about him, he wasn't a nice guy. It was a wonder Blake was.

"The media and a couple of reporters were there along with about two hundred faithful constituents. Dad said a couple of words, thanked his beautiful family, and shook a bunch of hands. And I got out of there as soon as I could."

I tried to find the bright side. "That must've been exciting, though . . . kind of?"

His bored expression was the answer. He reached for my hand, and we dropped the topic, leaving the rest of our drive in silence.

Once Blake parked, we walked into the brewery, and I was immediately overcome with the scents of yeast and wood. The walls and floor were cement, while the bar and tables were wooden, most of them covered in stickers. Four one-hundred-barrel fermentation tanks were in the back, separated from the tasting room by a waist-high wall that patrons placed their glasses on.

After perusing the chalkboard full of options, I'd found a seasonal ale that sounded pretty good, and I motioned for the bartender with an out-of-control beard. He introduced himself as Dominic and took our orders.

He handed me the tall, cool glass of beer, and I placed my index finger on the bar. "How long has this place been open?"

Dominic's face scrunched up as he thought. "We opened a little over three years ago now."

Once he had Blake's pint glass filled up, I asked another question. "Are you a brewer?"

"No, I help out here on weekends. My brother's the owner."

"Oh, is he around?"

Dominic nodded. "You want to talk to him? I think he's checking on one of the gauges in the back."

Once Dominic's back was turned, I faced Blake, who was sipping his lemon IPA. "How is it?"

"Yours is better."

I pinched his side. "You're just saying that. Don't do that. I want the truth."

"It is. Taste it." He handed me the glass, and I sipped.

It was a little too fruity for my taste. I liked the bitterness of the hops to come through more, but it was still good. I handed him my pale wheat to try in return.

"It's good."

I rolled my eyes, guessing how he would finish the statement. "But mine is still better?"

With his focus on the graffiti on the walls, he said a quick "Yeah."

I followed his attention around the room. It was cool, grungy, a little bit dirty, but in the best way possible.

"Man," I said, imagining my future, "I want this to be me."

He pointed to the two burly brothers. "You want to be that?"

"You know what I mean."

He laughed. "It will be you." He threw his arm around me and kissed my temple. "It has to be. You were meant to do this."

Deep down, I agreed. I felt it in my blood—weird to admit, having alcohol in my blood—but I was good at this. I loved it and had a passion for creating something that brought people together. As I scanned the room, I noticed everyone laughing, flirting, high-fiving, talking with heads bent together around pints of beer.

The idea of that possibly being my beer lit my soul on fire.

Just as I began to describe what I pictured for my own brewery, Dominic approached us with his brother, who introduced himself as Travis.

"First time here?" Travis asked.

"Yeah, but I've heard a lot about this place so I wanted to check it out for myself," I said.

Travis skimmed his hand over his long ponytail. "Happy to have you. What do you think of the ale?"

"Good." I nodded and took another sip. "Perfect for summer. And the tiny hint of pepper on the finish is nice."

"Caught that, huh?" Travis grinned. "Good palate you got there."

"Thanks. I brew, too."

Travis's smile positively lit up. Within the brewing community, we loved to meet one another, talk and learn, help one another out. "Oh, yeah?"

"Yeah. I opened up my own company a year ago. I'm in my garage for now, but working my way up. Hopefully . . ." I twirled my finger around in a circle indicating I wanted what he had.

"How's it going so far?" Travis put his elbow on the bar.

"Good."

"Better than good, right?" Blake said to me, then to Travis, "Her stuff is great. She's got this amber ale that's selling out at my gastropub."

Travis's eyebrows rose. "Your bar?"

"The Public." Blake nodded and moved his hand up my back, to my shoulder, and back down. Clearly possessive and proud. "Her beer's a hit."

Travis's smile faltered, and my stomach plummeted. "What's the name of your brewery?" he asked me.

"Out of the Bottle."

He stood up, putting two and two together, and wagged a finger at me. "I've actually heard of it. Pete's Tavern has your stout."

I swallowed down the sour taste in my mouth, hoping his next statement would be something complimentary.

"And your boyfriend is selling it, too? That's convenient."

My palms instantly began to sweat, my heart beating wildly in my chest. I had to defend myself. My company. "No. That's not—"

Blake piped up next to me. "Me having her beer has nothing to do with it selling well. No matter where it is, people are going to buy it because it's damn good."

Travis huffed at me, his thumb pointing toward Blake. "He your marketing director, too?"

I squeezed my eyes shut, praying for Blake to shut up and Travis not to jump to conclusions. This, right here, was *exactly* what I was afraid of.

"Listen, sweetie," Travis started in the most condescending tone known to women, "craft brewing is about what you can do with yeast and grain, not about who you sleep with. That won't—"

My vision and hearing went hazy as my body caught up to the spinning wheels in my head. Too many emotions to process coursed through my veins and my words failed me.

Blake's feet hit the floor with an audible thud when he stood up. "Whoa. Whoa. There's no need to talk like that."

I held my palm up to his face once my brain kicked in again, filled with rage. I could fight my own battles. "Travis, I know about brewing. I respect the craft. I spent two years in Germany learning it. Blake has nothing to do with how I got my start. That's all me."

"Yeah, well it seems good fortune has come by you pretty quickly. You've got your boyfriend in one bar, wonder what you did to get your account with Pete's Tavern. Hmm?"

I gasped. No one had ever accused me of sleeping with someone to get what I wanted, and it hurt more than I'd thought a false accusation could. This was exactly what I'd been afraid of. I'd done the one thing I said I wouldn't: gotten into a relationship with someone I worked with.

My jaw clenched shut with unsaid words, my eyes stinging, and Travis snorted in disgust. He spun away from me. Conversation over.

I shook away my unshed tears and turned from the bar, making my way out of the brewery as I heard Blake cursing at Travis behind me. Gray skies poured down rain, and I ran to Blake's car, my tears mixing with the falling drops.

I uselessly yanked on the locked door handle, desperate to get out of the rain and away from this place.

"Piper!" Blake called to me before his footsteps pounded on the pavement, and a moment later, he was next to me. "That di—"

I whirled around, my anger fixated on him. "I knew it! I knew this would happen!"

He blanched, but I didn't know why. I'd warned him. We had talked about this exact thing happening. "You knew I wanted to do this on my own, and that if we got together, people would think otherwise. And now, here I am, in the freaking pouring rain while another brewer thinks I slept with you and God knows how many other people to get my beer in their bars. Are you happy? Are you happy now that we're together and my reputation is ruined?"

"No, I'm not happy," he said, "but you have to know what he said isn't true."

"It doesn't matter!"

"What doesn't?"

When he reached for my hand, I shoved him away. "What went down in there was embarrassing. He's a colleague, and he accused me of sleeping my way through the brewing community. When word gets out, my career is going to be ruined."

"Your career?" He ran his hands through his wet hair before continuing. "Your career is your beer. And your beer is better than anything in that asshole's place." He held my shoulders, not letting me escape whatever pep talk he had prepared, but I didn't want to hear it.

I shook my head, eyes on the ground, too furious to look at him.

"He's probably jealous you've made a name for yourself in such a short time. It doesn't matter that I'm your boyfriend. It wouldn't matter if you dated the owner of Anheuser-Busch. It doesn't change the talent you have."

I backed away from him. An hour ago, I would've loved to hear those words from him, referring to himself as my boyfriend. But now I felt sick to my stomach.

"Come on," he said, finally unlocking the car. He opened the passenger door, tucked me in, and sprinted around to his side. We were both soaked, and I was miserable.

"Look at me."

After a minute, replaying the confrontation in my head, the fire had left me, only to be replaced by burnt ashes. My insides were cold and defeated, my fight gone. I lifted my eyes to Blake's, and he ran a hand over my dripping jaw.

"Can you honestly tell me you think you don't deserve what you've gotten in your career so far?"

I didn't answer. In the immediate aftermath of what had just happened, I felt like an imposter.

"You really think what you make isn't good enough to stand on its own? You think I only bought it to get you in my bed? Because, quite frankly, if you do, not only are you insulting yourself, but you're insulting me." His tone was biting, his words emphasized with stiff flicks of his hand. "Don't forget, I put everything I had into my bar, and I wouldn't do anything to damage that, *including* choosing to serve subpar alcohol."

I rubbed my temples. I believed in myself and my product, but God, it was so hard to start out. And with this footnote of Blake attached to me, I didn't know if I could recover. "This was a bad idea."

He put his hands on the steering wheel. "Yeah, coming here was a terrible idea."

"No," I corrected quietly. "I mean you and me."

CHAPTER 18

Piper

I needed to get my mind off my fight with Blake yesterday. I set down yet another case of Gray-Haired Lady and wiped beads of sweat from my forehead and upper lip. Brewing was simple biology; once you understood the fermentation process, it was relatively easy. The hard part was the physical labor: the lifting, pouring, moving.

Even though I was planning on speaking to him in person, it was impossible for me not to answer his text message asking if I was still upset.

My one-word answer:

Yes

Of course I was still upset. I'd been disparaged by another brewer. I'd put my whole future at risk by being with Blake, and I didn't know how to fix any of it, other than to work.

I was a one-woman band, grinding away eight to ten hours

every day, doing it all myself—the brewing, the packaging, the marketing. Nevertheless, I had big plans, and I wasn't going to let what happened yesterday affect me.

Or I'd try not to let it.

"You need help with that?"

I glanced over my shoulder to see Sonja in the open garage door. "Sure."

"I heard you grunting from the kitchen." She grabbed another full case and carried it to the trunk of my hatchback. Three cases later, my car was loaded and ready to drive over to the distributor tomorrow.

I stretched my arms above my head and wiped my hands on my T-shirt before sitting at the table I used for capping. Sonja leaned on the edge of the table and fiddled with one of the empty bottles. "The guys are coming over for dinner."

I tipped my head side to side, my neck cracking with relief. "The guys?"

"Bear, Connor, and Blake."

I groaned for a multitude of reasons, not the least of which being that I'd told Blake we were a mistake. "Since when are they 'the guys'?"

She blew her cheeks up and let out a rough exhale. "Since you got all googly-eyed over Blake. Since you introduced your best friend slash roommate to his friends. Since we all got drunk for my birthday and became BFFs for life."

I slid down in my seat, resting my head on the back of the chair. "Shit."

"What?"

"You know Blake and I had a fight. Why did you invite him over?"

Sonja shook her head at me like it should have been obvious. "First of all, you didn't even tell me what the fight was about. You just mumbled something about rain and a car, and then sulked in your room watching *Friends* for the rest of the night. Second of all, I wasn't going to invite the first two amigos over and leave the third out."

"You could've," I said lamely.

"And you could talk to Blake."

Sonja was right. She was always right. I hated that.

"So what was the fight about?" she asked, inclining her head in interest.

"This guy basically said I was sleeping with Blake and other owners to get my beer in their bars."

"*What?*" Sonja's eyes bulged, her shoulders rounding back into that fighter's pose I'd come to recognize.

I waved her off. "It's fine. I mean, it's not fine, but I stood my ground."

"So what happened?" She folded her arms over her chest.

I shrugged. "Blake didn't seem to make the connection of how us being together could be a problem for me."

"What are you going to do?"

I circled my hand in the air. "Apparently hang out with the guys while silently seething in the corner."

Sonja cracked a smile and patted me on the shoulder. "Terrific plan."

I pulled my T-shirt away from my chest, airing it out. I smelled like beer and yeast. "What time are they coming over?"

She set the bottle down and stood up straight. "Six."

"Sonja! It's five-thirty." I leapt out of the chair and ran out of the garage. I may have been mad at Blake, but I certainly didn't want him to see me in my ratty work clothes. "I have to shower and change and do my hair in"—I held up my cell phone—"in twenty-nine minutes!"

I sprinted into the house with Sonja's laughter as my soundtrack. I showered and changed in record time. I was slathering on tinted moisturizer just as loud footsteps clunked through the front door. Masculine voices carried upstairs, something about burgers on the grill, and I hurried through the rest of my makeup, putting my hair in a quick braid.

With an uneasiness in my belly, I forced myself to walk downstairs, greeted with waves from *the guys*.

"Finally," Bear said, lifting his beer to me. "Way to join the party late."

I noted it was the brown ale I'd been messing around with. I'd only made a few gallons and stored it in a keg. I didn't even have the recipe down yet, but he didn't seem to mind.

"Made yourself right at home, huh?" I jerked my chin toward his glass.

"Sonja told me to help myself." He pointed to the girl in question, who was seated cross-legged on the floor, drinking water with lemon. "Found it in the kegerator you have hidden in the basement."

"Hidden for a reason."

He threw me a grin before taking a big gulp of the brew. "It's good."

"It's getting there," I said, and turned to Connor, pointedly ignoring Blake's stare that felt like a laser beam on the side of my face. "How's it going?"

Connor tilted his head to the side. "Good. Hungry."

My lips tipped up in spite of my mood. "Man of few words."

Sonja stood up. "I'll get the salad started. Who's doing the grilling?"

Connor volunteered, and Sonja waved her hand toward the kitchen. "Come on, I'm starving. I missed my mid-afternoon snack."

"Uh-oh," Bear said with a smirk. "She missed her hourly two hundred calories. Someone call the doctor."

Quicker than a flash of light, Sonja struck her hand out to his bicep.

He grabbed his arm. "I'm kidding. You know I think it's hot when you talk calories to me."

He jumped back when she took another jab at him, and they playfully continued to shadowbox their way down the hall. Connor followed, leaving me still trying to ignore Blake.

"Hi, Sunshine." His voice was soft, even a bit apologetic, but I kept my eyes on the leg of the side table.

He stood up, grazing my hand when he said, "You look pretty."

"In this?" I rolled my eyes. I plucked at the old teal baseball T-shirt, knowing he was trying to get back into my good graces.

He brushed my braid over my shoulder. "You always look pretty. No matter what you wear."

I let out a begrudging "Thank you" but took one small step back. The way his mint-green button-down brought out the green flecks in his hazel eyes was distracting me from why I needed to stay away from him.

"Can we talk?"

"Didn't we do enough talking yesterday?"

He huffed. "No."

I assumed it was the lawyer in Blake that made him want to beat a dead horse.

"How about you show me where the magic happens?" Blake offered with his hands out.

I jerked back, my eyebrows pulling together. "You want to see *my bedroom*?"

His smile turned downright sinful as he reached for my waist. "Oh, I'm very interested in your bedroom, but I meant I want to see where you brew."

My cheeks heated, and for a moment I forgot I was supposed to be mad. "Oh." I toyed with the end of my braid. "Yeah, this way."

I led him past Sonja and Bear chopping vegetables in the kitchen and Connor fiddling with the temperature on our rinky-dink grill outside, down the short sidewalk to the two-car garage. I opened the side door and flipped the lights on. He let out a breath behind me that had me wishing we weren't in a cold garage filled with brewing supplies but upstairs with a nice, soft bed.

"Wow."

I glanced back at Blake, surprised at the awe in his voice. Working in here every day made me kind of blasé about it, but seeing it through his eyes, I could understand how it would be impressive.

Being in here automatically calmed me, and I pointed to the far side wall with the *Hang in There* poster. "That's where I boil."

"How much can you make at a time?" he asked, running his hand along one of the fermenters I'd elevated for easier access to the casks.

"Up to fifteen gallons, but I've usually got five fermenting." I pointed to the two tanks at the end. "I've always got the amber in those two since it's the most popular. I rotate the others through depending on what's selling."

I leaned back against the wall while he wandered around, inspecting everything as I answered his occasional questions, until he finally circled back to me.

"This is really incredible, Piper. To put this together all yourself."

I shrugged. "It's all I have for right now. I'll need backers if I ever want to be able to move out of here and actually open up a real brewery."

"This *is* a real brewery."

"You know what I mean."

He gave me an encouraging smile, but it melted. "Yeah. I know."

I'd put up a wall between us, sincerely scared my chances of achieving my dreams had been washed away with the rain yesterday. "Blake . . ." I started, emotion choking my words. "What if I've ruined everything?"

"Do you honestly believe that?"

I picked at the hem of my T-shirt until Blake stopped me with his hand on mine. "Talk to me, Piper."

"I think it's a strong possibility that rumors will spread about me. I already had to explain myself to Tim weeks ago, although I don't even think *he* believed me."

Blake put his hands on his hips. "Remind me who Tim is again."

"My old boss."

He snapped his fingers in recognition. "Right. What did Tim say?"

"He just . . . He told me he doesn't think it's a good idea for us to date, either."

"What does Tim know?" he grumbled.

"A lot, actually. A lot of people, business connections."

Blake waved me off, sparking my anger again. It felt like I was right back in Berlin with Oskar treating me like I didn't know what I was talking about. All that mattered was what he said. It didn't matter what I felt or thought. And I wasn't going to go through that again.

"It's easy for you to blow this off, but it's not for me. I hate having to always look over my shoulder, worrying about what people think of me. About how I dress or act. So go ahead, treat this like a joke, but this is my career. My *life*."

I turned away from him in a flurry, hiding the tears threatening to fall. I hated that he didn't understand how hard this was for me. After all this time of choosing my business over a man, I'd thought Blake was a turning point. That he'd be the one person who got it—got me—but his apathetic attitude toward my feelings proved otherwise.

"Just forget it, Blake." I turned around to him, keeping my shoulders back, feigning confidence. "Us being together is a bad idea."

"No." He shook his head, his hand in the air. "I object."

"What?" I huffed. "You can't . . . I . . ." My words failed. Between his serious expression and firm voice, I felt like I was in a courtroom.

"For as much as I hate hearing you say us being together is a bad idea, I hate even more all the crap you have to go through just because you're a woman. You think certain decisions you make will affect your career, and that makes you second-guess everything. But it's just not true. I'm not going to let anyone—not that dickbag from the brewery, not your old boss—let you doubt yourself."

He curved his hands around my wrists, his eyes so intent on me it was like he could see straight into me. Like he could see how afraid I was. I did want to be with him, but there were too many outside factors that I couldn't look past.

"I like you. A lot," he said sincerely. "And I know you like me. I also know you've worked incredibly hard to get where you're at, and you're going to get wherever you want to go because you'll earn it with that same ethic. It won't be because of me or anyone else. It's you. It has been you, and it will be you."

Compliments were hard for me to take in because sometimes it was difficult to believe in myself, and I darted my eyes away, ashamed to give in to those feelings of inadequacy.

But Blake, of course, didn't let me go. He brought my hands together, holding them up between us, and waited until I looked at him before saying, "I want to be with you. Whether you're making the best amber ale I've ever had or not. Is it a coincidence you do? Yeah. So what? I know what you're capable of. You know what you're capable of. Who gives a shit what other people think?"

"Because they can make or break me," I said.

"Okay." He shrugged. "Let's think this through. Let's assume Travis McTallywacker is indeed a douchebag who believes conjecture. He will most likely do one of two things." He held up the index finger on my right hand. "He will either stew about it with his meaty hands cooking up whatever lemon lager he makes, which is not as good as yours. Or"—he lifted my middle finger—"he'll take the ultimate juvenile way out and tell someone what he thinks has gone on between us."

He wiggled my middle finger. "Let's presume he goes

with option B because he's an asshole. Let's pretend he tells one, or two, or even three people. What are those people going to do?"

When I didn't answer, he filled in the blank. "Those people will likely ignore him because it's a rumor about a little known start-up, am I right?"

"I wouldn't say 'little known start-up,'" I said, and pursed my lips.

"There's that fight I'm used to." Blake bit back a smile. "And I wouldn't say that, either. You know why? Because your beer is *good*. How many times do you need to hear it? And from how many people?"

I let his words sink in before I spoke. "I know my beer is good. I don't need you to tell me. I don't need anyone to tell me. I know because all of my cases at the distributor sold out last week. Dave called me for double the amount; he said other bars are asking for it. I'm expanding faster than I can make it."

"Then what's the problem?" He threw his hands up.

"I'm afraid!" I yelled at him, then brought my hand up to cover my mouth, surprised I'd admitted that, let alone done it so loudly. "I told you I'm afraid," I said more quietly, collapsing into a chair. I was exhausted from keeping all of these emotions inside, and after finally speaking them, it felt like a weight had been lifted off me.

"What are you afraid of?" He tucked a few strands of loose hair behind my ear and skimmed my earlobe with his thumb before dropping it.

"Of failing. Of not being enough to run my company. Of not being enough for you." My voice cracked on the last word, and I hoped he didn't notice.

But he laughed. "You're kidding, right? You're the coolest, strongest, most badass person I know. You are way more than enough. I should be the one worried about not holding up my end."

He bent down and held my face between his hands. "You brew your own beer. You're the best girlfriend in the world. What can you say about me?" he asked with a lopsided grin. "That I've got majestic hair?"

I bit my teeth into my bottom lip, but I couldn't help my smile.

"I'm here for you—if you want me here, that is. But," he said seriously, "if you truly think us being together will hurt your future, then I'll walk away. I'll keep selling your beer at the Public, but I'll leave you alone."

The fact that he'd give me my space if I wanted it let me know he actually did understand how important it was for my business to succeed, and that I'd made a lot of sacrifices for it in the past. Turns out, I wasn't willing to sacrifice Blake, but before I could answer, he went on.

"I'd hate for you to give up on something we've barely gotten a chance to start."

I nodded and stood up, wrapping my arms around him. "Me too. What we have is worth it."

"I was hoping you'd say that."

I kissed his cheek before leaning back to look him in the eye. "I got a small glimpse of lawyer Blake, and he was super hot."

"Oh, yeah?" He chuckled.

I raised my eyebrows. "Uh-huh."

"Then let's go."

"What? Where?"

"Your bedroom."

I laughed as he tugged me out of the garage, past Connor, Bear, and Sonja in the backyard.

"Where are you two going?" Sonja asked as she handed a platter to Connor.

"Going to try some beer," I said, giving a quick excuse.

I ran toward the stairs once we were inside, and he followed after me, closing my bedroom door behind us. He took his shirt off as I hopped from one foot to the other, stripping my shorts off. He chuckled at my clumsiness and pulled me to the bed, kissing my forehead, cheek, nose, mouth, shoulder, any bit of skin that he could find, as he finished removing the rest of my clothes and then his.

He slid his hands down my back and thighs, my skin blazing under his touch. With every kiss and gentle caress, he shaped me, molded me to whatever he wanted. One hand dug into my hair, while the other rolled me underneath him, making me forget we'd ever had an argument.

After what seemed like forever, I lay on my side, and he pushed the hair out of my eyes.

"Do I look a mess?"

"No. You look properly ravaged," he answered against my lips.

I went quiet, and he frowned. "What's wrong?"

"Sorry for crying and being all . . ." I waved my hands around my head. "Yesterday."

He sat up suddenly, looking a bit annoyed. "No. Please don't make me into one of those guys who won't listen to a woman's feelings. And please, please, don't be one of those girls who is afraid to express herself. Don't apologize for it."

I tried to be strong in my daily life and not apologize for what I wanted, but I was self-conscious of coming off too emotional, or too bossy, or too weepy, or too whatever. It was a learned skill to not care what other people thought of me, and I was still working on it. Good thing Blake was around to help me.

"Okay?" He held his hand up for a high five, and I slapped it.

"Okay."

"And about what happened"—he kissed my palm then held it against his chest—"I know you think people are going to talk about you, but seriously, your beer speaks for itself. It doesn't need any defending, but I hope you know I will always defend you. Always."

"Always?" I smiled.

"Yeah. You're my girlfriend. You're first and foremost."

"I like the sound of that."

Then my boyfriend kissed me. "Let's go eat."

CHAPTER 19

Blake

Piper had taken to hanging out at the Public whenever she could. I was there almost every day because, even with two full-time managers, I liked to know what went on in my business. And that meant Piper was there with me, well on her way to being a permanent fixture.

She looked damn good as a permanent fixture.

I needed to finish up some paperwork, so I left her at the corner seat of the bar. The cocktail hour crowd hadn't quite filled out yet, and she'd sweet-talked Darren into making her some of his Reuben Bites. They were his newest creation, a current special on the appetizer menu. I'd come to learn Reuben sandwiches were one of Piper's favorite things to eat, and the little roll-ups were rapidly disappearing. I threatened to change the food's name to Piper's Bites, but she just did her casual Piper wave-off and went back to chowing down.

A little while later, I found her in the same spot talking to Missy, who was cutting up lemons in thin, even slices. From my hiding spot in the hallway, I studied Piper.

My girl's smile was contagious. My own lips turned up at whatever she said, and I wasn't even in the conversation. It was impossible to be in her presence and not feel included. She sucked you into her atmosphere, her happiness, and there was no other place I'd rather be. Being with Piper was like being spoiled with comfort. She was my well-worn blanket, my first cup of coffee in the morning, a cool breeze on a hot summer day. Her eyes, her hair, the way she played with the charm on her necklace—they were all my favorite things.

She clapped her hands once with a huge grin, excited about something, and talked animatedly, drawing invisible figures in the air with her fingers. Curious, I slipped onto the stool next to her.

". . . spent, like, five hundred bucks on a pair of cowboy boots," she said.

I butted into the conversation. "You have cowboy boots?"

She turned to me, surprise furrowing her brows. "No, Kayla does."

I traced one of her eyebrows with my thumb, smoothing it out.

Missy batted the air in front of my face with a napkin. "*Piper and I* were discussing Nashville. Jackie and I are going there for our anniversary."

Missy had married her longtime girlfriend last year. "When is it?"

"July 13."

"And you're going to Nashville, not some hideaway in the woods?"

Missy shrugged. "She likes country music."

When a patron called her away, I focused on Piper. "I didn't know you've been to Nashville."

"I've been to a lot of state capitals. It's on my parents' bucket list to see each one. Speaking of"—she held up her pointer finger—"my parents are going to Des Moines in a couple of weeks, and they're making a pit stop here."

"Okay." I grabbed a napkin to wipe a spot off the bar.

"Think you'd want to meet them?" Her high voice sounded like she was unsure of my answer, and I was almost offended.

"Of course I want to meet my girlfriend's parents. That all right? You ashamed of me or something?" I teased.

She threw her arms around me. "No. I just wanted to be sure you were okay with it. Meeting the parents, that's a big step."

It might've been a big step, but I didn't mind taking it. In fact, I looked forward to it. I angled my face, laying tiny kisses up and down the column of her neck. Funny how easily I'd forgotten how good she smelled, even funnier how much I missed her scent when she wasn't around. "Sunshine, I think you should know by now, I'd do just about anything for you."

Just as Piper's sweet lips met mine, Missy whistled. We both turned to her.

Missy had her chin in her hands, attention on us like a child watching a cartoon.

"Ah," she sighed, "young love."

I stood up, tugging Piper with me. "You sad about it? Now that you're an old, married lady?"

She blanched. "I am *not* old. Who told you that?"

"Your license."

I avoided the towel she threw at me and headed back to my office, towing Piper behind me. I shut the door with a soft click and threw my thumb over my shoulder. "She played softball for Oregon. Has a wicked arm. Nailed me once with a lime."

I touched the side of my head like the lump was still there. "I don't know why you're laughing. It's not funny."

She pressed her lips together, hiding her smile, and kissed my pout away, snaking her hands up the back of my T-shirt. Her fingers were cool against my skin, and after a long day hunched over my desk, it soothed my muscles. I nuzzled into the crook of her neck, neither of us quite kissing, while our lips barely trailed over each other.

Her mouth grazed my chin when she asked, "You ready to go over my stuff?"

The real reason Piper had shown up at the Public today was to go over her finances and business plan. Her goal was to open up her own brewery, and I wanted to help. But with her body pressed up against mine . . .

"Not really, no," I said, skating my lips across her cheek to her ear. "Maybe in a little while."

I cupped her thighs, guiding them up to my waist until she wrapped both of her legs around me. With her arms looped around my neck, I carried her the few steps across the room.

"I brought my laptop," she said, spying her messenger bag on the corner of my dark wooden desk. She reached for it, making one last-ditch attempt to get to the reason she was here.

We would.

But after.

"Mhmm." I carefully picked up the bag, without ever looking at it, and placed it on the floor. I dragged my teeth over her neck how I knew she liked.

And then she gave in. Without saying a word, she lifted her arms in the air, and that's all the hint I needed. I tried to lift her tank top over her head but couldn't. The thing had fourteen thousand straps crisscrossing along her back and somehow got trapped around her head and right arm on the way off.

The bun she wore on the top of her head drooped to the side, and the skin of her neck was blotchy from the scratch of my scruff. With one arm in the air, she looked drunk, and I chuckled.

"Don't just stand there and laugh," she said, giggling herself. "Help me."

"I don't know how." I fiddled with the shirt, trying to undo the mess of tangled straps. "You're wearing a death trap. I think I need the jaws of life."

"Just—"

Two quick knocks sounded on the door before Missy said, "Blake, your sister is here asking for you."

I groaned and fell forward, my head on Piper's shoulder. My sister, the destroyer of all that is good. The last thing I wanted to do was talk to her out there when we were just getting to the good stuff in here.

"Blake?"

"Yeah, I'm coming," I said toward the door even though I wasn't *coming*. Unfortunately. "You want to meet my sister?" I asked Piper, who was still twisted up in her top.

She pointed at herself as if to ask *Like this?*

"How 'bout we . . . ?" I guided her top off from the bottom hem. With a couple of tugs here and there, she was naked from the waist up, and I forgot all about what we were supposed to be doing.

I ducked my head down and bit her shoulder.

"We can't," she said, at once both trying to stop me from moving south while holding me close with her fingers in my hair.

"Yes, we can." I went to work on the button of her jeans.

She didn't put up a fight, and I scooted her to the end of the desk, allowing me to get a better angle. She looped her arms around me, her head falling back, and I nipped at her collarbone, dreaming of all the ways I wanted to take her in this office. On the desk. Against the wall. Over the—

The door burst open.

"What the hell?" I jerked upright as Piper gasped underneath. She covered herself, and I scrambled to pick up her shirt from the floor as my sister's shocked expression melted into a sly grin.

"You ever heard of knocking?" I yelled.

"How was I supposed to know you'd be back here with some random girl?" She said it like it wasn't her fault she'd interrupted us. Behind a closed door.

Once Piper had her bra and top back in place, I turned around to face Tiffany. "She is not some random girl, and anyone with manners would knock first."

She held her hands up. "Okay. Okay. No need to get snippy."

I ground my teeth together. She was impossible.

"Why don't you introduce me to your not-so-random girl?"

I glanced over my shoulder at Piper, whose face was tomato-red. I raised my brows silently, asking her permission, and she offered a faint nod and smile.

"Tiffany," I said, stepping to the side to let Piper stand up. "This is my girlfriend, Piper. Piper, this is my sister."

"Girlfriend?" she repeated, surprised.

"Hi." Piper offered Tiffany a handshake.

My sister appraised her with dark, critical eyes, reminiscent of my mother's. She barely grasped Piper's hand. "Hello."

"I'm sorry about—"

"Don't apologize," I told Piper. I crossed my arms, having absolutely no patience for Tiffany. "What are you doing here?"

Her brows narrowed in that way that made it seem like I was the stupid one. "It's Thirsty Thursday."

"Oh. Obviously." I couldn't believe my sister and Piper were the same age. Piper was mature, owned a business, and was a strong, independent woman. Tiffany still participated in college traditions and said things like "Thirsty Thursday."

"A couple of us from work are out for cocktails. I thought it was perfect we came here since I don't have to pay for drinks."

"You have to pay for drinks," I said with a roll of my eyes.

"But I'm your sister."

"And you can pay for your own drinks."

She stomped her foot. "Seriously? You're really going to make me pay?"

"Yes." If she was any other kind of person, I wouldn't have minded letting her order a few on me, but she was a spoiled brat who'd been here multiple times, always using me as her personal bank of alcohol.

She grumbled, and I motioned to the hallway. "Is that all you wanted?"

"Actually," she started, holding her cell phone up since it was fused to her hand. "I wanted to know if I could use your car."

"For what?"

"Madison's bachelorette is this weekend in Chicago."

"What about your car?"

She hesitated before answering. "It's in the shop. Had a little fender bender a few days ago."

I shook my head.

"Come on, Blake." She pouted.

"No. That's a six-hour drive. You can't even go six minutes without getting into a car accident."

"What am I supposed to do?"

"I don't know," I said, forcing her back toward the main room. "But find another ride. You're not using mine."

She whipped around on me just as we got to the bar. Her long, manicured fingernail pointed at me. "You're an asshole, you know that? Do you have any idea what it means to be family? You know, help each other?"

I brushed away her insinuation. Tiffany loved to play the victim. "Guess I shouldn't expect any Christmas gifts from you then. As usual."

She scoffed at me and turned on her heel to go back to the trio of men and one woman in her group. They were all dressed smartly, Tiffany the lone standout in a pink dress, a little short for the office, I thought.

I got Missy's attention. "Don't let her go without paying."

"Sure." Missy nodded, looking way too happy to have a mission for the night.

I pivoted around, heading back to the office. Piper was seated in the chair in front of my desk, laptop out.

"Sorry about that," I said, closing the door. "At least I learned a very important lesson." I pointedly locked the door.

She gave a little shrug and went back to whatever she was looking at on her computer.

I stood behind her, massaging her shoulders. "So."

"So, there's a two-story warehouse for sale that I love. I drove by it a couple weeks ago."

I bent down, checking out the pictures on the real estate website. I kissed her neck. "Looks good."

"It's nine hundred and fifty thousand." She pointed to the number on the screen, and I whistled.

"Steep." I curled my hands around her shoulders, slowly inching down to her chest.

"Blake." She turned to look back at me.

"What?" I played at innocence.

"No."

"No?" Five minutes ago we were hot and heavy; we could get back there real quick again.

"No."

"But—"

"No. Being interrupted kind of took the fun out of it."

"Fine." I plopped down in my chair with a heavy sigh. Tiffany knew how to ruin my day in more ways than one.

Piper placed her laptop on my desk. "She seems real nice, by the way."

I smirked at the sarcasm in her voice. "Yeah. A real peach."

"Has she always been so . . ."

"Childish?" I offered. "Juvenile? Foolish? Spoiled?"

Her gaze went up to the ceiling for a moment. "Yeah. All of the above."

I shrugged. "She's the baby. The apple of my parents' eye. She can do no wrong, according to them, and they feed into her ridiculous behavior."

"She kind of reminds me of that little girl from *Willy Wonka*. The one who wants a golden goose."

"Yup," I agreed, moving the laptop so we could both see. "That's exactly who she is. Now, what are we looking at here?"

Piper took me through her production calculations and projections. We also looked at her current budget, and what she wanted her budget to be when she expanded. We looked at costs of insurance, supplies and equipment, permits, and every other boring detail that went into making a brewery go. But this was the important groundwork.

We worked together to shape all the information into a business proposal so when she was ready, she could go to the bank for a loan. It took about four hours until we finished, but I could physically see her shoulders relax from the weight of the stress being taken away.

"Come on," I said, slipping her computer into her bag before looping it over my shoulder. "Let's go home."

"I'm exhausted." She yawned as we walked into the kitchen to leave out of the back door. "All that thinking took a lot out of me."

I waved good-bye to the staff and let Piper walk out to the parking lot in front of me, but I caught her wrist. "Hope you're not too tired. You owe me."

"I owe you?"

"Yeah. I believe the payment for helping you out with your business plan is two hours of naked Piper time."

She quirked her eyebrow. "And I believe you owe *me* for your sister walking in on us."

I clucked my tongue, shaking my head back and forth. "Call it a draw?"

"Okay."

We shook hands, and I snuck in a quick kiss before she headed to her car. "See you at your place in half an hour."

CHAPTER 20

Piper

I bounced on my toes by the luggage carousel, as groups of indistinguishable travelers with rolling bags, backpacks, earbuds, and heads bent down over cell phones passed me by.

Mom had texted about ten minutes ago that they had landed, and I couldn't be more excited to see her and Dad. Just as I was about to text her again, I saw my dad's head stick up above the rest. At almost sixty, he still had a full head of hair. It had started graying at the sides, but with his tall stature and angular chin, he could probably pass for forty-five.

"Dad!"

His head popped up, and behind his thin, wire-rimmed glasses his eyes lit up. "Pippi!"

I jumped into his arms, and he caught me around the waist. He kissed the top of my head. "I've missed you."

"I missed you, too," I said, then let go of him to hug my mom.

She kissed every part of my face while simultaneously smooshing me to her chest. Unlike my father, my mother was short, with a blond pixie cut. Looking at her, you wouldn't think she was fifty-six years old. Her skin was still mostly clear of wrinkles, save for the few around her bright blue eyes. I was convinced the Colorado mountain air kept my parents young and fit.

"Mommy," I cooed, feeling like a kid again in her arms.

"How's my girl been?"

"Good," I said, taking her hand. The three of us caught up while we waited for their luggage.

Dad told me he couldn't nap on the flight because he'd lost his beloved neck pillow, and Mom proudly showed off the new purse Dad had bought her for their anniversary last month. When the alert went off to let the passengers know their luggage was on its way, we immediately set off on our stupid, but decades-old, family game.

The person to get the most bags first won. I'm sure it started as a way to make it easier and faster to get out of the airport, but it had turned into an all-out Williams Family War. There was no actual prize to be won, unless you counted bragging rights, which just so happened to be enough for three constantly squabbling sisters.

After I was blocked from grabbing my dad's luggage by an older couple who moved slower than turtles, Mom ended up the winner, but I called foul since she had some teenage kid grab her bag from the belt. Dad gave her a high five and shrugged on his backpack.

I started toward the automatic doors outside, and Dad threw his arm around my shoulders. "Come on, tell me about this Blake guy while we walk."

My dad was good-natured, always pretending to be intimidating to boys when we were younger, but he was honestly too nice to ever scare anyone away.

"He's smart," I said, pulling my cell phone out. "He used to be a business litigation lawyer, but quit to open up the pub. He's trying to teach me how to swim." I showed Dad the picture of me in the pink floaties Blake had found, and he laughed.

"How's that working out?"

"Eh. He's gotten me to put my head under water."

"Baby steps," my dad said with a chuck under my chin.

My phone buzzed with a text from Blake. He'd made dinner reservations for the four of us at the Bachelor Farmer, a cool, mostly organic, Nordic-inspired restaurant.

"That's sweet," Mom said, reading the text when I showed it to her.

"How about I drop you and Dad off at the hotel, you take a nap or relax a little bit, then we can meet up later? Sound good?"

"Sounds great."

After dropping them off, I called Blake.

"Hey, Sunshine," he said when he picked up.

"You're the best, you know that?"

"I do, but I always like hearing it."

I laughed. "Also, not at all arrogant."

"I'd never dream of it." He actually sounded appalled at the accusation.

"I'm going to go home and clean up the house a bit since I didn't get a chance to this morning. I'm sure they'll want to come over to see Sonja and hang out."

"Hang out?"

"Yeah. I actually like my parents."

My mom and dad had always been the cool parents. Laid-back but firm, they never treated us like children. We did the usual things like staying out past curfew, but my sisters and I never got into serious trouble, and we were all really close. I'd come to realize as I got older that a family who all got along and spoke regularly was rather unusual. I couldn't be more appreciative of my parents and sisters.

He hummed on the other end of the line. "True. Do you need some help?"

"No, it's okay. I'll call you later."

"I'll be waiting."

We hung up, and I made a mental note to buy some extra special lingerie for my extra special guy. I hurried home to vacuum, pick up dirty dishes lying around, and light a few candles. Not that our house smelled bad, but between Sonja's sweaty sneakers in every corner and the residual hops and wheat smell permeating from the garage, our house didn't smell good. I had just enough time to shower and change before my parents showed up at my door.

"How'd you get here?" I asked, looking over my dad's shoulder to the random silver car at the curb.

"I have Uber now," he said, all proud of himself.

I ushered my parents inside. "I thought you'd lie down for a bit."

Dad kissed the top of my head. "Couldn't sleep when I'm just a few miles away from one of my top three favorite children."

"Well, gee, that's just about the best thing you've ever said to me."

He wrapped his arm around my shoulders. "I try."

Mom held her phone up. "Smile, you two."

Mom was forever snapping pictures. We'd only recently gotten her to upgrade from disposable cameras, and that was because we taught her how much easier it was to have them developed with the Walgreens app.

Mom smiled and pocketed her phone before checking how the house had changed since she'd been here last. Sonja had added funky mirrors along the back wall in the living room, and I'd bought the brown-and-teal rug for the floor. Her eyes caught on the plant on the side table.

She pointed at it. "A cactus?"

"Blake gave it to me on our first date. He said it reminded him of me."

Dad huffed. "A pointy, ugly plant reminded him of you?"

I turned the pot so they could see the budding flower. "A cactus blooms in the harshest of conditions. It's tough yet beautiful."

My dad's mouth moved into a begrudging smile. "Pretty slick."

"I know, right?" I laughed, and led them out to the back-yard, where we sat at the small bistro table, enjoying the late afternoon sun. Leo followed us outside, sprawling on his back for a tan. I took selfies with Mom to send to my sisters to make them jealous and talked shop with my dad. He'd always been enormously supportive of me. I don't know many fathers who'd be okay with sending their daughter off into the world to make alcohol.

My dad was.

"Hey, hey, hey, what's going on out here?" Blake said from behind me.

I jumped in my seat and whipped around. "What are you doing here?"

His dimple made a charming appearance as he shrugged. "Thought I'd call it a day a little early."

"And you thought you'd sneak up on us like a creep?"

"I heard your laugh from the sidewalk." He leaned down to kiss my cheek. "You look beautiful."

I moved slightly to kiss his lips, but kept it strictly PG. I turned back to my parents, who were both watching us with goofy smiles pasted on their faces. "Blake, these are my parents, Jamie and Christine. Mom, Dad, this is Blake."

My floppy-haired hero offered my parents a winning grin. "Nice to meet you both. Piper has told me a lot about you."

My dad shook Blake's hand. "That's funny, because she hasn't told us anything about you."

"Dad," I chided him.

Blake laughed congenially. "That's all right. There isn't much to tell. I'm just the guy who's hopelessly obsessed with your daughter."

My mom skipped his handshake and went right for the hug. "Don't listen to my husband. He's a fantastic liar. Piper's told us a lot about you, but come on, sit. I want to know more."

She pushed him into the chair next to her and I watched, bemused. My dad sipped his water with a slight quirk to his lips. My mother would have Blake occupied for the rest of the night. We stayed quiet as she questioned him for the next thirty minutes, and he responded with his usual charisma. Blake had her eating out of his palm by the time we left for dinner because of course.

My mom couldn't not love him. He was good-looking, owned his business, and had perfect manners. Between his obvious intelligence and healthy knowledge of Colorado trivia, which I was sure he spent quite a bit of time googling, Blake had won my dad over, too.

Blake was everything parents could want in a man for their daughter: brains, conviction, sense of humor, and most of all, respect for me.

He drove us to the Bachelor Farmer in his car, my dad in the front seat, asking all kinds of questions about the vehicle. I had no idea what they were saying, but I was happy they were getting along.

"He's so sweet," my mom said quietly, leaning over to my side in the back.

"Who?"

She rolled her eyes. "Blake, that's who."

"Thought you were talking about Dad."

She playfully poked my shoulder before launching into a story about Laurie and her husband, Jack, and their latest round of IVF. I listened absently while my eyes were on Blake. He'd gotten his hair trimmed so it didn't hang over his ears, and he was clean shaven. I could only assume he'd done it to impress my parents, and the thought made me adore him more.

He held my hand from the parking lot into the restaurant, and my brain wandered into the future as I watched my parents walking in front of us, my dad's arm around my mom's shoulders. They'd been married for thirty years and were still in love.

The idea flitted through my mind that I could have the same thing, and maybe it would be with Blake.

Once inside, Blake and I sat in the tall booth across from my parents in high-back chairs. "How did you two meet?" Blake asked after we ordered.

"We met in college, at a bar. I had my eye on this girl across the place all night. I noticed her platinum blond hair and tight pink pants."

"It was the eighties," Mom interjected.

"And all of her friends were watching so intently as she told whatever story she was telling, and I thought *God, I have to meet this girl.*"

Blake squeezed my knee, and I looked over to him.

He tucked a piece of hair behind my ear and tugged twice on my earlobe. "Sounds familiar."

"So when I needed a partner for pool," Dad went on, "I asked Chris."

"I liked that he was so tall," she said, and Blake and I laughed as Dad shrugged.

"Good genetics."

"Used the old let-me-show-you-how-to-play trick?" Blake joked.

Dad snorted out a laugh. "No way. My wife here is a ringer. She mopped the floor with all of us."

"Mrs. Williams, the pool shark." Blake high-fived my mom to her utter delight.

"But please don't call me Mrs. Williams. It makes me feel old. Call me Chris."

Blake nodded then turned to my dad.

"You can still call me Mr. Williams."

For one millisecond Blake's face went ashen, and Dad laughed. "I'm kidding. Jamie is fine. But remember that terrified feeling for later whenever you think you're about to make my daughter cry."

I covered my face with my hands. "Oh my God, Dad. You are the least funny person I know."

Blake drew me into his side. "I don't plan on it, but I'll remember. Don't worry, sir."

"Sir? I like that. Sir." He smiled down at my mom. "Why haven't I demanded all of my daughter's boyfriends call me 'sir'?"

"Missed opportunity."

"Totally."

We all laughed at my dad's goofy grin and enjoyed the rest of dinner with easy conversation.

After we'd eaten our fill, Blake pushed away from the table. "Excuse me for a second."

As soon he was out of earshot, Dad turned to me and tossed his napkin on his plate. "I like him, Pipes. I like him a lot."

Mom chimed in, too. "He's so sweet and attentive. When anyone talks, he really listens. That's a tough quality to find in someone. And the way he looks at you . . ." Her eyebrows rose as her words lingered in the air. "I can see why you love him," she said, instantly lifting my thoughts from some vague formations to a sudden, urgent stop.

"What? I don't—" I stopped.

Did I love Blake?

Since we'd started dating, I hadn't stopped to think about it. Sometimes it felt surreal, the way we were together, like we'd known each other our whole lives. We understood each other, found common ground, and respected one another. There was never an awkwardness or fear that this was one-sided.

I knew the way he looked at me was reflected back at him from my eyes, the same way I knew deep down he felt about me the way I felt about him. I never second-guessed that. But before I could talk to my mom about any of this, get her opinion on it, Blake was back.

He slid into his chair with an easy smile. "Anyone up for a beer at the Public? I've got a hankering for a Natural Red."

I palmed his face, pushing his lecherous smile away while my parents both agreed, with "I can't wait to see the bar" and "I thought you'd never ask."

"Let me just get the check," my dad murmured, and Blake momentarily flicked his eyes away from mine.

"I got it already. Don't worry about it."

I was positive my parents offered smiles and words of gratitude, but I couldn't have torn my gaze away from Blake even if I'd wanted to. His hazel eyes were more blue today, and he stared at me with such happiness and contentment I realized that if I could only look into one man's eyes for the rest of my life, I wanted them to be his.

The realization hit me like a physical blow. I loved Blake.

CHAPTER 21

Blake

I woke up early Thursday morning because of Piper's fidgeting at my side. Her constant writhing and wiggling to get comfortable were much less noticeable in my cozy king bed than in her tiny full, but they were no less annoying. Though I'd pretty much gotten used to snoring and crazy legs since we'd been staying at each other's houses every night for the past few weeks.

She had her own toothbrush and razor in my bathroom, and I had a couple pairs of clean underwear in one of her drawers.

Practically domesticated.

I threw my arm around her middle to settle her. "What are you doing?"

"I got a text from my mom." She fumbled with her phone.

Her parents had spent two days in Minneapolis before

they took off for Des Moines on Monday, and I had to say, I kind of wished they'd stayed longer. I loved hanging out with them. Her dad was a cool guy, a computer analyst with an outdoor obsession, and a semi-serious fatherly stare. I got to treat him to a round of golf the day before they left, which he really seemed to enjoy, and we got to talk about our mutual love for beer, the Apple Watch, and Piper. It was important for him to know I didn't take my relationship with his daughter lightly. I wanted him to be aware that I was in this for the long haul, and that he should expect to see me around. When I told him those exact words, he shook my hand and smiled.

Her mom, on the other hand, didn't need so much convincing. I didn't know why she had taken me under her wing like she had, but I hadn't minded. She liked me, and even more, liked me and Piper together, so whatever it was she saw in me and us, I could only hope to keep it up. She'd told me countless times how happy we looked together, and she was right. We were happy.

"What'd she say?" I asked Piper through a yawn.

"They ran into a man who split with his former brewery. He was a silent partner and was bought out," she said, reading from her phone. "They told him about me and gave him one of my beers they packed."

"That's cool." I tucked my head between her arm and rib cage, hoping she'd get the message and rub my back like she sometimes did in the mornings.

"Apparently they talked a good game because he's going to be e-mailing me later."

I sat up, the sheet falling to my waist, and grabbed my glasses from my nightstand, forgetting about the backrub. "What does that mean?"

"I don't know."

"Maybe he's looking to invest." My heart jumped in my chest. This was the break she'd been waiting for. "That would be incredible," I said with a kiss against her temple.

She bit back a smile, her eyes bright with optimism. "I don't want to get my hopes up."

"But isn't that what it sounds like?" I couldn't help the enthusiasm punctuating my voice. After all this time, after all of her hard work, I hoped this was her big break.

"I don't know. Maybe." She bit her bottom lip as her eyes lowered back to her phone. She reread the texts, and I could see the wheels in her head spinning. She needed a distraction.

I propped my hands on either side of her hips and eased my way on top of her. When she didn't put her cell phone down, I took it away, kissing her jaw.

She whined, "I was in the middle of a text back to my mom."

"And I'm in the middle of trying to seduce you. No cell phones allowed."

She made a soft sound of protest, and I licked at her ear then down her throat, forcing her legs apart with mine. She stretched her neck, silently telling me to move my lips to the spot she liked best, while surreptitiously reaching for her phone. She slipped it out of my grip and lifted it in the air behind my back. I assumed to continue texting her mother.

Sneaky move.

I sat back on my heels, coming to terms with the fact that there'd be no morning delight for me.

"Fine. Let's get breakfast." I had the morning off before I needed to be at the pub. "Come on," I said, squeezing her big toe. "To the Original Pancake House we go."

For the first time since I'd known Piper, it had taken her more than twenty minutes to get ready. All because she didn't want to leave her cell phone for longer than a few seconds. I understood her anticipation, but her nervous energy had nowhere to go.

She hopped around my bathroom, tying her hair up in a ponytail then letting it drop back down a whopping three times. Her legs bounced in the car while she held her phone between her hands as if it were going to run away at any moment. Even while we ate, she picked the phone up, put the phone down. Waiting. Waiting. Waiting.

I tried to keep her mind off the incoming e-mail. I played tic-tac-toe on the napkins with her, told her stupid stories about me, Bear, and Connor, even passed on that dumb joke about the pirate who walks into a bar with a steering wheel in his pants and says, "It's driving me nuts." She'd smile or laugh on cue, but her eyes never strayed far from the screen.

When we got back to her house, I couldn't take it anymore. "You have to relax. I have three hours before I need to go into work, and we're going to spend them *Gilmore Girl*-ing."

"*Gilmore Girl*-ing," she repeated with a laugh. "You're wonderful."

We sat together on the couch with her feet in my lap and her head on the other end of the sofa, and I streamed my Netflix account onto her television.

Toward the end of the second season, it was clear to me Rory was going to dump Dean. "I don't know why she'd pick Jess over Dean," I said, pointing to the television. Dean was a bit of a doofus, but wanted the best for Rory. Jess was a douchebag. I shook my head. "Nice guys always finish last."

"You love this show," Piper taunted. "Admit it, you love *Gilmore Girls*."

I waved her off. "I do not."

"Just like you never watched an episode of *Sex and the City*, right?" She poked me in the side with her foot, bringing up the memory of the day we first met.

She climbed into my lap and swept my hair off my forehead. "You're a nice guy."

"Yeah?" I wrapped my arms around her middle, bringing her flush against me, her legs on either side of my hips.

"Yeah. You took me out for pancakes this morning"—she dragged her fingers down the back of my neck—"bought me chocolate peanut butter ice cream without me having to ask"—down my chest and stomach—"and changed your toilet paper to the kind I like instead of the brand you used to buy." Reaching the hem of my T-shirt, she snuck her hands underneath the cotton to tease at my skin. "All really nice guy things."

My muscles involuntarily twitched under her touch. "I do try."

"Mhmm," she hummed into a kiss, her lips tasting of the cantaloupe she'd been nibbling on. "And I want you to finish first."

I didn't understand what she meant right away; I was too busy pulling the thin strap of her tank top down to pay attention, until she ground down on me.

My body responded immediately, hardening against her.

She slipped off me and knelt on the floor, looking up at me with both a sweet smile and sexy bedroom eyes. I couldn't keep my own gaze off her as she unbuttoned my dark chino shorts and yanked the zipper down.

God, I loved that. The ownership we had over each other with familiar touches and silent communication. I hadn't ever had that with anyone before, and I didn't want to have it with anyone else. I wanted Piper to be the only woman to ever own my body and heart.

Watching her expertly work me with her mouth made the pleasure ten times better, and I tugged on her hair, feeling the telltale burn deep down in my belly. She rubbed her hands up and down my thighs and leaned back. "Nice guys finish first."

"Your turn." I growled and wrapped my hands around her elbows, snatching her up from the floor and onto my lap once again. I viciously went after her throat, using my teeth and tongue to torture her as much as she'd tortured me.

I drew a line from her neck to her collarbone, and the telltale wiggle of her hips in my hands let me know I was on the right track. The shirt she wore was no match for me. I jerked it and her bra out of the way to get to her, but just as I lifted her off me to reach for her shorts, her phone dinged.

And I was back at square one. No matter how much she tried to ignore it, I knew her mind was on her phone two feet away. Her mouth was no longer as pliable. Her body no longer lax under my hands.

"Go on," I said, my hands going slack against the couch. If her brain wasn't 100 percent into it, neither was I.

She scooted off me, and fixed her tiny shorts and put her shirt straps back in place before she grabbed her cell. "It's the e-mail."

Her eyes widened at me, and my stomach dropped. If I could have absorbed her angst, I would have, but all I could do was be there for her.

"What's it say?"

She read it silently to herself, the index finger of her left hand constantly twirling a lock of hair.

"You're killing me, Smalls," I said, trying to lighten the mood while I read over her shoulder.

"Dear Piper," she started. "I was given your contact information by your parents. We met blah, blah, blah," she said, skipping down to the important stuff. "A few years ago, I invested in the DeLio Brothers Brewery, which has been running successfully since 2013. Last year, I parted ways with the brothers, on good terms, but have spent the last six months making plans to open another craft brewery in Des Moines. I have the capital and resources to invest, but I need the talent. From my research of your website, the pitch from your lovely parents, and the sample of your beer, I am very interested in speaking to you more about the possibility of bringing you on in this endeavor."

She slowly turned to me, a small curl to her lips, when she said, "He wants me to call him. He's already bought the lot and has all the permits."

"That's great." I pressed a kiss to her lips, my elation swiftly plummeting to worry when I put two and two together. "In Des Moines?"

"What?" she asked against my mouth.

"You'd have to move to Iowa."

She jerked away from me, her eyes clouding to a moss green as they darted back and forth between my own. The reality must have just hit her, too, because she opened and closed her mouth. "I don't . . . think . . . I . . . well, I don't know."

I nodded in agreement, but we both knew what the truth was.

If she wanted this investment opportunity, she'd have to move to another state.

"Yeah, we'll cross that bridge when we get there," I said, but I hoped to God we'd never get there.

And didn't that make me a jerk?

I was supposed to be Piper's number one supporter, but here I was praying this would work out for *me*. I didn't want to give her up, but if she took this offer, I'd have to. And I'd have to do it with a smile on my face.

I pressed play on *Gilmore Girls* and tried to ignore Piper next to me, happily typing away on her phone.

I crossed my arms and pretended I wasn't sulking as I watched Dean publicly break up with Rory at the dance-a-thon. Who knew I'd become so emotionally involved in fictional characters' lives?

"You okay?" Piper asked, running her fingers down my arm to link her fingers with mine.

"Yeah." I pasted on a grin, but she saw through it. The suspicion in her gaze was clear, and no matter how much I tried, I couldn't hide my disappointment at her future plans. It may not have been set in stone yet, but you didn't have to own a crystal ball to see what was going to happen.

CHAPTER 22

Piper

The conversation with Bob Oakden lasted more than two hours. The passion in his voice was evident as he told me about his history in the business. He'd earned his money in his younger days in commercial real estate, and once he turned fifty, he'd decided he wanted to explore other options. He loved beer and wanted to get involved in brewing, which led him to invest in a small start-up.

Bob was the type of guy who followed his gut, or at least that's what he told me when he offered me the deal: a partnership to open a brewery in Des Moines where we'd split profits in half. He was willing to put up almost all of the starting cash, but he wanted a piece of Out of the Bottle in return. He sent me over a business offer and contract, and pictures of the beautiful old brick firehouse he'd bought with the intention of gutting the inside for a brewery.

It all sounded ideal, and I obviously had a lot to think over.

I told him so, and he kindly offered to put me up in a hotel if I was interested in meeting with him in Des Moines. Once again, I told him thank you and that I'd consider it.

But once I hung up, fear got the best of me. I had a lot of information and questions floating around my brain, and I couldn't digest any of it.

My room suddenly became too small, the lights too bright, and I had to get out. I changed into mesh shorts and a T-shirt, and threw on sneakers before knocking on Sonja's door. "I need some fresh air."

I knew she had been up early this morning to teach a class at the gym and only had an hour or two of downtime before she had to go back, but I needed her.

She tossed her phone down to the bed. "Wanna go for a run?"

My brain was so fried, I actually answered, "Yeah," and hopped down the stairs toward the front door. Sonja joined me a minute later in her neon-green sneakers, Nike shorts, and matching top, looking much more adept at this running business than I was.

"Let's go this way." She started us off to the left, heading in the direction of the park.

I concentrated on putting one foot in front of the other, breathing in through my nose and out of my mouth like Sonja reminded me. The only positive effect of running was that I was too focused on the fire in my lungs to think about the chaos in my brain. I took one step, and then another, and then another, until I couldn't catch my breath.

Sweat rolled down my temple, and I slowed to a stop with my hands on my hips. "Hold on. Hold on."

"We've haven't gone a mile yet," Sonja said, doing the annoying thing where she kept running in place as if she wanted to rub it in my face that I had failed so spectacularly at keeping up.

"Why are we doing this again?" I asked once I had enough air in my lungs.

"Because you said you needed some fresh air and some time to think."

I bent over, studying pebbles on the ground as I fully caught my breath. "Oh, yeah."

Sonja headed down the road, walking at an easy pace, and I followed her dutifully. We went about half a mile before she finally asked, "So, you going to tell me what happened with the phone call or not?"

"He wants to invest."

She knocked her shoulder into mine. "I knew you'd get it."

I smiled.

"Why do you look all"—she pointed to my face—"wonky?"

I batted her hand away. "I don't look wonky."

"You do. Why?"

Why? That was the question.

An opportunity like this was what I'd been working for, so shouldn't I have jumped at the offer?

A few years ago—hell, even a few months ago—I would've been making plans, packing up, buying a plane ticket, but now there were too many things, too many people slowing me down.

"I'm not sure what to do. I mean, this is a huge, huge leap for me. Out of the Bottle would finally have a home, but I'd have to split ownership with Bob. I can't take that proposal lightly. Or the move, for that matter. Right?"

"Let's think about this logically with a pro and con list. Give me a pro."

"Pro. Okay." I named the first thing that came to mind. "Out of the Bottle would be a fully functioning brewery with state-of-the-art equipment for increased production."

"Definite pro." She nodded. "Con?"

"I wouldn't be in control anymore. I'd have to run all of my decisions past Bob. He knows what he's doing and is clearly industry savvy, but I've been solo for so long, I don't know if I'd like having a partner."

"Totally understandable. Pro?"

I shrugged. "I've never been to Iowa, so I'd get to live in a new place. Meet new people."

Her eyebrows narrowed slightly at that, not quite a glower, but close enough. "Con?"

"I don't think those new people would be as cool as you." I grabbed my best friend's hand and leaned my head down on her shoulder.

"Obviously. No one *ever* is as cool as me." She pointed at me. "Pro?"

"Not as cold there."

Sonja inclined her head. "True. But you got used to these winters after a while, huh? Con?"

I retied my hair into a messy bun, wicking the sweat back. "I'd have to start all over again, move, find a place to live."

"That does suck. Think about all the packing you'll have to do. At least you'll have some strapping young men to help you this time."

Speaking of strapping young men, Blake's face popped into my head, not that he had ever left, but I'd been trying to keep him out of my decision. I was a business owner, and I needed to decide what was best for me and the business. This had nothing to do with him.

Except, it had *everything* to do with him.

"Des Moines is only three hours away," I said, determined to stay positive. "Close enough that I could drive back, or you could come there." I didn't have to mention Blake's name for Sonja to hear it in my voice.

She frowned ever so slightly before replacing it with a smile. "Yeah." She nodded, the usual assurance filling her voice. "Three hours is nothing."

I shot my hands out to the side, the truth thundering in my head because I didn't think even Sonja believed the words that had just come out of her mouth. "It's three *hours* away!"

"I know! Do you have to move?" Sonja wailed, hanging on to my arm. "I'm so happy for you, I really am, but I hate that it's not here."

She had given voice to every thought racing through my mind. I thought being outside, talking it through, would help, but it had only led to more confusion.

The more confused I became, the angrier I got with myself. I prided myself on my independence, on always doing what *I* wanted to do, so I hated that I couldn't do that now. That I couldn't make a clear-cut decision.

"Let's review," Sonja said, taking off on a quick trot. I had to follow as she went on. "The good things about this choice are that Out of the Bottle would have backing, you'd finally be able to make your own beer in a place that wasn't our garage, and you'd be out there in the world. Bad things: you'd have to consider your new partner, move to a different state, and leave me. And, you know, Blake."

I'd tried to convince myself that if I didn't say his name, I could pretend it wasn't true.

There was no Blake Reed in Des Moines, and he entered in on the list with an underline and an exclamation point.

And I had officially become someone I promised myself I wouldn't. After my relationship with Oskar ended, I'd decided I would never let another man influence my decisions. I'd never let a man get in front of my dreams. I'd never give up who I wanted to be or what I wanted.

But here I was thinking of doing that exact thing.

I pushed forward, chugging along as fast as I could. "I'm not going to not take the offer because of Blake."

"I . . . think that makes sense."

"No, it doesn't," I huffed out. "It's a double negative. It doesn't make sense. None of this makes sense."

I ran so slow that Sonja turned around and walked backwards faster than I was going forward.

"Blake wasn't supposed to happen. I wasn't supposed to fall for the guy who sold my beer. I wasn't supposed to have to choose between him and my dream."

"I know this probably isn't at all helpful, but I'll support whatever you decide, and I'm sure Blake will do the same."

"You're right." I rubbed at a cramp in my side. I wanted her to tell me what to do, not leave it all up to me. "Not helpful at all."

"Let's go." She steered me down the street, circling back to the house. It felt like a million miles until we arrived at our front door, where I promptly fell to the ground in exhaustion. The run may not have helped clear my head, but it made me physically too tired to even think about my decision.

Sonja pulled out a house key from a hidden pocket in her shorts and unlocked the front door. Leo's tail lazily swung in the window as he gazed outside at me. That fat cat actually had the nerve to taunt me while all he did was eat treats and sleep.

"Here." Sonja tossed me a water bottle, but it fell to the grass with a thump when I didn't catch it.

"What time do you have to go in to work?" I asked, reaching over for the water.

"About an hour. I'm there until late tonight. What are you going to do today?"

"The same thing I do every night, Pinky, try to take over the world."

Sonja didn't laugh at my joke, and I sat up.

"That's Brain, from *Pinky and the Brain*."

She shrugged.

"*Animaniacs*. You never watched it?"

"Nope."

I slapped a hand to my head. "I knew you lived under a rock, but I didn't know it was a giant boulder. It was a cartoon series on weekday afternoons. Arguably the greatest cartoon of the nineties."

"Arguably," she repeated, raising perfectly tweezed eyebrows. "I'll look into it when I have time."

But she never had the time. That's why she never got any of my pop culture references. Because while I was parked in front of the television, binge-watching *The Big Bang Theory*, Sonja was off working or working out. Maybe for my next birthday, I'd ask her to spend the whole day with me, in her pajamas, watching every old cartoon I could find. She'd hate it.

Then I remembered that if I moved to Des Moines, I wouldn't be home for my next birthday, and my exhaustion couldn't cover up my apprehension anymore. I slowly stood up and made my way inside and upstairs. I flipped my sneakers off into my closet and picked up my cell phone from where I'd left it on my dresser.

There were a few texts from Blake.

Let me know how the call went.

I thought you had the call at 9, is it still going on?

Three hours? Damn, I hope you're hatching a plan for world domination.

I'm meeting Bear for lunch, want to come?

The last message was about twenty minutes ago. I texted him back.

Just got in from a run.

When he didn't get back to me, I hopped into the shower and changed into clean clothes before heading out back to the garage.

My sanctuary.

The one place I didn't have to think.

I got out my bottle capper, a simple machine to make the job easier without having to pay the thousands of dollars for an inline capper. Capping bottles was a menial task, but I could focus on it without exerting much energy, and soon I got into a rhythm.

I sang along to the Band of Horses album I had playing through the Bluetooth speakers, and thought about absolutely nothing except for how the labels might look on a darker glass bottle Bob had suggested.

That was until my phone rang.

And I knew it was him.

I wiped my hands on a rag and picked my phone up to find I was right. It was Blake.

I didn't have it in me to answer, so I let it go to voicemail and waited another twenty minutes until I pressed play on the message.

"Hey, Sunshine. We missed you at lunch. A couple of high

school hockey players recognized Bear and wouldn't leave the table. We ended up hanging out with a bunch of sixteen-year-olds. It was actually kind of fun."

I snorted at his reluctant laugh.

"I'm just calling to check in. See what's up . . . and I miss you. That's crazy though, right? I slept in your bed last night, woke up with my arms around you, and kissed you before I left for work this morning five hours ago."

I'd probably have laughed if my skin hadn't heated up at the warmth in his voice.

"I shouldn't miss you yet," the message continued. *"That borders on creepy stalker."*

I bit back a smile at his crazy train of thought.

"But I do. And I had to tell you. I miss you every day, no matter how long we're apart."

"It's not creepy," I said, forgetting for a second this wasn't actually him I was listening to. "It's sweet."

"Anyway. Call or text me later. Let me know what's going on. I'm closing tonight since Missy's not feeling well, so I'll probably just head home. Unless you tell me otherwise. Talk to you later. Bye."

The message clicked off and instead of deleting it, I replayed it, letting his voice calm me.

Hey, Sunshine.

I miss you.

I shouldn't miss you yet.

But I do.

And how could I move away after that?

CHAPTER 23

Blake

My cell phone rang just as I pressed send on a new produce order. I hoped it was Piper since she'd never called me back. My nerves had gotten the best of me, and I imagined that all kind of things had gone wrong.

It had only been a day, but I didn't know why she couldn't call me or answer my texts. At this point, it was difficult for me to concentrate on anything, and it was Piper's fault. I wished it was for a better reason than me being annoyed at her, but I tried to let it go as I picked my phone up.

Mom flashed on the screen.

And I became annoyed times two.

I hadn't talked to my mother in weeks. Avoidance was easier than dealing with all the anxiety and anger that came with the guilt trips, but if I let it go to voicemail too many times it would only be worse.

"Hey, Mom."

"Hi, darling."

"What's up?"

"I was calling about Sunday. Your sister informed me yesterday that you have a girlfriend. Is that true?"

I scratched my eyebrow with my thumb. "Uh. Yeah."

"Why haven't you said anything?"

"I—"

"Why wouldn't you want to introduce her to your family?"

"Well, I didn't—"

"Blake, I don't appreciate you keeping secrets from us. Especially one about a woman in your life. Tiffany said you seemed awfully . . . taken with this girl."

"Piper. Her name is Piper. And, yeah, I like her a lot."

Like was such a stupid word to use. I didn't just like Piper.

I adored her.

I cherished her. Even when she didn't call me back.

I treasured, idolized, and worshipped her.

I loved her. But the first time I said those words certainly wasn't going to be to my mother.

"Why don't you bring this Piper to dinner?"

I paused, thinking this through. If Piper was going to stay in my life, she'd have to meet my family eventually. But there was a sinking feeling in my stomach that it wouldn't matter soon.

"I'll see if she's available."

"Wonderful." My mother's voice dropped down an octave, telling the truth behind her dubious superlative. "I'm very interested to meet this girl after what your sister has told me."

"Okay," I said, wrapping up the conversation. "I'll let you know either way. Thanks."

"Bye-bye, darling."

As soon as I hung up, the sinking feeling in my stomach bottomed out as my mother's words hit me.

I'm very interested to meet this girl after what your sister has told me.

My sister had only met Piper because she walked in on us about to have sex in my office. They were in each other's presence for a minute, maybe two, at the most. What could Tiffany possibly have said to my mother?

And what had made my mother say that sentence in *that* tone?

I pushed away from my desk, checking the time. It was almost six o'clock on a Friday night, the beginning of the night, but I didn't feel like sticking around any longer. Missy's bug had turned out to only be a twenty-four-hour thing, and she was feeling better and already back behind the bar. Between her, Abe, and Lou, the newest bartender, they didn't need me looking over their shoulders. Plus Darren had the kitchen covered.

I grabbed my keys, waved good-bye to everyone, and ducked out with one destination in mind.

When I rang the doorbell and no one answered, I figured Piper must be out back. I took the usual trek to the backyard to find the garage open, and I spied a flash of red through the doorway.

Sticking my head in the door, I found Piper cleaning up some of her supplies in the utility sink while she had one of her brew kettles boiling and a cask being filled from a fermenter. She had time to brew but not to talk to me?

As I watched her do three things at once, I imagined how much easier it would be when she had a staff and a bigger place. Something larger than a twenty-by-thirty garage. I wanted that for her. I wanted her to be successful, I wanted it more than I wanted it for myself. I could tell from her rounded posture that she was tired, and it made me feel bad for being so put out over a phone call.

"Hey."

She jumped at the word and swung around, brandishing a filter as a weapon. Her eyes softened from their previously wide fright. "Jesus, you scared me."

"Sorry." I stepped closer. "How's everything going back here?"

She shrugged. "The usual. Got another batch of the grisette cooking."

"How are you? You never got back to me."

"I know."

"How come? You don't like me anymore?" I said jokingly, but it came out flat.

"I was just so exhausted yesterday."

She barely met my eyes when she said that, and I didn't like it. Whatever was bothering her had the hair on the back of my neck standing up. The eerie feeling from earlier while talking with my mom came back.

I wanted to comfort her, but something was off between us. "So tell me what happened with Bob."

She took her time capping off the cask as she replayed the phone call. But she wasn't as excited as I'd thought she'd be, and I didn't understand why until she told me what he wanted—an equal partnership in the company.

"Oh, wow." It wasn't unheard of or unreasonable to make this kind of deal. If Bob was backing this company, he'd want a stake in it. It made sense, but it also made me cringe. Out of the Bottle was Piper's. Even though this would be a huge break, it would mean Piper giving up a piece of her dream. I couldn't imagine what she was feeling.

"I know," she said, correctly reading the tone of my reaction as she turned off the propane burner. "I told him I needed a few days to think about it."

"And that's what you've been doing since yesterday?"

She turned to me slowly, a heaviness to her face even though a smile peeked out. "Pretty much."

I had no words to make this decision any easier, and I didn't want to flood her with any more apprehension, so I offered her my open arms. "Come here."

She walked into me, resting her head on my shoulder, wrapping her arms around my waist. I held her tightly, kissed her head, and rubbed at the tension between her shoulder blades. We stood like that, breathing together, for a few moments.

"Want to Netflix and chill?"

"Yes, please," she murmured against me.

"Order in?"

"Yeah, but first I have to shower. I'm all sweaty."

She didn't tell me to follow her inside, but I did anyway, stalking behind just out of reach. She took the elastic band out of her hair, and her hair fell down her back as she reached the bathroom. She knew I was there, but acted as if I wasn't, and suddenly I was the guest to a private show.

I sat on the closed toilet lid, openly observing everything she did. She turned the water nozzle on and held her hand under the spout for a few seconds, testing the temperature.

She took off her sneakers and tossed them to the side before removing her socks, all the while offering me the view of her ass. Next, she dragged her jeans off, revealing every inch of the creamy skin of her legs, and dropped them in the laundry basket. Then came the best part, because I loved it when she crossed her arms over her abdomen to leisurely pull her shirt over her head in the most provocative movement of all time.

With a flick of her fingers, her bra was off, and in one quick swoop, her underwear hit the floor. I scarcely got a good look at her body as she carefully stepped into the bathtub with one hand on the wall before stepping behind the transparent plastic shower curtain.

With a restraint I didn't know I had, I tore my eyes away and cleared my head of all lewd thoughts. "So, I talked to my mom today."

"Yeah?" The snap of a bottle echoed in the room, followed by the sweet scent of her sun-ripened strawberry shampoo.

"I have dinner with my parents on Sunday, and they want you to come."

"They do?"

The surprise in her voice had me regretting my decision to not introduce her earlier. I didn't want her to think they hadn't wanted to meet her. "Yeah. My mom said she's really interested to meet my girlfriend."

A few long seconds passed where I thought maybe she'd say no.

The water turned off and the curtain flicked open to reveal my beautiful Piper in all of her naked glory. She gathered her hair up over her right shoulder and wrung it out as rivulets of water flowed down her arms, over her breasts, down her stomach.

"Blake?"

I lifted my eyes up to her face. "Huh? What?"

"I said could you give me that towel, please?"

"Oh. Yeah, yeah." I handed her the green-and-pink towel. "I couldn't . . ." I shook my head, refocusing, and a smile tugged at the corner of her lips as she wrapped the plush cotton around her body, hiding all the good stuff from me.

"You're cute when you're flustered."

"I can't help it. You're gorgeous."

She grabbed a smaller towel from the rack and did some

kind of magic trick to keep it on top of her head, and then treated me to the *Piper Lotions Her Legs* show.

She rubbed the white lotion into her thighs and calves in circular motions, and I hummed, gaining a new appreciation for Bath & Body Works cucumber melon. "Do you want to go on Sunday? Dinner's at six."

"Yeah, I'd like to finally meet the infamous Senator and Mrs. Reed."

I let out a relieved breath and followed her into her bedroom.

"What am I supposed to wear?"

Just as I was about to answer, she dropped her towel.

"You look pretty outstanding naked."

She barked out a laugh, and finally began to look like herself. Her eyes sparked with trouble as color bloomed in her cheeks. She deliberately sashayed to me, entrancing me. I fell backwards onto the bed and reached out to her.

"You smell so good," I said, bringing my lips to her neck when she lay down next to me. I skimmed my hands up and down her body, feeling how tense she was. Knowing what was on her mind, I wanted her to relax.

I nipped and licked at her until she moaned, and I was fully assured she was thinking of nothing else but this moment. I moved over her pink skin and bright eyes. I needed more of her.

We slowly and tenderly kissed until we pushed the sheets from the bed and my clothes were off. On our sides, I caressed her leg, lifting it over my hip, aligning our bodies.

Piper had gone on birth control, but we still always used condoms to be safe.

"Piper." I curved my palm around her jaw, sucking on her bottom lip. "We haven't talked about it, but can we . . . ?

"I need to feel you," I said, skimming my hand from her jaw down her neck, over the slight curve of her breast, to her waist.

She nodded. "I need to feel you, too."

She hitched her leg higher on my hip, opening herself up to me as I guided myself into her. I needed a moment to soak it all in. The way she felt, the way we moved together, how she looked—I wanted to remember all of it. There was nothing sweeter than her warm breath against my cheek, her heat pulsing around me, and her eyes staring into mine. This was everything. My past, my present, and my future. All in this woman.

She closed her eyes and kissed me with a sigh. I did the same, losing myself in her body. I pressed my forehead to hers, rolling my hips slowly. Moving together and apart, we found this intimate, unhurried rhythm that was as torturous as it was heavenly. This was making love.

When she kissed me, it was like she tried to breathe in my air. She stared into my eyes, serious and sort of sad. It felt a little like she was trying to take it all in, like it was our last time.

But I could never give her up, not after this. Not ever.

We found our high together, my body buzzing like an electrical current passed through me to her and back. By the time we came back down, we were both breathing hard, and I managed to peel myself away from her to look in her eyes.

I wanted to say a million things, not the least of which was *I love you, please don't go*, but I didn't think it was right to ask her not to follow her dreams, or appropriate to bring it up now, just after we'd had sex. Quite possibly the best sex we'd ever had. The best sex anyone had ever had.

I kissed her nose, grinning down at her. We were both flushed and sweaty and a bit of a mess. "Want another shower?"

"Sure." She propped herself up on her elbows, a tired smile twisting her lips. "But no funny business."

I stood, holding my hands up in innocence. "I make no promises."

CHAPTER 24

Piper

The following Sunday, I fretted for an hour over what to wear, changing into almost every outfit I owned before finally deciding on a funky purple-and-pink flowered dress that flared at my waist. It had a little bit of frill on the neckline and gave off an I'm-a-sweetheart vibe, which I thought was the goal when meeting the parents.

I slipped on black flats and swiped on lip gloss before I headed downstairs to where Blake was laid out on the couch, one arm behind his head, the other draped over Leo.

"Is this okay?" I asked him, twirling in a circle.

"You look perfect."

"And look." I shoved my hands into the dress. "It has pockets."

He playfully rolled his eyes at me. "Congratulations."

I tossed my light pink cardigan over my shoulder, because even though we were well on our way into summer, I wasn't sure if spaghetti straps were appropriate for the Reed family dinner.

"Are you sure this is okay?" I asked, looking down at my outfit.

He stood up. "Yeah, it's fine."

"That doesn't sound reassuring."

"You're beautiful," he said with a kiss to my cheek. "My parents are . . ."

He trailed off as he opened the front door, and I stepped outside before turning to him. "You parents are what?"

"Assholes, I told you before. I know you're nervous about meeting them, but I'd be surprised if they said more than a few sentences to you. I'm the black sheep, remember? I'm sure all of their attention will be on why I'm wearing shoes without laces."

I dragged my eyes down Blake's long body, covered in a fitted button-down rolled to his elbows, slim light blue pants, and tan boat shoes, looking every bit the preppy boy he tended to cover up, and I laughed.

He always knew exactly what to say to calm me down, and I rose up to kiss him.

Blake kept his hand on my leg as we drove, only periodically removing it to change lanes on the highway or fix the air vents. We didn't talk much, and the Iowa offer had a lot to do with it. I didn't know if our reasons for avoiding it were the same, but I was thankful he didn't press me on the issue. I needed to make this decision on my own. For right now, though, I was focused on making a good impression on his parents.

I hadn't grown up in the Twin Cities area, but I was aware of the St. Paul neighborhood Blake grew up in. It was where all the elite lived, in these grand old houses. I couldn't take my eyes off them as we cruised down Summit Avenue.

"Oh my God, look at that one." I stretched my arm out of the window to point to the Old English–looking mansion. "And that one." The one with the balconies. "I want that one." The gray stone house was a beauty.

He laughed beside me. "How many millions do you have in savings?"

"Think they'd take a down payment in beer?"

"Doubt it." We pulled into the breezeway of a grandiose redbrick mansion that seemed more suited for Victorian New England with its wraparound porch and peaked roof.

My nerves ratcheted up. Blake's family came from serious money, and I was suddenly more unsure of myself than I'd ever been. Would there be a lot of forks to choose from at dinner? Should I have worn a longer dress? What did I do when I met his family? Handshake? Kiss the ring?

He took my hand as we walked up the forever-long sidewalk. The front door had one of those heavy knockers, and I was a teensy bit disappointed at its plain oval shape. A lion or some other ostentatious decoration would have suited the rest of the place. "Looks a bit like Richard and Emily's house in *Gilmore Girls*, doesn't it?"

He shrugged. "I guess."

He rang the doorbell and a woman in a plain navy dress answered. She introduced herself as Sandra, and I was caught off-guard it wasn't one of Blake's parents ushering us inside. But then again with all this money, I should've expected they'd have someone working in their house.

Gleaming hardwood floors and a Persian rug greeted me in the foyer, along with a tall grandfather clock and an exotic plant of a kind I'd never seen before.

There were too many opulent decorations to look at all at once, but a marble table caught my attention. It had a little gold antique trinket on it, next to a framed black-and-white photo of a couple, I assumed from a few generations ago. Old money, for sure.

There were more corridors than in a *Scooby Doo* cartoon, and I wondered if maybe a ghost or two had made a home here. There had to be at least thirty different rooms in this house if the number of doors in this *wing* was any indication.

Sandra led us to a room with a chimney and elegant picture windows. It smelled like citrus furniture polish, exactly what I assumed a picture from a design magazine would smell like in real life.

"Darling." A tall woman with cropped dark hair stood from a thick leather chair that creaked under her movement. With nude heels and a sleeveless cream-colored dress, she looked every bit the senator's wife. She kissed both of Blake's cheeks. "How are you?"

"Good," Blake answered flatly. "Mom, this is Piper." The

gentle pressure of his hand on my back propelled me forward.

"Hi. It's so nice to finally meet you," I said, going in for a hug, but she stuck her hand out. The forward motion between the both of us had her fingers grazing my boobs.

Great first impression.

I laughed it off, but her thin lips disappeared into a straight line.

"I'm sorry." I shook her hand, but it was weird now. "Mrs. Reed."

She didn't correct me on using her last name, so I assumed that's what I'd be calling her. Formalities.

Her dark gaze briefly studied me, and I resisted playing with my hair or biting my lips under her scrutiny. "Your home is lovely."

"Thank you." She brought her attention back to Blake, a pleasant smile on her burgundy-painted lips. "Your hair is long again."

Blake ran his fingers through it, but the movement was all wrong. His posture looked as if a pole were stuck up his ass.

"I like it long," I said, opening my big mouth.

Mrs. Reed flicked her eyes to me, and it was difficult not to cower. "Yes, well, this shaggy mop-top look doesn't do anything for his handsome face. He's a grown man, after all, not a teenager."

Blake exhaled deeply through his nose, and I felt the urge to stick up for my man, even if it was only about his hair, but my reply died on my tongue when Mrs. Reed raised a challenging eyebrow. As if she *wanted* me to argue, maybe give her a reason to hate me.

I wouldn't.

She pivoted, and her steps echoed on the hardwood as she walked toward the center of the room. Tiffany sat on the couch, one leg crossed over the other, her head bent over her cell phone. Mrs. Reed tapped her knee for her attention. Tiffany spared Blake and me a passing glance. "What's up, big bro? Pippa?"

"Piper."

Tiffany slowly lifted her head. "Hmm?"

I may have had to keep my mouth shut with Blake's mom, but I didn't need to take it from his sister. "My name is Piper."

She shrugged. "'Kay."

I'd like to say I was shocked by her flippant and obviously purposeful dig, but I wasn't.

Blake stepped on her toes as he walked by.

"Ouch. Shit, Blake."

"Language," Mrs. Reed warned.

Blake apologized with a quick "Oops. Sorry," and offered me a one-shoulder shrug. It was no *Oops.*

"Jacob, we have company," Mrs. Reed said as she picked up a martini with one olive from a glass side table.

A man in a crisp dark polo shirt and ironed khakis came around the corner with the *New York Times* stuck under his arm. With his wavy hair combed into place and gray-blue eyes behind dark-rimmed glasses perched on his nose, he was strikingly attractive. An older version of Blake.

It was hard to reconcile the stories Blake had told me about the man who stood in front of me now, a gracious smile on his face. "And who is this?" he asked Blake even though his focus was still on me.

"This is my girlfriend, Piper."

"Piper, that's an unusual name."

Okay, he might've been an older version of Blake, but he was definitely more intimidating. From his encapsulating handshake to the thick tenor of his voice, this was the kind of man who commanded attention. And right now, I was the sole focus of his.

"I guess," I said, not knowing how to respond to the semi-accusation.

"Would you care for a drink?" Mrs. Reed asked, after sipping from her martini.

"A beer would be great," I said cheerfully.

A snort sounded next to me, but I didn't dare turn to confirm it was Tiffany, my eyes on Mrs. Reed when she ever-so-slightly cringed before putting on a phony smile.

"We don't have beer."

I cleared my throat. "A water is fine."

Mrs. Reed nodded and flicked her eyes up behind me. "Sandra, a water for Piper."

I couldn't imagine how Sandra worked here, under Mrs. Reed's harsh stare and Tiffany's passive-aggressive noises. Mr.

Reed had yet to say anything more than a greeting to me, and I was actually grateful for that. Five minutes with Blake's family, and I couldn't raise my arms, sure my pit stains were enormous.

Sandra returned a minute later with an ice water. I thanked her quietly and sat down next to Blake on a stiff-backed love seat. There wasn't much in this house that looked or felt comfortable. I was surprised there weren't parts cordoned off, furniture meant only to be seen and not used. Like a museum.

"So, Piper," Mrs. Reed started. "Tiffany told us she met you at Blake's bar."

My cheeks heated remembering how Tiffany had interrupted us. I hoped his sister had glossed over that part.

"Yes. Only briefly," I said. "But I'd like us to get to know each other better."

Mrs. Reed hummed into her drink while Tiffany ignored me, typing away on her phone. Blake dropped his arm on the back of the sofa behind me, sending me an encouraging but toned-down smile. He knew how nervous I was, and how hard I would try to make his parents like me, but already it felt like a losing battle.

"How exactly did you two meet?" Mrs. Reed asked, pointing between me and Blake.

"At the Public."

"Oh. At the bar a lot then, hmm?" Mrs. Reed sipped her martini while Mr. Reed let out a low sound, a mixture of a snort and a huff.

"Piper is a local brewer." Blake wrapped his hand around my shoulder. "Her beer is some of the best around."

Mr. Reed lifted his eyes at that, focusing on me over the rims of his glasses. "You're a beer brewer?"

"Yes."

"How did you get into that hobby?"

My fingers tightened on my water glass as my stomach tied in a knot. "Brewing isn't a *hobby*. It can be for some people, but it's my job. I work out of a nanobrewery now, but I have plans on expanding my career."

"You two make quite a pair, don't you?" He tossed his paper down on the table in front of him, and it landed with an audible smack that reverberated through my body. This was not going well at all.

Blake stood up and walked over to the wet bar, leaving me to decipher that comment alone. I was saved from having to come up with a reply by Sandra telling us dinner was ready. Mr. Reed motioned for me to go ahead of everyone else. I did, even though my paranoia that they were talking about me behind my back was impossible to ignore. I took the chair Sandra pointed to, and I began to wonder if maybe she was a very lifelike robot as opposed to a breathing human.

I sat up straight, shoulders back, hands in my lap, trying desperately not to seem out of place. I kept a smile on my face as Mr. and Mrs. Reed settled in their seats at opposite ends of the long dining room table. Tiffany eyed me from her position across from me, and finally, to my relief, Blake sat down next to me, a dark amber drink in his hand.

Our salmon and pasta dinners were served on silver-rimmed fine china, and thankfully we each had only one fork. I picked mine up to eat a bite, but froze at Mrs. Reed's throat clearing. Her left eyebrow was raised in a high arch, her hands folded in front of her.

"We pray before meals in the Reed household."

"Oh, I'm so sorry." I dropped my fork, and folded my hands like a good little girl. If there was something I could do to fix how this night was going, I had no idea what it was.

Mrs. Reed said some prayer that had Blake shaking his head. Guess he wasn't exaggerating when he told me stories about his parents.

"It's okay," he whispered to me, but I wasn't so sure about that.

I waited until everyone else had had their first bite before I took mine. We ate in silence, punctuated with the tinkling of glasses or the scraping of utensils against plates. I didn't know if these family dinners were usually so quiet, but it made me uncomfortable. My family dinners were filled with laughter, stories, and lots of smiles.

This was torture. Filled with antagonism and serious stares.

"How's your job going, Tiffany?" Mr. Reed finally asked. "Any more mention of your promotion?"

Blake quietly sighed next to me as he sat back in his chair, taking another sip of his drink.

"No, but I'm assuming I'll hear something at the end of the summer."

"What do you do?" I asked.

Tiffany tossed her hair over one shoulder. "I'm the executive assistant to the assistant vice president at Harper and Marks."

"What does that mean?"

Blake leaned in close to me like he had a secret, but spoke loud enough for everyone at the table to hear. "It means she's Dwight from *The Office*."

I let out a giggle. Dwight was one of the funniest characters on that show, the office fool. Self-important but clueless.

"What are you laughing at?" Tiffany shot at me.

My smile dropped. "Nothing. Blake just said—"

"You're just a beer wench," Tiffany said with a nasty curl to her lip.

"Tiffany," Mrs. Reed hissed. "That's unkind. Even if she is only an alcohol maker."

Mr. Reed did that huffing guffaw, which it didn't take long for me to learn was his way of expressing condescension.

I trapped my napkin in my fists, hoping to keep my voice even when I said, "A brewer. People who create beer are called brewers. And I've gone to school to become a master brewer."

"Piper apprenticed in Germany," Blake said then, staring at his sister. "She supports herself doing something she loves. She's not *only* an alcohol maker." He finished his words with his gaze on his mother.

"Right." Mrs. Reed held her martini glass up to me in a toast. "She's not only an alcohol maker. She's Blake's girlfriend, too."

Her words had an underhanded tone to them, and my hackles rose.

"About that." Mr. Reed patted his mouth with his cloth napkin before he turned to his son. "Frank's daughter just moved back home. We were thinking maybe you two could meet up."

"Oh, Amanda is perfect." Mrs. Reed clapped in glee. "That would be wonderful if you two could work something out."

My jaw dropped. These people were actually telling Blake to go out with another woman. In front of me.

Blake rested his hand on my knee underneath the table. "No. And I'm offended you'd even bring that up. Especially here. Now. In front of my girlfriend, Piper. I'm not interested in Amanda, or whatever it is you think she can do for you."

Mr. Reed propped his elbows on the table, still focused on Blake. His face held no emotion when he pointed at me and said, "Well, she won't help us win an election with her *master* brewing. What do you think they'll say about her? About us?"

My eyes stung with tears. I honestly had never been so insulted in my life. I'd done absolutely nothing to deserve this kind of treatment, like I was some piece of trash under his shoe. Worse, Mrs. Reed was nodding along, with her pinched face.

"Good thing *we're* not running for office," Blake said, pushing away from the table. His chair screeched loudly against the floor as he grabbed my hand, forcing me to stand. "C'mon. Let's go."

Mrs. Reed opened her mouth, and I cringed inwardly at whatever she was about to say, but Blake cut her off with a hand up. "Don't even start. You've done this. Anytime you let Dad talk down to me. Anytime you chose to let Tiffany do whatever she wanted. I gave you so many chances to be my mother, yet you turned a blind eye to me. So now I'm doing the same to you."

He stalked out of the house, but not before throwing an "I'm done with this family" over his shoulder. I had to jog to keep up. With the tight hold of his fingers around mine, I feared my arm might come out of its socket. Then again, maybe that would take the sting out of what had just happened.

He opened the passenger door for me, and after I slid into my seat, he slammed the door shut. I jumped at the force of it. His jaw jutted out in anger as he took his spot behind the wheel, tension coming off him in palpable waves.

"That was horrible. Your parents are horrible," I said, wiping away a tear trailing down my cheek.

He didn't say anything, and his silence irked me even more.

"They hated me from the beginning."

"They hate everyone. You're not special." His voice was eerily calm, like his father's, and my tears slowed as resentment rose inside me.

I knew he was upset, too, but his words only added to my already emotionally wrecked state of mind. "I tried to be congenial. I tried to be what they'd want in your girlfriend."

He flicked on the turn signal. "Yeah, well, maybe you shouldn't have tried so hard."

I stared at his profile in shock. First his family, and now him? "Why are you acting like this?"

"I'm not acting like anything." His monotone words had me wondering what had happened to my sweet boyfriend.

"You are. You're acting like this is my fault."

He let out a long-suffering sigh but didn't say anything.

"I know you don't care since you deal with your parents all the time, but that sucked for me, Blake."

"You don't think I know that? I care, Piper. I fucking care," he said, slamming his hand on the steering wheel. "If I didn't care about what they were saying, I wouldn't have left. You think it's easy for me to hear the shit they were saying? It's not. But it's also not worth the fight, either."

"So you're saying I'm not worth fighting for?" I didn't mean to yell, but the words poured out of me. I was on the cusp of making a major life decision and uprooting everything I knew, and here he was, basically saying he didn't care enough to fight.

He stopped at a red light. His nostrils flared. "Don't twist my words."

I threw my hands up, feeling like I'd fallen into another dimension. "I'm not, but that's what you said."

He shook his head. "It's not worth fighting with my parents over *anything*. They won't listen. Trying to reason with them is like reasoning with a brick wall. What they said back there was disgusting. You and I both know it, so don't think it didn't hurt me. Because it did. I love you, Piper. I've been fighting for you from the beginning. I've supported you one thousand percent in everything you've wanted to do. I mean, for Christ's sake, I was the one who got your beer at Pete's Tavern and Monkey Bar. I stood up for you with the douchebag at—"

My brain stalled to a sudden stop at his words. "What do you mean *you* got *my* beer at *bars*?"

Just when I thought this night couldn't get any worse, a fiery comet had landed in the middle of this emotional tornado, destroying everything in a quick and single strike.

And my beautiful, charming boyfriend, who somewhere in that rant had said he loved me, disappeared and broke my heart into a million pieces.

CHAPTER 25

Blake

O h shit. I definitely hadn't meant to spill *that* secret.

I'd seen Piper annoyed. I'd seen her angry. But I'd never seen her quite this furious. Her eyes wide and dark. Her fingertips curled toward me like talons. Her face pulled into a glaring frown.

I stuttered out a few words, the reason for her sudden rage clear. But after that dinner, I didn't have enough patience or sanity to have this argument. I just wanted to go home and lose myself in my girlfriend and not think of anything other than how good she felt.

"You can't drop a bomb like that and then not explain it. What did you do?" she demanded with her palms up.

The sun was just about to set, the sky a rainbow of navy, violet, pink, and orange behind Piper. If I hadn't been in the middle of this nightmare, I'd have pointed out how beautiful it was. How gorgeous she was in this moment. "What do you mean?"

"You're too smart to play dumb. You said *you* got my beer into other bars. We made a deal in the beginning. I didn't want to go out with you until *I* had gotten into two other bars. It was important for me to make it on my own. But no. You had to go get involved. You overstepped your bounds, Blake. And it's *not* okay. This is my company. Mine. You had no right to throw your weight and influence around."

"You're talking like I'm Michael Corleone or something."

"Don't make a joke out of this," she snapped.

"I—"

A horn honked three times behind us, cutting off any other clever comeback I had. We both looked over our shoulders at the car then up at the green light. I let out a breath and swirled around in my seat to drive through the intersection.

She mumbled something under her breath, and I glanced at her. "What?"

"I said I feel like I'm back in Germany with Oskar."

That almost made me laugh. "You feel like you're back in Germany? What does that even mean? What does your ex have anything to do with this?"

She shook her head. "You don't get it. To be second-guessed, given advice that you didn't ask for, told how you should act differently or just give up completely . . . that's what I deal with all the time. That's what Oskar did to me. And that's what you did to me, too."

For a moment, I was stunned into silence. That's honestly what she thought of me? "How can you compare me and Oskar? I want you to do what you want to do, he didn't." A minute ago, I had just told Piper I loved her, but the part she cared about was me helping her business. That was backwards. "I want you to succeed, so yeah, I helped you along a little bit. What's wrong with that?"

"Everything is wrong with that. Why don't you get that I need to do this on my own? After everything, you did the one thing I asked you *not* to do."

"I thought I was supporting you. I didn't think it was that big of a deal."

She growled, pulling at her hair. "Oh my God. I had to sit on your parents' uncomfortable chairs while they basically said I wasn't good enough to be in their company, and then I find out my success is all because of you. I couldn't feel more worthless if I tried."

"That is absolutely crazy." I took the corner a little hard, and my car bounced when all four tires hit the street again. I swore, I couldn't understand why Piper thought so little of herself sometimes. "I thought we had this issue all ironed out."

"You've been lying to me this whole time. Our relationship is based on a deal you broke."

"I didn't break our deal. I helped it along." It was a flimsy excuse at best, but at this point it was my only defense. I had supported her the best way I knew how.

She pointed a finger at me. "Don't try to lawyer your way out of this."

"I'm not trying to lawyer my way out of anything, but I am trying to explain what happened. I can't defend myself if you won't listen."

"You wouldn't have to defend yourself if you didn't do anything wrong to begin with!"

This twenty-minute ride back to Piper's house was starting to feel like twenty hours. I couldn't get there fast enough, and the guy in front of me wasn't even driving the speed limit. "Come on," I yelled through the windshield. "This is . . ."

My words trailed off. My brain was driving on all cylinders, but it had no direction. I had no idea what to say to Piper to make this better. I had no idea if I *could* say anything to make it better. Her arms were crossed over her chest, her gaze fixed out her open window, and I figured it was best to wait until we got to her home to talk about it further.

I hadn't even fully slowed down in front of her house when Piper opened her door. "Piper! Jesus."

I shut the car off and followed her to the front door. "Piper."

She refused to acknowledge me, and when I reached to open the door, she turned abruptly in the entrance, halting me.

"I need to think."

"Okay." I held on to the door with my right hand, moving to step inside again.

Piper was immobile. "Without you."

Those two words cut me in half. That wasn't us. We talked things through, we worked together. We were a team.

"Can't we talk for a little bit?"

She gazed at the toe of her shoe for a moment before she stood up straight, pulling all of her long red hair behind her shoulders. "I think you've done enough talking."

I immediately wanted to argue. I had points all laid out in my head, reasons for us to sit down, but logic wouldn't help this situation.

"Talk to me, please. Nothing's changed between us." I stared into her hardened eyes. "Has it?"

"Everything's changed," she said quietly with a shrug, one that looked as if she had the weight of the world on her shoulders. "I don't want to be reliant on you or anyone. And you made me, whether you realize it or not. You took away my independence."

"I didn't mean for it to be like that. I thought I was help- ing. I never intended to hurt you."

She ignored me, and each second she didn't smile or take my offered hand was a dagger in my chest. "Don't do this," I pleaded, unsure of what I was even begging for. *Don't turn me away. Don't let this come between us.* "Please."

"I don't think we should be together anymore," she said with finality.

"Don't say that. Come on, you're upset, I get it, but we can get through this." In my previous life, I'd won more cases as a lawyer than I could count, and been to court more times than that, but this was one fight I wasn't sure I could win.

"There is no *we*, Blake. There is you and me, and I'm not even sure I want to have us in the same sentence."

I'd lost the trust of the one woman who'd become my world, and hell if it didn't feel like I'd lost part of myself, too. I blew out a breath, hoping I'd be able to take another one. "That's it then? You're giving up on us?"

"I'm not giving up. I'm moving on." She turned and went inside, and I stood frozen, staring at the white paint peeling on the corner of the front door.

Just a few hours ago, I'd kissed her, tasted her mint toothpaste. Two days ago, we'd been together, nothing between us but our sweat and skin. Weeks before that, I'd met her parents, told her father I was in it for the long haul. And before that, on the windy and cold first day of April, when Piper first walked into my pub, I'd thought she was like no one I'd ever met. I thought I knew deep down she was special, that she would be special to me.

And now we were nothing?

I wanted to scream, punch something. I wanted to riot. And with the way my heart beat so hard in my chest, my body even protested.

I pounded on the door. "Piper, please, please open the door."

A second passed.

Two, then three, and then a hundred more without any answer. I let my forehead drop to the door. When I had gone to those bars so many weeks ago, I simply went to talk to them, put a bug in the managers' and owners' ears about her beer. I didn't convince them to do anything. I didn't make any deals or contracts. All I did was support a woman I believed in very much by talking about her in a positive way.

And why was that so bad?

I hit the door with the side of my fist once more and stomped back to my car. She'd get over it, she'd have to.

And then it struck me like a blow to the head.

She didn't have to. Because there was Iowa.

I didn't want her to move. I wanted her here with me in Minneapolis. But after today and the flat good-bye she'd offered, I had a feeling she'd made her decision.

Iowa.

I fucking hated Iowa.

I jerked the car key, turning the ignition over, and pressed the Bluetooth on. Connor picked up on the second ring. "Hey, what's up?"

"What are you doing right now?"

"Uh, nothing, why?"

"Piper just broke up with me." My stomach churned, saying those words out loud, and I wanted to vomit.

"Oh." A ruffling of some sort sounded in the background, then "What do you feel like drinking?"

"Anything but beer." It hurt to even think of the drink that had brought Piper and me together.

"All right. I'll be at your place in a bit. I'll call Bear."

I disconnected the call, heading home in a fog.

I flicked on the lights in my apartment, illuminating the evidence of my life that had just shattered. A pair of Piper's shoes were next to the door, the charger to her laptop haphazardly thrown on the couch. I went to my bedroom to change, glossing over her clothes in my laundry basket and the black hair tie on the dresser. I ignored the small hand lotion bottle tipped over on the floor by the nightstand because she'd tried to toss it there and missed.

"Goddamn it," I moaned, hitting the doorjamb. My world was filled with Piper. She was in every vein of my existence. I'd bleed out if I tried to extract her, and no Band-Aid would help.

I flopped onto the couch and turned to whatever stupid movie was on TV. I didn't want to think about anything. I wanted to be numb. And just in the nick of time, a couple of hard knocks echoed from the door.

"It's open," I said from my spot on the sofa.

Bear walked in with pizza boxes in his hand, and uncharacteristically had nothing to say. No smartass remark, no big jovial hello. Just a nod of his head as he stepped over my legs that I hadn't bothered to remove from the coffee table.

Connor had the bag from the liquor store. "I didn't know what you wanted so . . ." He placed down a bottle each of Bankers Club vodka, Old Crow whiskey, and some tequila I'd never heard of. "What's your poison?"

"Are you actually trying to poison me with this cheap stuff?"

He shrugged and pulled out a bunch of mixers from his bag. "What's the difference when we're drinking to get drunk?"

"Good point." I grabbed the blue Gatorade and the vodka, and proceeded to mix a drink every high school kid would envy.

"What happened?" Bear asked, offering me a slice of meat lover's.

"I don't know," I said before biting into my pizza. I swallowed and wiped my mouth with the back of my hand. "We went to dinner at my parents' house, which was a total disaster, and when I have the motivation, I'm going to light them up. I'm so done with them. How they treated Piper was the straw that broke the camel's back."

Connor poured some whiskey into his soda. "That's why she broke up with you? Because of your parents?"

"No." I gulped down my Blue Blast concoction. It was disgusting. "Yes. I think. I don't know."

"Which one is it?" Bear asked with a mouthful of pizza.

"Both, I guess. We left but got into this big fight because she said I don't support her. I told her I've always supported her and tried to do everything I could for her. She flipped out when I said I went to Monkey Bar and Pete's Tavern."

"You went to Monkey Bar and Pete's?" Connor got up to look through the cabinet by the sink and returned with three shot glasses.

"Yeah. I wanted to introduce them to Piper's beer."

"And she didn't like that?"

"No." I tossed my dirty paper plate onto the table. "I told you. She flipped out."

"I'm just trying to understand the whole story," he said, pouring tequila into the glasses.

The three of us did the shots, and I sat back, happy to have the burn start in my throat on its way to my belly and out to every part of my body. Burning the pain out of me.

I plowed through another three pieces of pizza and two more of the disgusting Blue Blasts drinks, until I realized Bear still hadn't said anything. Bear sat there quietly eating and drinking whiskey straight up. I kicked at his knee. "What do you have to say about all this?"

"Nothing, really."

I laughed. "Nothing? You always have something to say. What is it, huh?"

"I was afraid of this happening. You two getting divorced. Who gets the kids? The beer?"

"That's all you care about? While your best friend since freshman year of high school is sitting here crying into his vile vodka and blue Gatorade—"

"Hey, man, don't blame the drink," Connor piped in.

I flicked my middle finger at him, my attention still on Bear. "What do you really have to say about it?"

He ran a hand over his face, his eyes scanning the room before landing on me. "You said she didn't like that you did everything for her, so why are you surprised she's mad you went to talk to the bars?"

"It wasn't that big of a deal," I said, aggravated that my friend was taking her side.

"It's a big deal to her."

"I was just trying to help her."

"But clearly she doesn't feel like you did. She feels like you took something away from her. She's hurt and angry. You can't be mad at her for feeling that way."

I slunk down on the couch, focusing on whatever Tom Cruise movie this was. *Mission: Impossible II*, I thought, but it was hard to tell between my level of sobriety and all the fighting. All the missions seemed impossible.

Like finding my way out of this hole I'd dug myself into with Piper.

Impossible.

"She doesn't think she's good enough," I said with a smack to the couch, finally acknowledging her words out loud, like maybe if my friends heard them, too, they'd be able to help me. Because I didn't know what to do. "It's ridiculous. She's the most remarkable woman I've ever met. She's funny and smart and good-looking."

Connor readjusted the hat on his head. "Yeah. She's pretty."

"Nice eyes," Bear said, and I pointed at him.

"Only smart thing you've said tonight."

He tipped his drink toward me. "Don't get upset with me because she's pissed at you. I only pointed out the same thing she did. You've made it, man. You've got the Public. She's still working for her dream. How do you think it felt to hear she got her first steps to it because of someone else?"

"What does it matter? I got some of my capital from my trust fund."

"It's pride." Bear sat forward. "You hurt her pride."

I hadn't thought of it like that. Easy for me to think it wasn't that big of a deal, but for someone starting out in her precarious situation, I guess I could understand how it might feel. After all, that's why I distanced myself from my family. I wanted to strike out on my own, lose the Reed name, build my own future. I should've understood Piper's wants from the beginning, but I was too blinded by my own want. I didn't take hers into consideration.

"I told Piper I loved her. I told her and she didn't care. And now she might move to Iowa, and there's nothing I can do about it."

"You could apologize," Bear offered.

"I tried to."

"Try harder," he said.

Connor refilled the shot glasses. "I think she's so mad because she loves you, too. If she didn't, she wouldn't care so much, right? Isn't that the key? The opposite of love isn't hate, it's apathy."

Bear slapped his thigh with a loud chuckle. "McGuire for the win. Who'd have thought?"

Connor raised his shot glass before downing the contents. "We've all loved and lost. Some of us just hide it better."

For one short second, I forgot about what I was dealing

with and felt bad for my friend, who'd experienced his own heartbreak. He'd been through a tough spot, had his heart stomped on, but then I thought of Piper.

And the organ that used to be my heart cracked all over again.

My only hope was Connor. He eventually got over his misery, so I would, too. The only bright spot in this stinky pile of shit.

CHAPTER 26

Piper

There was a soft knock on my door. After writing, deleting, rewriting, and deleting again the angriest text I could think of, I fell asleep crying to the *Titanic* soundtrack. Because the only thing sadder than what had gone down last night was Jack freezing to death in the Atlantic Ocean while holding Rose's hand.

I picked my head up, wiping the mascara from around my eyes. "Yeah?"

"You all right in there?" Sonja asked from the other side of my bedroom door, then poked her head in.

I sat up, my throat all scratchy when I said, "I guess."

"You look . . . good."

"Don't lie to me."

She sat next to me on the bed. "You look like shit."

I ran my fingers through my tangled hair. "I feel like shit."

"Bear told me what happened."

I shouldn't have been surprised, and yet I was. Sonja made herself at home next to me under the covers and asked, "What happened?"

"What did you hear?"

"Bear and I were going to go for an early morning run today, but he canceled when word got out that you broke up with Blake. Sounded like an all-hands-on-deck situation. I'm pretty positive they all got drunk last night."

I searched the bed for wherever I had left my cell phone last night. I found it tucked between two pillows. There were twenty-two text messages. All from Blake. And all after midnight. I could practically see him getting drunker and drunker as the night went on.

"Yep, they did." I read the messages out loud. "'I think I get why you're mad at me, but I'd like to talk to you about it. Please call me.'"

"What time was that at?" Sonja leaned over to see the time by the blue bubble.

"Twelve-sixteen. And a few minutes later he wrote, 'Please don't ignore me. It's killing me.' About twenty minutes later, 'You're killing me, Smalls.' And a GIF of Ham saying that." I showed it to her.

She took the phone from me, scrolling through all of his texts. "He's determined, if nothing else."

I had used to adore his persistence. Now I found it tiring. I took my phone back to reread the messages.

Remember our first meal at the Pancake House? You got the chocolate chip pancakes. I knew from that day I wanted to be with you.

I won't stop trying to fix this, no matter how mad you are at me.

Im not going 2 bed until u call me. Call me. Call me. Cll me.

Pepper, please. forgive me?!?

While I was crying in my bed last night, Blake had gotten drunk enough to send me grammatically incorrect and misspelled texts. And it made me even angrier. He'd betrayed me by going against my wishes, but it also made me feel inferior, patronized. His words reminded me of Oskar. *Why don't you want me to take care of you? You should be happy I want to.*

It was exactly like Oskar, but worse because it was Blake. My Blake.

I'd experienced the imposter syndrome before, but now it was multiplied by a guy who couldn't even bother to spell-check his texts.

I didnt mean to hurt u. Your my sunshine.

I clicked on the link he'd sent me with that one, which opened up a YouTube video of Natasha Bedingfield's earworm "Pocketful of Sunshine." I rolled my eyes and quickly closed the link, silencing the song.

Remember that song? It's so annoying, amiright?? I'm write. But it remind me of u. not cause your annoying but because i got a pocketful of sunshine.

Its you. Your my pocketful of sunshine.

Then the smiling emoji with sunglasses.

These ridiculous messages continued until three in the morning, when I could only guess he finally passed out. His last text being:

Why won't you ducking talk to me!

I tossed my phone aside and laid my head on Sonja's shoulder.

"So, what's the real story?"

I inhaled deeply, pushing my lungs to expand for the first time in what felt like twelve hours, and told my friend the whole sad story of last night. She nodded along, cringing or sometimes mumbling a curse until I got to the part about Blake going to Pete's Tavern and Monkey Bar.

She held her hands up. "Wait. What?"

"He said he was the one who got my beer in those bars. He supported"—I added quotes around that word—"me from the beginning."

Sonja blinked away from me. Her arms crossed over her stomach, and she tilted her head. "I followed you up until now. Tell me why exactly you broke up with him?"

"I've worked too hard for too long to let some guy take the credit. My company's barely off the ground, but finding out I didn't even make it this far on my own was a punch in the gut. And Blake was the one to deliver it."

Fresh tears sprang into my eyes, but I shook them away before they could fall, determined to focus on my anger instead of the hurt. "And then he told me he loved me, like that was going to make it all better."

Hearing those three words didn't make it better. It made everything infinitely worse. Because I couldn't hate him if he loved me.

Sonja grabbed my shoulders. "Whoa. Whoa. Whoa. He told you that?"

"Yeah."

"He actually said 'I love you'?"

"Yeah."

"And what did you say?"

"Nothing. We were screaming at each other. What could I say?"

She rolled her eyes. "Oh, I don't know. Maybe 'I love you, too'?"

I waved her off. "No. No, I'm not going to tell him that."

"But it's true," she said, and God, I'd never hated my best friend more than in that moment.

"Can we take a step back for a second?" she asked, kicking the covers off her legs. "There is nothing I respect more than your drive. You have this independent, go-it-alone streak in you a mile wide. If I actually used the psychology degree I have, I might suggest it's because you're a middle child, but that's neither here nor there."

I took a swipe at her, but she bobbed out of the way with a grin.

"You want to run this company your own way, and I get it. We all get it, but sometimes you need a little help. I honestly don't think Blake went to those bars to do your work for you. He went to help you because he believes in you, like we all do. What does it matter who spoke to the owners, whether it was you, Blake, or the guy at the distributor? You're all working for the same outcome, yeah?"

I nodded.

"Blake has been behind you since day one, even if it was

in a way you don't like. I don't think you should punish him for that."

I grabbed the pillow from behind my head and threw it at her. "Ugh. Stop making sense."

Sonja folded the pillow in her arms, offering me a sad, understanding smile. "Why? Because knowing you want to be with Blake will make the decision to move to Iowa harder than you want it to be?"

I stared at my friend, hating her more now than a minute ago. I covered my face with my hands, my shoulders shaking as my built-up tears took over. Sonja pulled me to her, letting me cry into her neck. I got a few words out in between sobs. "I don't want to miss an opportunity because I'm afraid to leave a boy."

She shushed me. "I know. I know."

"I'm afraid to leave Blake. I've never felt like that before."

I felt Sonja nod, but she didn't say anything as I cried out all of my frustration, trepidation, and loss. I broke up with Blake because I couldn't handle making this decision, and if I didn't have one to make, there would only be one answer.

Yet this didn't feel any easier. This was infinitely worse. Like I'd lost a part of me last night.

I lifted my head and wiped my face. "Don't I owe it to myself to go to Iowa?"

Sonja's brown eyes were smudged with tears. "I don't know, Pipes. No one can tell you what to do. You want to be the one to make all the decisions? That includes the tough ones, too."

She was right. I had to make this decision on my own.

I crawled out from under the covers. Sonja raised her brows at the dress I was still wearing from last night.

"At least you looked cute." She stood up and hugged me before leaving the room, humming "Pocketful of Sunshine" under her breath.

I turned to the mirror and took stock of my appearance. I hadn't washed off my makeup last night, and it had smeared down my face. My cheeks and nose were red from crying, lips and eyes puffy. I felt like I'd slept for a thousand years, but could lie right down and sleep for another couple hundred. My limbs were heavy, and my heart beat erratically in my chest.

As much clarity as I had after talking with Sonja, there was still so much left I had to figure out. Namely, what was I going to do?

I opened my laptop and pulled up my e-mail. I owed this to myself. At the very least, I had to try.

CHAPTER 27

Piper

I followed the trail of the Principal Riverwalk, listening to Bob point out different things around us. The deep timbre of his voice enveloped me with warmth, mingling with the heat of this Des Moines weather.

"Is it always this hot?" I asked, tying my hair up in a ponytail.

He laughed. "Beautiful, huh?"

My phone told me it was ninety-three degrees, and we'd been walking around downtown for more than an hour. I wasn't used to such high heat and humidity. Or all this walking.

"And how about this?" Bob asked, extending his hand toward the bridge in front of us. "Gorgeous."

I held my hand up to shield my eyes since I'd lost my sunglasses somewhere in my hotel room. It was about 250 miles from Minneapolis to Des Moines, and I hadn't planned enough drive time, especially since I had to stop about an hour into the drive because I'd chugged a venti iced coffee before I left. Bob and I had planned on meeting outside my hotel at five, but since I was running late, I'd tossed my overnight bag on the floor for a quick change, leaving a variety of my things—including my sunglasses—lying there as I closed the door behind me.

"Mmhmm." I reclined my head to follow the arch all the way up. I didn't think bridges could be *gorgeous*, but he seemed into it and I didn't want to be rude to my host.

"It's the Iowa Women of Achievement Bridge," he said, leading me toward the middle of said bridge, where we paused to look at the little waterfall beneath us. "This is a popular tourist spot. You know, with all the art and everything." He pointed his thumb over his shoulder, in the direction we had just come from, where we had passed a modern art statue. "Imagine being able to walk by this every day."

I looked around me. Parents holding hands with their little kids. A couple of teenagers on skateboards in the distance. An older couple a few feet away, kissing sweetly. The sounds of the river below us and the color of the open sky above was . . . "Pretty awesome."

Iowa wasn't what I'd thought it would be like. Or, at least, Des Moines wasn't. It was hip and growing, changing economically and culturally. Well, that's how Google had put it.

"So, now that I've given you the royal walking tour, can I buy you dinner?" Bob's smile was contagious. He was a congenial guy with a tan and a rounded belly that told me he enjoyed living his life.

"Sure."

"I've probably talked your ear off. Eating and drinking are the only ways to shut me up."

I laughed. "I don't mind."

On the walk back to his car, I began to try to visualize myself living here in this "big small town," as Bob called it. I'd assumed Iowa was all cornstalks and waving wheat, which it could be, but Des Moines was nothing like that. It was full of life and color, with huge graffiti murals and an art society club. The more Bob told me about the city, the less I needed to be convinced I'd like living here.

He had just about finished his spiel about the cost of living when he parked at a meter along a street. "This part of the city is known as the East Village. I wanted to bring you to it because a lot of new restaurants and bars are cropping up here. Two breweries opened last year. And you need to see your future competition."

I liked that Bob had so much confidence in me. And even though I knew he was playing it up to sell me on this place, it felt good to be chased as opposed to me always doing the chasing.

He led me down a few blocks, and I peered into the window fronts of stores, a mixture of furniture places, art galleries, cafés, and chic clothing stores. If I was going to be honest with myself, this was the perfect city to open a craft brewery. My excitement took me by surprise.

Over dinner, Bob actually asked me about myself. He wanted to know about my family and what kinds of things I enjoyed. Of course, he always brought it back to Des Moines and how my sisters would love to visit. He already knew my parents loved it since he had met them here. He told me about the music festivals and the art house cinema that played old black-and-white films all the time.

"It all seems terrific," I said. "Yet, I have to tell you it was a difficult decision to come down here to meet you. Not that I didn't want to, but it's hard to think about moving away from what I know."

"But you've done it before. I mean, you lived in Germany. I don't think moving here is anywhere near as hard as moving to Europe."

"You're right," I said with a smile, but I put my elbows on the table so I could cover the way my mouth involuntarily dipped down. It wasn't what I'd be leaving. It was *who* I'd be leaving.

But maybe this was what I needed. A fresh start.

I cleared my throat. "So, when do I get to see your space?"

"You mean our space."

I winked at him. "You run a good game, Bob, I'll give you that."

"I was thinking tomorrow, after you've gotten the feel of the area and I've convinced you why you should want to move here."

"You're doing a pretty good job so far."

He nodded. "How's about we go for a drink?"

"I thought you'd never ask."

Two hours later, I was back in my hotel room. After being thoroughly wined and dined, I lay on the bed, staring up at the ceiling. It was easy to pretend I was here on vacation and not to make a major life decision, but now that I was alone, the gravity of this situation hit me full force. I was either going to move to Iowa and start all over again with a business partner, or I was going stay in Minnesota and continue to go at it alone.

I reached for my phone, which was burrowed deep in my purse, and turned it on after having had it off all day so I could be fully present with Bob. Multiple notifications rang out as it came to life. There were a few texts from my mom checking in, a couple of emoji-laden messages from Sonja, and one voicemail from Blake, which I refused to listen to.

With the hurt and confusion already clouding my thoughts, I feared hearing his voice would send me reeling either back to him or far away from him. I wasn't ready to do either.

Instead I opened Twitter to find I had been mentioned again by BeerasaurusRex, this time in a veiled attempt at spreading a rumor.

@BeerasurusRex had heard through the hopvine that a little start-up was starting up some romance in exchange for taps. His tweet concluded:

Not cool, bro. Not cool.

What was this, *Gossip Girl*? And who the hell was this

guy? My first thought was Travis, but more likely he was just some guy who'd spoken with him. No matter, I hated them all.

I slapped my phone down on the nightstand, more furious than ever. Maybe now *was* the perfect time to get out of Minneapolis.

The next morning, I explored more of Des Moines by myself before meeting Bob at an older brick building in the market district. He was standing next to the firehouse sign out front.

"So what do you think?" he asked, arms open wide.

It was so stereotypical firehouse, I thought a Dalmatian was going to run out from the garage door. I didn't hate it, but it wasn't really my style. "It's . . . nice."

The inside was narrow and still had the pole from the second floor in the middle of the place. I curled my arm around it. "Too bad this will have to go."

Bob's brows squeezed together. "It will?"

"I . . . just assumed."

He shook his head and explained his ideas for the layout, keeping "the integrity of the firehouse." He wanted a bar in the front and a wall up in the back to separate the space into two rooms, and that's when he began to lose me.

"You want to wall off everything so the patrons can't see what's going on in the back?" When he nodded, I looked off to the area, picturing where I'd be working every day, with the actual craft piece of the brewery hidden. "What happens if someone wants to see the process?"

"They can pay for a tour."

"Pay for a tour?"

"Extra income," he said, clearly having everything already figured out. "When they come in, they're coming to a bar. But they can pay for the extra experience of the tour. They'd get a free drink at the end, but I think it adds a little mystique to the place rather than having it all hanging out. Besides, who wants to see all that all the time anyway?"

"Me," I said with a huff.

He laughed, but I wasn't kidding. Craft brewing was all about the process. And for the first time since I'd arrived yesterday, I began to think Bob and I weren't on the same page.

After walking the perimeter of the building, Bob brought me back to the front. "Now that you've seen everything, I wanted to hear your thoughts about the name Firehouse Brew."

I froze. This was new to me. "I had no idea you wanted to change the name."

"Well, we're going to be partners, open up a new LLC. I think it's only appropriate to start from scratch."

I tugged at the end of my braid, gnawing on the inside of my cheek.

"You don't like that name? We can come up with something else."

"It's just that I've been working on my brand for a long time. My recipes, the name . . ."

"Right, but now we'll have our own brand."

I inhaled, trying to pretend I didn't mind everything he was saying to me.

"I've got the permits and the crew ready to build us a brewery. All I need is a brewer."

I nodded.

"You've just got to sign on the dotted line."

"You gave me a lot to think about. I'm going to think about it."

"Of course. Of course." He squeezed my shoulder. "Take your time. But don't take too long," he said with a chuckle. "I've got a business I want to get up and running."

I nodded and with a wave headed out the door. Off in the distance, sirens went off, and I couldn't help but feel they were an omen.

CHAPTER 28

Blake

Piper hadn't texted me back. Not that I really expected her to after my drunken rambles. But she hadn't returned my phone calls, either. I'd left her a voicemail every day since Sunday. Coherent messages. Pleading messages. Reasoning messages.

I thought maybe she'd change her mind. We were in the heat of the moment, we'd both said things we didn't mean, but if she hadn't taken the time to get back to me by now, I had to assume it really was over.

Although, if we were really and truly over, I wanted to end it face-to-face. Not with raised voices or while we were arguing. I wanted to look her in the eye and hear the words.

I took my time getting ready, in no rush to get to where I was going. I hadn't bothered to shave in days, and my scruff had started to fill in pretty well, but in the name of wasting time, I got my razor out. If I was going to lay my heart out on the line once and for all, I might as well look my best doing it.

I put on a polo, gray shorts, and a pair of boat shoes. Piper's favorite pretentious, preppy look she always pretended to hate. I didn't bother calling ahead because I knew she wouldn't pick up. It was probably for the better anyway. If she knew I was coming, she might leave.

On one hand, I understood her avoidance, but on the other, I hated it. It wasn't fair. I deserved more than a fight in a car. I deserved a proper good-bye from the girl I loved.

I swallowed the lump in my throat as I dropped into the driver's side seat. The radio automatically turned on, but I snapped it off, not wanting to remember Piper's pitiful off-key singing next to me.

My apartment was only a few miles from her house, but this trip seemed to take forever, and by the time I finally pulled up to the curb in front, I'd practiced the speech I wanted to give seven times.

With feet weighted like cement, I stepped onto the sidewalk. I had trouble lifting my attention up to the house and kept my gaze down, noticing things I never had before. The patch of dandelions in the middle of the small lawn. The uneven slope of the grainy concrete pavement. The dirt on the white railing that needed to be cleaned, as well as the windowsills.

And just as the thought came into my head to rent a power-washer to do it, I remembered.

Fixing things around this house wasn't my job anymore.

Doing favors or nice deeds just because I wanted to was out of the question. That was what a boyfriend did. Something I was not.

I knocked on the door, and when no one answered, I rang the doorbell. A minute passed, so I walked around the side of the house, but the doors to the garage were all closed up. If she was working, she always kept them open, but to be sure, I opened the side door.

The lights were off, and no Piper to be found.

I checked the time on my phone. It was after three, and I had no idea where she could be, but I wasn't leaving without seeing her. I made my way back to the front of the house and sat on the stoop. I texted Missy and Darren to tell them I didn't know what time I'd be at work and settled in to wait.

I spent the first hour playing on my phone.

I spent the second pacing.

The third, I sat in my car, charging my phone.

And finally, during my fourth hour of godforsaken waiting, Sonja's little Toyota pulled up behind me.

"Blake?" She stepped out of her car. "What are you doing here?"

"I'm here to see Piper, do you know where she is?"

Sonja frowned and slowly closed the distance between us. She hesitantly raised her eyes to mine, her voice quiet like she was afraid to say it. "She's in Iowa."

I didn't know how long it took for a person to die once their heart stopped beating, but I didn't feel connected to this world anymore after hearing that.

"She left on Tuesday. Drove down."

"Tuesday?" I got out, grasping at pieces of the story for something to hold on to. Today was Thursday. She'd been in a different state this whole time.

"She said she had to go, and didn't think she'd be able to if she talked to you. I'm sorry. I'm so sorry, Blake."

As quickly as my heart had stopped beating it picked back up, galloping away. A pain shot down my chest and through my rib cage. I waited for an audible sound, imagining my bones breaking, and when it didn't happen, I pressed my hand to my breastbone, making sure I was still whole.

Sonja stretched up on her toes, hugging me around the neck, but I didn't have the energy to wrap my arms around her. I sunk into her. Like deadweight.

I was deadweight.

"She was really torn up about it," she said, as if that would comfort me.

It didn't.

"I'm sorry. She said she owed it to herself to see what it was like." She slowly backed away from me, but kept her fingers on my shoulders, anchoring me.

"I guess that's all there is then," I said. I'd get no final discussion. No time to look in her emerald eyes. No brush of my fingers around hers, no kiss good-bye.

Piper wasn't mine anymore.

I combed my hands through my hair, shaking off Sonja's light grip. I stepped away from her, needing to get out, get away. I spun around to my car, but I felt Sonja's gaze on my back the whole time. I didn't acknowledge her, I couldn't right now. I kept my eyes ahead, always ahead. It was the only way I could keep it together.

Outside the windows of my car, people walked downtown, laughing and smiling, all enjoying the late evening. Most people were headed into a long Fourth of July weekend. Fireworks popped in the distance already. The parties had begun.

And I wanted nothing to do with it.

I tore into the Public through the back door, one single raise of my hand to the staff on my way to the office, intent on working. I'd get some paperwork done, inventory the bar and kitchen, maybe reorganize my filing cabinet. Everything and anything to keep myself occupied. But when I poked my head into the hallway, I found the bar packed.

I jumped in to help out.

"You all right?" Missy asked as she poured two lagers from the taps. "You look a little crazed."

If she only knew. I gave her a single stiff shake of my head and got to work.

I'd refilled the ice twice and changed one of the kegs before I had a chance to help the servers clear some of the tables off. By the quick look I'd gotten at the POS system, we'd be well over our target this week. One thing to celebrate, at least.

By ten o'clock the crowd had thinned out a bit, and I wiped my forehead with the rag I had tucked into my back pocket.

"You almost look like a real bar back."

My head whipped toward the voice. The one I could pick out of a crowd and would most likely remember for the rest of my life.

Piper.

One corner of her mouth tipped up to form the smallest of smiles. Her hair was up in one of those knots that I could never figure out. Her face was flushed like she'd run here, and she held a reusable shopping bag in her hands.

She bit her lip before asking, "Can we talk for a minute?"

My vocabulary momentarily flew out of the window, and I mumbled some sort of agreement. She waited for me to come around to the opposite side of the bar before stepping up next to me. She smelled delicious, a combination of her usual fresh wheat scent and something new, sweet like sugar.

I didn't know whether to be excited by or dread the fact that she stood in front of me. My hand rose to her waist of its own volition, but I pushed it in my pocket to keep from touching her. I pointed down the hallway. "Let's go to my office."

She followed me, and I closed the door behind her. She kept close to the wall, holding the bag to her chest. I assumed she had brought the stuff I left at her place, officially cutting off all ties. And I thought I could handle it, but I couldn't.

I wasn't ready for the end.

To stave off the inevitable, I changed into a clean, dry

shirt. I kept a few T-shirts in one of my drawers for occasions when I got dirty working or, like this case, had beers spilled down my back. I shucked my wet polo and yanked on the plain black shirt. Out of the corner of my eye, I caught Piper staring at me.

I pivoted to fully face her, and her gaze slid up slowly from where it hovered somewhere around my hips. The sudden brightness in her eyes lit a spark deep inside me. The pull between us was still there, the attraction real and palpable. My pulse thrummed, steady if not nervously, and I sat on the edge of my desk to keep the jittery energy from escaping.

The faster we got this over with, the better. "I wa—"

She stopped me with a tiny step. "Can I go first?"

Her body was still closed off, her feet pressed together, her knees noticeably wobbling. In fact, when I focused on her fingers tucking the lone lock of hair behind her ear, they shook ever so slightly.

I once again kept the visceral need to go to her at bay. Things needed to be sorted out between us, and touching her wouldn't help anything.

"Sonja told me you were at our house waiting for me." When I nodded, she took one more step to me. "Why?"

"Because you didn't return any of my calls or texts, and I figured if we really were broken up, I wanted some closure."

Her throat bobbed on a swallow, and the longest moments of my life ticked on before she spoke. "I wanted to talk to you, but I couldn't. I would've chickened out of going to Iowa, and I needed to."

The earnest pleading in her voice broke my heart all over again. No matter how things ended between us, I'd never want to keep Piper from doing what she needed to do.

"I know," I said, dropping my hands to the desk as a reminder to keep them to myself.

"I went to talk to Bob in person, see the space, understand what my opportunity cost was."

A chuckle unwillingly left my throat. "Look at you, using economic terms like a pro."

"I learned from the best," she said, coming a mere three inches away from me. It physically hurt to have her so close and not kiss her, hug her, anything. I already despised the words about to come out of her mouth, but this was what I needed in order to move on.

"I owed it to myself," she continued, her eyes shining under her lashes, "to see what I'd be giving up. In the end, having a brewery out of state wasn't worth giving you up."

For the second time today, my heart stopped, and it took me a long time before I sucked in another breath, frozen in anticipation of her next words.

"I'm sorry I didn't tell you I left, but if I hadn't gone, I'd always ask what if, and I didn't want that shadow following us around." She bit into her bottom lip, her eyes focusing on the wall behind me, the ceiling, and then the floor. "If there is still an us, I mean. I realize I might be too late, but I want to be with you. I love you, and I should've—"

"Piper." I interrupted her, fearing for my health. It couldn't be good for the body to have so many close calls to a heart attack. "Can we sit down?"

"Oh, yeah. Sure, sure."

I held her hand as we sat in the two chairs in front of my desk. I turned hers so we were face-to-face. There was no hiding anymore.

"Can you say that again? The part about how you love me?"

She breathed out a giggle; it was the best sound I'd ever heard, besides, of course—

"I love you, Blake."

I held her beautiful face between my hands and kissed her perfect mouth that had uttered my most favorite words.

"I want you to know what happened with the other bars," I said, pulling my mouth away from hers.

"I don't care."

"Yes, you do, and it's important you hear my apology. I'm sorry that I ever made you feel disrespected or that I made your work seem irrelevant." She leaned into me, but I wouldn't give in until she heard the truth. "I didn't go to those bars specifically for you, it just sort of happened. I ran into Pete at the distributor, we got to talking, and one thing led to another. Monkey Bar was a place I used to frequent all the time, and I'm still friendly with Susan and Eddie, so when I stopped there for a drink one night, I put a bug in their ears about you. I didn't say anything other than your beer was phenomenal, and they should give it a shot. That's it, I swear. I didn't—"

"I know you didn't mean anything by it," she said, interrupting. "It's hard for me not to have self-doubt, but I know you'd never intentionally do anything to make me feel less than. I know that. It's difficult to forget about history, but me and you are brand-new. We both deserve to get what we want."

She kissed me, and I let my hands roam over her hair and the back of her neck since I could now. In between short bursts of her mouth on mine, she said, "I'm sorry I acted the way I did on Sunday. I was overwhelmed and hurt by what happened."

"You should know I told my parents in no uncertain terms that until they can respect me and my decisions I will not be taking part in any related Reed family events. No dinners, no holidays, and obviously no election BS. I don't want you to have to worry about them on top of everything else."

"You're sure?" she asked, a bit of doubt coloring her tone.

"Yeah. I can't control what family I was born into, but I can control my life and decide if I want them in it or not."

"Well, if you're happy, I'm happy."

"I'm happy," I said. "But I want to hear about the last few days for you."

She pursed her lips and looked away. "I was looking for an excuse not to stay. I had it in my head that if I stayed here and didn't take Bob's offer, I'd betray my dreams."

Since she was practically there already, I hauled her to my lap. "I swear I'll never ask you to stop. I'll never ask you to give anything up for me. I want you to be whoever and do whatever you want."

She curved her arms around my neck, running the tip of her nose against mine. "I know. And before I left on Tuesday I went to the bank and spoke with a nice woman named Mary Ellen, who helped me fill out some forms about a loan. She called me this morning to tell me that I got it."

My jaw dropped, anticipating what she was going to say.

"It's enough to buy a small building in Prospect Park and get me up and running."

I started to tell her how awesome that was, but she stopped me.

"And I already hired my first employee."

"Yeah?"

She nodded, trying to hide her smile.

"My new PR guy is Thomas Behr."

I laughed. "No shit."

She shrugged one shoulder. "Who better to sell my beer than Bear?"

"That's brilliant." I shook my head at her. "You did all this and you didn't tell me."

"No, because this is *my* business. I needed to do it on my own. And you need to swear to me no interfering. You can make all the decisions about my beer in your bar, but no more favors, okay?"

"Cross my heart." I drew an X over my chest and kissed

her again, imprinting my promise on her with my lips and tongue and teeth.

She smiled, and that was it. We had said all we needed to say to each other. I'd missed this girl, and I wrapped my hand around her neck, leaning her head back so I could kiss down her chin and throat with my lips and tongue. She meekly fought against me, pushing at my shoulders. I bit into the crook of her neck then sucked a mark into her skin, and she shrieked.

"Wait, wait." She shoved me away and leapt off my lap. "I have presents for you."

She picked up the bag, and thankfully it didn't contain any of the things I'd left at her place: including but not limited to contact solution, my favorite Twins T-shirt, and the old-school Adidas sandals I'd thrown on one night when I'd been in a rush. What she did take out of the bag was a Tupperware container full of Funfetti cupcakes.

She offered it to me. "I stopped at the grocery store on the way home tonight. They were either going to be celebratory or drown-my-sorrow treats."

"Well, I hope you made a double batch. We have a lot of celebrating to do," I said, before plucking the lid off and diving into one of the cupcakes, while she grabbed the next item from the bag. I licked the vanilla icing from the corner of my lips and wiped my hands off before taking the poster from her hands. I slipped off the plastic wrap and unrolled it to reveal a simple message.

"I thought maybe you could add it to your collection,"

she said, angling her head to the giraffe poster she'd given me when the Public opened.

"Absolutely." I grabbed the tape from my desk and stretched up to put the poster on the wall. I stood back to admire it. One sentence written over and over again in neat cursive. *I love you.*

I repeated the sentiment in her ear as I looped my arms around her. She grinned, but didn't let me kiss her yet. "One more." She bent down for the last item, a growler. "I've been working on this recipe for about a month. I want you to be the first to try it."

"It's new?"

"Yeah. I'm thinking of calling it Buzz Cut."

I scooted out of the office for two glasses from the bar and returned holding them up triumphantly. "I'll let you do the honors," I said, putting them down on my desk so she could pour. "What is it?"

"It's a barley wine," she said, passing me one of the glasses. "The ABV is eleven percent."

An eleven percent alcohol by volume. Holy Jesus. "Good buzz then, huh?"

"Hence the name."

I clinked my glass to hers before drinking. I kept my eyes on her and was transported to the first day we met, when I did this very same thing. This woman—this funny, intelligent, and bright woman—was here with me, and I couldn't get enough. I slammed my glass down, grinning. "Fill me up again, Sunshine."

EPILOGUE

Piper

I can't believe my baby is finally open." I didn't know what it was like to have an actual baby, but I'd wanted this for so long I was physically, mentally, and emotionally exhausted. It was almost exactly six months from the day when I turned Bob down in Des Moines and came home to Minneapolis, deciding to go it on my own. And here I was, opening Out of the Bottle Brewery.

"I can't believe *my* baby did this!" My mom tossed her arms around me.

"You did good, Pippi. Real good," Dad said before sipping from his beer in the specially designed glasses by Kayla. My whole family had flown in for this, but I'd taken my parents in the back to have a moment alone with them.

"If it weren't for you two always being so supportive, I don't think I ever would've been able to do it on my own."

"Honey, I am so proud of you." Mom couldn't stop kissing my cheek. "You are proof you can do anything when you put your mind to it."

My dad actually got a little teary-eyed when he bent down to kiss the top of my head. "I love you, Piper." He patted my back then sniffed and cleared his throat. "I think I need a refill."

Mom rolled her eyes. "That one. Always so emotional."

I laughed and followed my parents toward the front. I'd purchased a small warehouse, about two thousand square feet. The entire front wall was made of windows, so everyone walking by could see inside to the gleaming stainless steel brite tanks along the wall. Opposite them was the bar, where visitors could try any of the brews, then have a seat at one of the numerous picnic benches to play games like Clue or Jenga. Out the back, there was an open cement lot that I'd fenced in and strung lights around. It was too cold right now to be outside, but there were a few people milling about eating snacks from the food truck parked on the corner of the street.

It was pretty fantastic. And it was all mine.

My pride overflowed.

"There you are," Blake said, coming up behind me. "Everybody's been asking where you were."

"I'm here. In my brewery." I smiled. "I can't stop saying it."

He kissed my cheek. "You don't have to."

He pushed me to where Bear and Sonja were behind the bar, my makeshift bartenders for the day. Sonja handed me a beer while she threw a face over my shoulder at Blake. They'd become awfully friendly in the last few months, but the secretive smile she shared with him was a bit unnerving.

Charlie, my newest friend and Connor's frenemy, hugged me. I'd moved in with Blake pretty soon after we'd made up, and Charlie had needed a place to live after accepting the head coaching position for the Otters. She was a female football coach. It was almost unheard of. Needless to say, Sonja and I immediately took this badass chick into our mini-sorority.

"This is pretty impressive," she said with a slight Georgia accent.

"Thanks for coming."

"Of course. Wouldn't miss it for anything. Except for a statewide playoff game." She lifted her glass of the Blonde with a wink, and I laughed.

"Where's Connor?"

"Who knows with that boy."

"I thought you two were . . ."

"We're coworkers. We teach and coach in the same school. That's it."

I nodded, knowing exactly what she meant when she said *That's it*. I'd said the same about Blake and me.

"Gather round," Blake said, motioning to Connor, who was shooting daggers at Charlie, closer to us. Bear wiped his hands off and poured him and Sonja two small glasses as well. "I just wanted to say a quick little something."

"Quick?" Connor joked.

"Yes, quick." Blake elbowed him. "But I wouldn't be making jokes about length of time if I were you."

"Yeah, just length," Bear added.

All of us girls looked at one another and shook our heads.

"First of all, I wanted to thank you for being here to support Piper, but also for being great friends. You're all more than friends, you're family." He held his glass aloft, and all of us did the same before drinking.

I took a few sips of the amber ale before I noticed it. Something moving around at the bottom of the glass. Without thinking, I stuck my hand into the beer and fished it out. Confusion, surprise, and then elation all crashed onto me like my glass on the bar.

"Oh my God."

Blake took the ring from my wet hand and bent down, drawing the attention of most everyone around us, but I couldn't focus on anything other than the man staring up at me.

"Sunshine, you are the strongest woman I know and I couldn't imagine my life without you in it. Will you marry me?"

I'd often thought about Oskar and how he affected me, and admittedly, he'd influenced my decisions for a while. I never thought I'd want to get married, or I thought that if I did, it wouldn't happen for a very long time. But life had other plans.

Blake was my missing puzzle piece that made everything better. He was my lobster.

"Yes!" I yanked him up, kissing him everywhere. "Yes. Yes. Yes. Yes."

Applause roared around us, but all I heard was Blake saying, "I love you," over and over again. Once I stopped jumping up and down, he slipped the ring on my fourth finger.

"I'm so shocked," I said, placing my hand over my heart as it beat wildly. "I think I need a beer."

Blake handed me a new beer. "On the house. I know the person who makes it."

"Oh yeah?"

He nodded. "I like her. She's pretty okay."

A little laugh escaped me. I felt drunk.

Drunk in love.